FREY

MELISSA WRIGHT

The Frey Saga

FREY

MELISSA WRIGHT

FREY

PROLOGUE

I stood in the center of a council chamber I had never seen before. A vast library lined the walls, interspersed with decorated frames and ornate mirrors. A great vaulted ceiling rose overhead, embellished with intricate carvings and painted in exquisite detail. Across the empty space before me was an elaborate table that seated six leaders of High Council, my executioners.

No, not executioners. I was being absurd, surely. *How bad can the punishment be for what I've done?*

Guards stood behind me, within arm's reach on either side. To the left of them were council members, and as I glanced right, in walked the dark stranger who'd come into my life only days before I had managed to destroy it.

Chevelle stood at attention, facing the council table. He did not acknowledge me.

I could hear others enter behind us, presumably witnesses, and I wondered if my tutor—my only possible ally in this ordeal—was among them.

Even she might not be able to save me from this fate. *It's over*, the voice in my head kept telling me. *This is it.* But I was getting ahead of myself.

1

(DAYS EARLIER)

T hat morning, I was out of the house early. I'd wanted to avoid my aunt, who was determined not to let me forget what a burden it had been to take me in, even if it used every spare ounce of her energy to do it.

The thought annoyed me as I rushed up the path and through the village gate, keeping my head down. No one generally went out of their way to speak to me, but I wasn't one for taking chances. The other elves didn't have much use for one who wasn't able to contribute, and my lack of magic and skill usually put me far from their minds, except for Evelyn of Rothegarr, with whom I'd nearly tussled the day before. She'd gone into a bit of a coughing fit right before it had descended too far into unpleasantness, and I'd been saved from my own dark thoughts about how to deal with her.

When she'd gotten to the village, though, she'd progressed from coughing to choking and, according to my aunt, had blamed the whole thing on me, as if I could work magic.

I slipped around the village and through the tangle of brush behind Junnie's house, darting past a trellis and toward the door. As I ducked under the hanging ivy, my foot caught on a vine and I stumbled forward, cursing as I nearly ran into a boulder—a boulder wearing a shirt.

Gradually, I tilted my head back and blew my too-long bangs aside to peer up, first at a strong chin and stern mouth, and then at the darkest sapphire-colored eyes I'd ever seen. A lot of elves had blue eyes, but always bright and shimmery. These were of the deepest blue. *They must appear black in the shadows.*

The thought made me flush.

He turned from me without a word and disappeared in a few long strides. I watched him go. With his short dark hair, dark eyes, and a large, strong build, he certainly wasn't from this clan.

Behind me, Junnie cleared her throat. "Freya?"

I hadn't realized she was watching me from the open door. "Who...?" I trailed off.

"You needn't bother yourself with him." She could see that I would. "Chevelle Vattier. He's from a northern clan. He'll be here only a short while. Council business."

That brought me back to my mission. "Fannie said there was some trouble with Evelyn?"

"Yes." There was something in her tone I didn't recognize. "She's fine now."

"Yesterday, I saw her."

"Yes." She half-smiled. "Don't worry yourself, Freya. Come, now. Let's study."

I hesitated. Evelyn had mentioned me, but not accusingly, and surely, there was more Junnie could have said. But she only placed a gentle hand on my shoulder and led me inside.

4

Junnie was older than I but remained striking with the blond hair, blue eyes, and thin features that seemed to be standard-issue among the village elves. The Council had assigned her as my tutor, citing my advanced age as the reason I couldn't learn with the others, but I suspected it was my stunning lack of ability that had landed me there.

"So," I said, forcing a smile, "what's on the agenda for today?"

She avoided my gaze, straightening the deep-blue sash that tied her tunic. "How do you feel about studying the lineages?" She knew I hated trying to memorize endless pages of names and dates, and she didn't seem surprised by my groan of complaint. "Well, let's get to it, then," she said, leading me toward the back room through the tiny living area.

She didn't have or need a great deal of space. Much as I was, Junnie was practically alone. Her family had all received the calling to serve elfkind. I didn't know exactly what that meant, only that the elf usually left with fanfare and seldom returned in fewer than a hundred years. It was apparently a very honorable thing, though Junnie never seemed proud.

Just off the living area was the study, which was larger than the front room, stuffed full of documents and lit by a pair of dim oil lanterns. Dust covered the decrepit scrolls and books lining the walls, but aside from a well-used worktable, the room was clean. Settling onto my usual stool, I leaned forward, elbows on the carved edge of the table to prop my head up for the monotonous hours to come.

I went back over our conversation, trying to find some meaning in the lack of information from my tutor. I recalled the dark-headed stranger and became distracted.

Junnie's books of lineages distracted me too. I would have

time to worry about Evelyn later. In the meantime, I had my chance to find out about Chevelle Vattier.

After leafing through a dozen or so volumes, my determination began to falter. There were many lineages, but I needed something on the northern clans, something on Vattier, and Junnie didn't have that. I would need a library, maybe even the council library. I shivered—I definitely wasn't sure about that. Even if I worked up the nerve to sneak in, I didn't have the magic to search documents quickly enough to find what I was after, as the council members did. I would have to stick to the village library.

I explained to Junnie that I wanted to leave early to collect various plants so I could easier identify the species the way she'd always urged me to. I expected at least a speculative gaze, but Junnie was distracted, scratching away at a scroll with quill and ink. I knew better than to go directly to the library. The village was small, and word wouldn't take long to get back to her, so I took a rambling, rarely used path out of the village and found myself wandering idly through the trees. Eventually, I came into an abandoned, overgrown garden, where I did not attempt anything useful like identifying the species but instead tried again to grow with magic.

Evelyn, daughter of a council elder, had caught me trying with a thistle the day before and had quite plainly informed me I was to be punished. But I was tired of being the only one who couldn't do it. Of course, I'd been warned not to practice without supervision, but I didn't see what harm could come if I wasn't able to do anything more than light a lantern. Her disagreement with that assessment was what had started the argument, and though I felt alone in the field, I couldn't help but glance around for her presence.

I concentrated first on one weed then on each of the

others, attempting the same tingle that came when I sparked a small flame. I had no luck for hours, but soon, a small thorn tree and a couple of noxious strains began to mature in response to the magic. Not much, but there was enough of a change to prove it was working.

I stared at the plants in awe.

All that time, I'd thought something was broken in me, that something had happened when I'd lost my mother, but maybe Junnie was right. Maybe I just needed to get my focus and to work until the magic came through.

Then I thought of Evelyn accusing me of practicing magic, and my panic rose anew. I stood, kicking dirt over the offending plants.

I ran back toward the village, brushing the evidence of my foray off the legs of my trousers. My heart raced as I straightened my hair and cut through the trees toward the village center. I would go to the library. It was safe there.

But then I remembered why I was going and hesitated. It felt wrong. I had no good reason for researching Chevelle Vattier, except I was curious. *There's nothing wrong with being interested, is there?*

Heat crept into my face for no good reason, and I picked up my pace to the old tree that housed the library. I knew my shoulders were drawn in, and I was glancing around too often, but I couldn't seem to help it. It felt illicit. I felt guilty.

Twice, I imagined a set of dark eyes on me, and a pricking sensation ran over my spine. I was going to have to pull myself together. I was being ridiculous. At that rate, I would have been fawning at him and flipping my hair like Evelyn by sundown.

When I finally walked into the library, I remembered why I didn't go there to study lineages. There must have been a thousand volumes and tenfold more scrolls on the main level alone, and I had no magic to lead me in the right direction.

I sat for hours, exploring the early texts, stories of the river clans and their battles with the Imps of Long Forgotten, firsthand accounts of the Trials of Istanna, and the long lineages of the eldest families. In all those records, there was nothing about a Vattier and nothing on the North.

A whisper roused me from my studies, and I realized it was late, so I decided to give up until the following day. Rising unsteadily, I heard the whisper again, but it was only the wind.

I glanced backward. Papers scattered on the floor. I surveyed the library, but it was practically empty. Someone on a higher level must have caused the pages to fall. I bent over and read the closest document. It was an account from the northern clans—I was stunned. I managed to stash the papers in my shirt then attempted a casual exit, convinced I should read them at home to avoid getting caught.

I'd made it out of the library and almost to the gate when I noticed a dark figure half hidden by a wide tree. It was Chevelle speaking with a councilman. He turned his head, glancing toward me, and I was caught by his eyes.

I was ashamed to admit I was staring. Worse still, I'd stopped walking to look at him. Color rose in my cheeks as I turned away. I couldn't understand what was wrong with me. The pages stuffed in my shirt felt like fire against my skin. It felt the way it did when I tried to lie.

I quickened my pace, stumbled on a root, and glanced back to see if he had noticed. But he was gone. I didn't know whether I was relieved or not.

My mind went over the encounter again as I made my way home. He'd had such a stern expression and such an intense gaze, but I thought I knew why: because I wouldn't stop staring at him.

IT SEEMED that my aunt Francine always knew when I didn't want to be bothered and went out of her way to ensure that I was. I quietly entered the house, hoping to slip off to my room, but there she was, smack in the center of the sitting area, drunk as a two-day jamboree. She had the same dull blond hair and muddy-brown eyes as I did, though mine were specked with green. She stopped me on my way through and forced me to sit and be her audience. I watched her as she rambled. She never mentioned Evelyn again, so neither did I. All I could think of were the papers I'd hidden away.

After a long evening of ducking her verbal jabs and listening to her theories on the Council's secret conspiracies, I finally made it to my room. With a flick of my fingers, light flooded the tiny space. I took a quick inventory: the seal on my wardrobe was intact, my drawings were still scattered across the floor, and the stash of walnuts remained on the table beside my bed. My mother's pendant hung from a woven-leather chain above my pillow, shooting refracted beams across the bed, and I smiled as I sat beneath it.

Scanning the pages I'd brought home from the library, I tried to find some order. I sorted them as best I could onto the worn comforter and sat rigidly while reading, unable to fathom why the document had me so anxious. For days, I'd been on edge.

The first pages contained the usual detailed description of the record-keeper, including his lineages and how he'd come upon the information. He was apparently a scribe for

Grand Council and was responsible for copying scrolls and adding new information from their various local libraries for each of the northern clans.

Some of the information was suspect, such as gossip from the neighboring fey guild about strange activities and reports from travelers about deserted villages—or maybe they weren't deserted. One description seemed to imply the village was empty not only of elves but of all evidence that it had ever been inhabited. There were maps of mountains and forests I'd never seen, showing each village and town. Curved lines of azure representing rivers and streams cut through the page, and I had a pang of regret for not studying maps with Junnie.

The next pages were a copy of the record-keeper's report to Grand Council about his findings, including his conclusion. There were missing pages, but something dreadful had happened, for certain. His official report should have been factual and serious, but the description was loaded with fear. Even his script became shaky as it reached the final word, *extinction*. All of the northern clans were gone, according to his account. Something had wiped out an entire region.

I wondered why that wasn't something I'd learned in my studies or been told in stories.

The last pages were lists of clan members, in order of family names. There must have been thousands, but pages were missing there too. F, G, L, N, and V were just gone.

As I reached the end, I took a deep breath. I had gotten so involved in the terrified man's story and page after page of family names that I had forgotten why I was reading in the first place. I sighed. Of course, the pages with the V names were missing.

I felt a small stab of guilt for the selfishness of the

thought while looking over such loss and tucked the pages under my mattress.

Lying back on the bed as I looked up at my mother's pendant, I closed my eyes, trying to remember her. I could see her face, her straight nose, her gentle smile. Her long hair waved around her shoulders, stray locks caught by the wind. She wore an embroidered white gown with bell sleeves and a low-cut neck. Her pendant hung there. It started to refract light, but there was only darkness around my vision of her. The wind picked up, and her dark hair began to whip back and away from her face. She was smiling gloriously, her arms outstretched. The pendant started to glow, and the darkness cracked. The wind was howling. I could barely see, or maybe something was covering my face. When I screamed, the sound was lost. I tried again, but suddenly I was blind, mute, and still. And yet I knew everyone was dying, running and screaming and dying.

I jerked upright in bed, gasping, my ears ringing. My face was damp, and as I wiped it, I was surprised to find it was not tears but blood. My nose was bleeding.

It took another moment to get my bearings. My bed sheets were a tangle, and my clothes were disheveled. It had only been a dream. I had fallen asleep looking at my mother's pendant, trying to remember her, and somehow combined it with the disaster I had read about the northern clans. *Just a dream*, I reminded myself.

Shaken, I sat up, struggling to collect myself. I reached up to remove the pendant from the hook and squeezed it tightly in my fist. It felt good, like a connection, and I slid the leather chain over my head, pulling the pendant down to rest on my chest. It felt right there, and I knew I should have been wearing it all along.

As I let go, I realized I'd gotten blood on my hands, so I headed to the hall and poured water from the pitcher into a ceramic basin. Staring into the mirror was not my favorite pastime—it mostly made my head hurt. But I had to clean the blood from my face and straighten the nest of hair on my head.

When I leaned forward, a flash caught my eye. For a moment, I thought the pendant was reflecting light from somewhere in the dark hallway, but my brain must still have been muddled from sleep. I examined the stone more closely and saw blood smudged there as well, so I rinsed it clean.

I lingered there, clutching it tightly—it was a comfort to hold. It seemed to warm something deep within me. I vowed to keep it on as I shook a thought from the dream away and headed for the door.

It was a gloomy day, and I didn't miss having to squint against the bright sunlight. Early as it was, I decided to take the long way to town, meandering through the fields and thinking of all that had passed in the last few days until I reached a patch of weeds that reminded me of Evelyn's taunting. I felt a momentary spasm at the thought of her choking in the pit of my stomach. Then I remembered growing the weeds in the garden, and I was suddenly in a rush to get to Junnie's.

I rapped our special knock, and in a heartbeat, Junnie was opening the door. "Morning, Frey. Early start today?"

I was determined. "Yes. I want to practice growing."

She glanced at the pendant against my chest. She was silent for a moment as she looked into my eyes, almost searching, probably worried I was sad or missing my mother. "Not today. It seems I have business with Council this morning." Her mouth turned down in a grimace.

"Oh." It wasn't like I didn't have plenty to do—I would just head to the library and try to find the missing pages to the northern clan documents. "Well, I'll see you then." I smiled at her and headed around to cut through the village.

I took my time to allow her to make her way to the council building. As my feet scuffed along the path, I heard angry whispers and glanced up to find their source. A council member was leaning toward a dark figure, wearing a harsh expression and pointing out fingers on his other hand. *Counting reasons for his argument?*

He turned his head as if scanning for an audience. He found one—me. As his eyes hit mine, I had the feeling I was intruding and that I should look away, but something kept me staring.

It was him again: Chevelle Vattier. I swallowed hard and forced myself to continue walking, determined not to trip. As the path wound closer to them, I became excruciatingly aware that it was going to split, heading either to the gate or to the library. I still hadn't decided how to make my escape when Chevelle turned back toward the councilman and spoke something low, cutting the conversation off. The councilman shot me a quick look before storming off.

Chevelle remained standing where he was, his back to me. I had to make a decision. I could walk within feet of him to continue to the library to research him, or I could run home and hide, coward that I was. My stomach tightened. It was ridiculous. I kept walking.

He turned to me, scarcely a few feet away. "Good morning." He nodded as he spoke, his voice as smooth as velvet.

My body seemed to angle itself toward him of its own accord. I mentally cursed, but I could recover—I would just keep going in the same direction, as if I was on my way to the village center, because I *was* on my way to the village center. There was no need for him to know it was to research someone associated with the Council, someone like him.

I tried to respond to his greeting but felt choked and instead only nodded, my jaw clenched. I kept on the path, not daring to look back in case he was behind me. I was convinced he was. He wouldn't have been taking the back way to Junnie's, and he wouldn't have been leaving the village without a pack—he was likely going to a council meeting. He was certainly right behind me, following me into town.

Somehow, I made it to the library without tripping or looking back, though I was nearly overcome with the temptation to turn at the door so I could see him one more time. I didn't know what was happening, only that it was far past time to pull myself together.

The library steps curled around the interior of the tree, shelves cut into every space above and below, and tables, racks, and patrons were scattered about the remaining areas. I found a dark, empty corner on the third level and relaxed onto a seat, leaning against the inside wall of the old tree and taking in the scent of ancient paper and binding materials.

After a momentary pause to blot out my latest incidence of poor self-control, I decided to attempt to locate the missing pages by magic. I had, after all, succeeded in growing only days ago. I concentrated as hard as I could, and though nothing flitted out of the shelves and onto my desk, I had a strong feeling I knew where the documents were, mostly because I knew the approximate area from where they had fallen the day before. I made my way over then took a few volumes and scrolls back to my secluded table. I was able to find several documents on the northern clans and even one of the missing pages of names—L.

I had spread them out on the table and was studiously examining them when a shadow crossed my desk. I realized someone was standing there and distractedly glanced up to see who.

My instinct to breathe deserted me.

It was Chevelle Vattier.

2

Chevelle stood there, staring down at me as I leaned halfway across the table of documents concerning the northern clans to conceal that I was researching him. I tried not to betray myself by glancing at the papers, but the only other place to look was at him.

He didn't look away. I had no way of knowing if he'd seen the documents before I realized he was there, and I stared at him, frozen for what seemed like an eternity. I was unable to decipher his expression or guess how I should explain having the documents. Words abandoned me when I opened my mouth to speak.

He finally broke the silence. "Freya."

He'd used one of Junnie's pet names for me. I couldn't believe how much I liked that.

He reached out his hand. "I am Chevelle Vattier."

I nodded a slow, stuttering nod.

He wasn't smiling. His face was unreadable. "I am an old friend of Junnie. I saw her at Council this morning. She was disappointed that she has been too occupied by clan business of late to guide you. I offered to help her—to help you."

The stranger I had been obsessed with was going to help me with my studies. I melted, sliding down into my chair. He was still holding his hand out to me. My back pressed against the wall, and as he took a step forward, I became wholly aware of how small and isolated the library space I had chosen was.

He turned his outstretched hand palm up, indicating the stool beside me, as if that had been his intention all along. "May I?"

I nodded once, and he slid onto the stool, facing me, not the table spread with documents.

I still had not spoken.

His dark eyes moved to the pendant against my chest then quickly back to my face, as if he had committed an indiscretion.

We sat there for a few more moments, but my words would not return, not with the imposing stranger inches before me.

When he finally spoke again, I realized his offer of help wasn't a request. "Let's begin with histories." He flicked the middle finger of his left hand, and a thick ivory tome flew from a shelf, opened, and floated steadily between us, as if on a table. There was something so wrong about it, but I couldn't say why.

I pushed away the urge to question an associate of Council, instead asking, "Chevelle?"

He smiled. It was only one word, but he understood. I was asking if I could address him in the common parlance, not the official titles and formalities of Council that he might have been used to. He tilted his head in a nod.

We sat tucked in the narrow space behind a small library table for hours. He pulled books between us and returned them to the shelves, never once glancing at the papers referencing the northern clans, spread out beside us. Nothing we studied touched on the histories of those clans—there was nothing of his histories, nothing of mine. But conversation had become easy as soon as I had spoken that first word, as soon as I had said his name and he'd smiled in return.

I found myself leaning toward him as he spoke, actually paying attention at times, for he had a pleasant voice and an unusual dialect. He wove histories as if they were stories of his childhood friends instead of useless facts, and I became enthralled. It felt as if we were alone there in the quiet corner of the third level, the occasional murmur below and whisper of flipping pages the only other sound in the dim setting. A small knothole made a window in the wall across from me, and some light from the cloudy day occasionally came through, putting Chevelle's face in shade. I had been right— his eyes appeared nearly black in the shadows.

I leaned forward, listening to him as a small gray bird landed on the lip of the knothole and chirped once. Not many animals feared the elves. It seemed curious about what we were doing.

It chirped twice, and I winced at the annoying cheeping, working to focus on Chevelle's story.

Then it chirped three more times. I gritted my teeth, but I could not block out the irritating sound. It broke into a melody that pierced my ears, and I barely restrained a growl of frustration as I cursed the devilish thing. That was when I heard the hollow thud of its body smacking the floor.

I jerked upright. My ears were still ringing from the harsh song, but the bird lay dead on the wooden planks below the window. Chevelle started to turn to find the source of the muffled thump, and before I realized what I was doing, I flicked my right hand, and the bird's body flopped behind a shelf and out of sight. When Chevelle turned back to me, I stared right into his eyes, as if I had not seen or heard a thing, wondering why he wasn't still explaining the histories of Grah. He glanced past me... or maybe at the crown of my head, as if he was avoiding my eyes. *My lying eyes.*

I was too worried about being caught to feel guilty about the bird, to think about its soft gray feathers or the wing that was bent awkwardly beneath it. I didn't know about where Chevelle was from, but in the village, one didn't just kill birds, especially not for singing.

After a moment, my tutor continued the lesson, but his demeanor had changed. He watched the book, and occasion-ally his gaze wandered from my face, back up and out of focus just above me. But he did not look directly into my eyes as he had before. It bothered me, and I didn't think it was because of my conscience.

When he reached the end of the book, it returned to its home on the shelf, and he stood, placing a hand briefly on the top of my head. It was only a momentary touch, but elec-tricity surged though me. A flash of confusion or frustration passed over his features too quickly to identify. He looked into my eyes one last time as I sat stunned and speechless, my skin still tingling from the contact.

"Enough for today," he said, nodding as he turned, his long strides taking him from my view.

I sat motionless as I watched him go and remained so for some time. I hadn't realized how exhausted I'd been.

When I finally rose to leave, I stashed a few more of the northern-clan documents under my shirt. My head was swirling with all that had happened—not simply my new tutor, but the magic. On my way out, I walked past the shelf that hid the body of the dead bird. I'd never been able to move objects, but it seemed that I had done it without thinking. It wasn't just that, but the weeds and thorns in the old garden bothered me too. I needed to see Junnie.

The door was partially open when I reached her house, so I peeked my head in and called for her. When she didn't answer, I slipped in to check the back room.

As I walked through the sparsely decorated living area, I passed a carved mirror on the wall and noticed something off in my reflection. I knew I was flushed—I could feel the frustration and worry—so I stopped to get a closer look. There *was* something not right with my complexion, but what was really off was just above my face. I squinted, leaning toward the mirror as my hands reached up seemingly of their own accord.

The first quarter inch of my hair was blackened. I parted my hair in a different area and then again, but the roots of my hair were dark over my entire scalp. My fingers began to tremble against my skin. I could come up with no plausible explanation for the change. "Junnie," I called again.

She didn't answer. The study was empty. I let out a shaky breath and glanced around. Nothing was out of place except for a thistle on the table. It was thriving but unplanted. I examined it closer. It was rather large, and though the blooms looked healthy, the exposed roots were black, seemingly rotted. I didn't understand how a plant could survive without soil and with such decay. I scanned the table, but it was the only plant there, aside from Junnie's potted ivies and flowers, which hung as they always had.

At my touch, the thistle leaves crumbled, my skin tingling

with the unfamiliar feel of my own magic. I watched its ashes fall, landing on scattered seeds and bulbs, and realized in horror what it meant. It was the thistle I had grown. *The garden*.

I rushed out, leaving the door open as I had found it. I hurried from the village, almost running under the cloudy skies, trying to remember where the abandoned garden was located. It wasn't hard to find because of its new size, but if I hadn't been half expecting and half fearing the excessive growth, I might not have recognized it. Each strain I had attempted to grow was flourishing. Noxious weeds were taking over the meadow.

I stood there, overwhelmed, frozen before the changed garden. I had to press my eyes closed to *not* see. Light rain began to fall as I raised my head to the sky, drawing in a deep breath. The cool water trickled down my face, calming the heat of my pulse, but it didn't clear my head. I still couldn't understand.

A painful fear shot through me at the thought of the destroyed thistle on Junnie's worktable, and I tilted my head forward to run through the growth. Vines, thorns, and leaves turned to muddy ash as they touched my outstretched arms, wet with rain. When I reached the edge of the garden, I stopped to kneel, digging my fingers deeply into the soil to form a trench. When I saw the bare roots, black and rotted, I was suddenly exhausted. It was too much.

It took me to a familiar, mindless place, and I turned to walk home, void of any sensation save the slow rain on my skin.

When I entered the house, Francine was there, but I trudged past her on the way to my room. I barely took notice of her expression and the suspicion in her eyes as she took in my mud-streaked clothes and dripping hair. I didn't speak—I was spent, and I just couldn't make myself care. In the darkness of my room, I collapsed onto the bed. I didn't bother lighting a flame. I wanted to be alone, and in the dark, I felt more so. I closed my eyes, dropping asleep to the thrum of falling rain.

I AWOKE gasping from another dream of my mother and destruction. The rain had stopped, and the sun was rising, so I wiped the sweat from my brow and went to the hall pitcher to splash my face. The dark roots of my hair were stark in the mirror's reflection, and I recalled the dream. The memories of my mother were fuzzy, but I'd always thought she'd had light hair, beautiful and golden like Junnie's. In the dream, though, it was as black as the roots of my hair had become.

I stood there for a long moment, staring at the darkness, then spun as I made another stupid, rash decision. Slinking past Fannie's room, I headed for her makeshift vault. She kept all the things I wasn't allowed to touch in that room, which was supposed to be off-limits, not that I'd bothered to explore it before. There was a large flat stone, covering where it hid in the floor, which I'd never been able to move. But that was before.

I wasn't sure how the magic had worked with the bird, but I knew it had, so I dropped to my knees, held my hands above the stone, and closed my eyes, concentrating with everything I had. Nothing happened right away, and my mind wandered a bit with thoughts of what might be inside and how I wanted to see and needed to touch my family heirlooms, the things that had belonged to my mother.

The stone lid scraped across the floor as it shifted. It didn't go far, but I didn't need it to move much. I reached down and drew out a small leather pouch, its bronzed decorations weathered and worn. I laid it aside, reaching back in. My fingers closed around a tube, probably a scroll case. I started to take it out when I heard a wheezing growl behind me. I froze.

The stream of profanities that followed was long and harsh, and part of it sounded as though it was in another tongue. I released the tube and turned slowly toward Fannie, who was red-faced and shaking. She stepped toward me, and I slid the pouch that lay against my leg behind my sash. She didn't seem to notice.

The blow was quick, and I hadn't seen it coming. My head turned with the contact, whipping back toward her before I had a chance to rein in my shock and anger. Fannie's eyes lit with anticipation, as if she wanted me to fight back.

I had never even talked back to Fannie. I didn't have the size to fight her, let alone the magic, and she was conniving. When I'd first come to live with her, she had sent me to Council repeatedly, complaining of my behavior. I had undergone hours of evaluations under the scrutiny of council members, exams and trials, endless questions, and black blots on parchment that made abstract shapes. "What do you see, Elfreda?"

I'd known what they'd wanted to hear, something about butterfly and flower species. But I was so resentful to Fannie for putting me there that I usually saw a black blob of death consuming her. "A Monarch," I would say instead.

She looked beyond me at the few inches of open floor, and I took the opportunity to bolt past her and down the hall, straight out the door at full speed. I ran from the house, ignoring the paths—other elves would be no help to me. I kept running until I was certain she wasn't coming, and then I collapsed at the edge of a meadow, breathless. I dropped my face into my hands and might have wept if I hadn't been so fueled by fear and adrenaline.

"Freya?" a soft voice asked.

I looked up, startled.

Chevelle stood just in front of me. He dropped to his knees and reached out to touch the mark across my cheek left from the slap. Shame flooded me, and I turned my head to hide the evidence, but he cradled the side of my face.

3

"Freya," he repeated in a softer voice as he lifted my chin. He appeared concerned as he glanced from the welt to my eyes, and I struggled to keep the tears that were welling from falling. I'd not had a caring touch from anyone for so long that I didn't know how to react. And I was ashamed. Fannie had authority over me, but I wasn't a child. It was only that I had nowhere else to go. I couldn't leave.

"You'll need to learn protection spells."

"I-I can't..."

"We won't tell Francine or the Council," he promised, and I didn't miss the way he said her name. "We won't even tell Junnie," he added softly.

I didn't understand. Cold moisture from the ground seeped through the material covering my legs, and I shifted, fidgeting as I looked up at him. "I mean I can't do magic. Just useless stuff like lighting candles—"

"Then we'll start with fire." Chevelle lowered his hand to mine and stood, pulling me up and toward the center of the clearing.

Once we'd distanced ourselves from the tree line, he stopped and turned back to me, still holding my right hand. My eyes followed his as he looked down at our clasped hands. A cool blue flame lit on my right sleeve.

Immediately, I jerked my free hand up to extinguish it, but Chevelle took it and stopped me from smacking at the flame, which had already disappeared. "No," he said. "Use the magic. Feel it."

I nodded, and he returned his gaze to our hands. He couldn't have been much older than I, but his hands dwarfed mine, and it made me feel suddenly and fleetingly like a child again.

A spark lit at the hem of my left sleeve and slowly worked its way up my arm. I wanted it off of me, needed to put it out. When I concentrated on that, the flame flickered. It flared again, and Chevelle squeezed my hands. *I have to be able to do this.* I focused hard on the base of the flame as it wavered then fell back toward the hem, where it finally choked off. I glanced up at Chevelle. He looked pleased.

"Again," he said as he stepped back and released my hands.

The meadow seemed to open as a circle of fire grew in front of me. I tried to see past it, through the flames to Chevelle, and then it was gone. He moved farther back, raising his right hand so a stream of fire followed it, arcing in my direction. I was afraid I wouldn't be able to extinguish it before it hit me. My feet were frozen in place. I could only think of one thing: *fight fire with fire.* I flung my arm toward the incoming stream of flames, and a tongue of fire akin to a dragon's shot out and collided with it.

I was shocked. I'd only used my power to light candles

and lanterns. I'd had no idea I could produce such a vicious plume of flames. I looked at Chevelle.

"Yes," he said, exalted. He raised his arms above his head to construct a massive circle of blazing heat. When his eyes returned to mine, he smiled. He liked playing with fire. Then he shoved the fireball toward me with frightening speed.

I threw both hands in front of me, palms forward, and forced out the largest mass I could in response. Chevelle flicked his wrist, and the flame dodged up and angled back toward me. I shook my hands frantically, spitting sharp bullets of heat at it, hoping to break it up. But he pulled his hands apart, and the thing split, each side curving toward me. There were suddenly two, and they were closing in fast.

I leapt forward just as they collided where I'd been standing, and I lost my footing while I watched the fireworks behind me. Spinning into a tumble to keep from landing flat on my face, I rolled to my feet, thrilled from the fire play and from the magic. I let out a breathless laugh, and Chevelle joined in, though in all fairness, he might merely have been amused by my fall.

We spent the next several hours there in the meadow, sculpting my craft. The exercises grew increasingly more difficult, but it seemed Chevelle was only toying with me. He must have had experience with fire magic, because the flames he produced behaved like an obedient dog. Mine, on the other hand, were about as compliant as a wet cat.

Exhausted by the day's work, I began to sway a bit. Chevelle led me to the base of an old willow tree, and I slumped against the trunk, sliding down to lie on my back. Chevelle reclined against the tree, his legs coming to rest just above my head in the soft grass.

I gazed through the immense mass of leaves and branches overhead and breathed deeply. I felt the need to explain the welt, and my eyes rose toward him as I lightly touched my cheek. "I was searching for my mother's things…"

He stared straight out into the meadow, not responding, so I returned to watching the canopy of leaves.

"I can't remember her," I said. I hadn't discussed it with anyone before, but once I started talking, I couldn't seem to stop. Without his response, I kept on, explaining my dreams —purposefully leaving out the part I had read about the northern clans—and closed my eyes in an attempt to see them more clearly. I was recalling the details of her dark hair blowing in the wind and the feeling of being trapped when my thoughts faded into the blackness of sleep.

I AWOKE in my own bed, the room dimly lit by a single flame suspended above my table. A flash of embarrassment hit as it dawned on me that Chevelle must have placed me there—he must have seen where I lived, my room. And then I smiled because he had left me a flame.

I stretched my entire body, rejuvenated from the rest. I was unsure how long I'd slept, but it looked like the sun was rising again, and I wanted to be out of the house before I ran into Fannie.

It was probably too early to hope to see Chevelle. I'd spent the last two days with him, but he hadn't revealed anything of himself, and that only made me more curious. I retrieved the documents I'd hidden after my day with him at the library to find out whether they added anything to the report from the council scribe. There wasn't much new there, mostly more names, but I did notice a watermark on one of the pages. I held it up to the light to see better. There was a council marking and something else.

I dug out the first pages from under my mattress and examined them. The pages directly from the record-keeper's report all included the same council mark plus a string of characters. I tried to decode them and realized that one of the symbols was likely a page number, and the others were probably locators. I felt like a fool. They were just like the codes used in the library, only more elaborate. No one really used the ciphers—they weren't needed with magic, but they had been added to many of the pages when the fey had started tracking clan histories.

I was holding in my hand the information I needed to find the northern clans in the council's library. My stomach tightened, but I found myself getting up and heading toward the village, regardless of the consequences.

I argued with the impulsive part of myself the entire way to town. *I shouldn't do it. I couldn't. But I am. I am going to do it. And if I get caught, I can claim ignorance. The entire clan thinks I'm an imbecile, in any case. Maybe I'll just see how close I can get. Maybe I'll just try...*

And then I was there, standing in front of the council building then walking in. My attempt at stealth was poorly executed, but no one ever seemed to pay much attention to me, anyway. I casually leaned around a doorway to see into the next room, where a small group of villagers stood, blocking my way. They spoke in low voices, and as I tried to figure a way past, something seized my attention.

"Evelyn has been a model citizen... doesn't seem right..."

My nerves twitched as the worry caused by her supposed accusation returned. I remembered the risk I'd put myself in to go there. I strained to listen but could only pick out parts of the conversation.

"Well on her way to becoming a council member... if anyone should leave..."

"Yes, but who can trust him..."

"Why can't we simply banish... who knows if the spells will even hold... dark magic can't be trusted..."

I struggled to hear them, irritated that they were talking so quietly, and the harder I listened, the more I perceived a dull, buzzing hum. My ears popped. And then, at once, the group began to scratch at themselves feverishly, clawing at forearms, abdomens, and necks. Each wore an uncomfortable, even frightened expression as they hurried out of the room and into an inner council chamber.

It was more than a little strange, and I glanced after them as I made my way through the newly vacant room, but I was distracted by the sight of the library door.

I had no way of knowing if there was a protection spell on the entryway. When I walked through, there were no obvious repercussions, and I assumed that, with so many council members around, they must have thought it unnecessary.

The council library was overwhelming. It housed copies of all the books in the village library as well as hundreds more that were too delicate or important for public use. And according to my aunt Francine's theories, they held secret documents containing things they didn't want commonly known there as well.

The walls were stark white like carved marble, and the room felt cold and empty despite the abundance inside. I found a shelf to hide behind and placed my pilfered documents on the floor. I examined the shelves in front of me, looking for a match to the symbols, and found the sections to be arranged by groups, with each shelf divided into categories. I walked the library in search of the section for either of the characters listed in my documents and was about to give up when I noticed some encased racks in the center of the room. I checked the small section. The symbols fit.

I smiled, thinking it had been easy as I slid my fingertips across the volumes on that shelf. My fingers tingled as they crossed a thin section of pages bound together. I slid them out just as I became aware of some sort of commotion that sounded like it was getting closer.

The tingle hadn't indicated that I'd found what I was looking for. It was a protection spell. I ran.

As I shot through the rooms, all I could think of was not getting caught. I shoved the pages under my shirt before I made it through the last door. The village was crowded with elves oblivious to my horror. The protection spell must have alerted only Council. I ran from town and pushed through the brush at the edge of the village, taking the shortest direction out of the boundaries. I kept running until I became winded then hastily searched for some kind of shelter. Burrowing deep in a briar patch, struggling to catch my breath, I wrenched the wad of papers from under my shirt, buried them in the soil beside me, then waited for my punishment to come.

But no one was coming. I was naïve to think they would chase me like hounds on a fox. They had magic—they were High Council.

I stayed in the patch of briars for most of the day,

cowering despite myself, but as the sun lowered in the sky, I crawled out on my belly to start the long walk home.

It was late by the time I reached the tree, and I was tired enough that I didn't care as much about being caught. I didn't even know if they knew who broke the seal, if they knew I was the guilty party. But I was still quiet as I entered the house then my room and slid into bed.

THE NEXT MORNING, I slipped out early to call on Junnie. When I reached her door, it was cracked open again. I pushed it aside and scanned the front room, to no avail. I walked through to check the back, but still found nothing. Junnie was exceedingly clean and organized, so I couldn't tell if she'd even been home. I wandered to the front door and was surprised by a tall figure there. The elaborate robe and tassels of a decorated council member blocked my way, and the fear returned.

"Elfreda."

I cautiously dipped my head in respect.

"Juniper Fountain has received the calling."

I stared at him in disbelief. "What?" But then I shook off the question, because I had heard clearly enough. The more important question was, "When?"

He grimaced at my disrespectful manner. "Not long."

Not long? Not long ago? Not long from now? I felt sick. I knew I was testing his patience, but I had to keep pushing. "Where?"

His mouth tightened. "That is council business, Elfreda. That is Juniper Fountain's path, not your own." He stepped aside and rolled his hand to encourage me out. "Make your way."

I pushed past him feverishly, starting for town. But I quickly recalled the incident at the library and turned, heading home. I remembered my run-in with Fannie over the vault and realized I had nowhere to go. A pain throbbed deep in my chest. An instinct pushed at me, and I ran for the clearing where I'd learned magic with Chevelle.

He was there, waiting for me. The pain in my chest dulled a little, or maybe it was overwhelmed by a new pressure. I crossed to him slowly. Junnie was all I'd had since I'd arrived, and she was gone. For a hundred years, she would be gone. I wanted nothing more of Fannie, nothing more of any of it. I didn't know what I would do, but by the time I reached Chevelle, I knew that I wanted to retrieve my mother's things from the vault and leave that wretched place behind.

I made my stance more formal to match his. "I want to learn transfer magic."

His mouth tightened, and he turned his head in a half shake.

"You taught me fire," I argued.

"For protection, Freya."

"Please," I begged.

He hesitated.

I didn't know how to convince him. *Is it too soon for me to learn? There's an order to the spells, and one must earn the knowledge. If I go too fast or out of sequence, I could endanger myself.*

"There is no hurry," he said, clearly trying to persuade me.

"There is," I insisted. "I am running." I didn't know why I chose that word. I wasn't bound to the place. "Leaving" would have sufficed, but it felt like running, like escape. I knew I was trapped. Someone would stop me. *Yes, I'm running.*

My head swung to locate a noise at the edge of the clearing behind me and I saw long robes... two council members. My throat went dry, and Chevelle grabbed my shoulders as he said in a low voice, "Home, Freya. Run."

I didn't hesitate. I sprinted straight home without looking back.

The house seemed empty, but I didn't check. With my heart pounding, I went directly to my room and closed the door behind me. The single flame still flickered above my bedside table, and as I walked closer, I noticed a package on my bed. I spun my hand and lit the room to better see. It was a wide ivory box tied with tweed. There was a small note under the knot.

Dearest Elfreda,

I must away without saying goodbye. I am sure you cannot understand, but please trust in me. Don this immediately. —J.

I tugged at the tie, and the string fell away. I sucked in air as I opened the lid. It seemed that I couldn't quite catch my breath anymore. Reaching inside to draw out the long white gown, I could not fathom Junnie's reasoning—she must have gone through much to get me the package. Numbly, I stared at her words while I unfastened my shirt and sash. The pouch I had rescued from the vault fell to the bed. *How had I forgotten that?* I kicked off my shoes and pulled my top and pants off before sliding the gown over my head, straightening the length with my hands. The corset laced tightly at my waist, and the plunging neckline was lower than anything I would ever wear.

I retrieved the leather pouch from the bed to examine the contents, but before I loosened the binding, I heard a crash behind me. Three council guards had busted open my door. I tucked the pouch under the long bell sleeve of the dress as they crossed the room to seize me by the arms.

4

In the center of the council chamber, I waited for my trial, listening as they called my full name. I had always hated it—to be named for the ancient word for "elf" was bad enough, but the flowery string of words that followed just made me cringe. I had never known my father, but given that they were traditionally responsible for choosing the names of their firstborn, I blamed him for it.

"Elfreda Georgiana Suzetta Glaforia stands before High Council..." The formal tone of the speaker severed my rambling thoughts, dragging me back to a frightening reality. *What will they do to me? How bad could the punishment be for sneaking into a library and stealing a book?* Maybe it wasn't even about that. Maybe Fannie had told them I broke into the vault. But they were my family's things too, so it couldn't be that bad.

She could lie.

I swallowed hard. Maybe it was about something else entirely. Maybe a dead bird.

A guard approached me. I had been drifting again, lost in

thought. *What had they said?* The council leaders were focused on the pendant at my chest, where it lay exposed against my skin in the V of the low-cut gown. They had ordered the guard to remove it. I didn't understand why they would want my mother's pendant, but I knew better than to ask. I knew what would happen if I spoke before being instructed.

The guard stood facing me, both hands poised to take the leather chain over my head as I stared on insensibly. His touch lingered, and I glanced down, surprised to see that he had a firm grip on the necklace but wasn't lifting it—*couldn't* lift it. I looked to the council leaders as the guard turned toward the table and decisively stepped away from me.

"The crystal will not be removed," he said. Though he spoke only to the elders, it set into motion a wave of murmurs that filled the room, reverberating up the high ceiling.

A council elder silenced the witnesses then trained his gaze on me. "Who instructed you in fusion?"

I didn't have an answer. I'd never heard of fusion. I wasn't sure what to do, and I looked out of desperation toward the only person in the room who'd ever helped me. Chevelle was watching me, surprise clear on his face. Whatever I'd been accused of, he hadn't expected it.

The council elders mistook the exchange as an answer. "Chevelle Vattier, you have led this fusion?"

His head whipped back toward the council table, and he shot out a forceful "No."

They focused once more on me. "I ask again, Elfreda. Who taught you the magic to seal yourself to the crystal?"

I was at a loss. I stood helplessly as Chevelle spoke up. "Elfreda." He'd used my given name, I hoped simply because we were in a formal setting and not because of whatever horrible thing I had been accused of. "Where did you learn how to fuse the pendant with your blood?" he pleaded.

Fuse the pendant with my blood? What is he talking about? I heard someone behind me: "How did she know to keep it from being removed?" And someone else: "Who even left it with her?"

It came together then, the feeling I'd had when I'd awakened and placed it around my neck, the part of the dream I'd shaken off as I stood before the basin washing up, cleaning the blood from my hands and from the pendant. I wanted to explain, to tell them what I'd seen in the dream, but it was foggy and half-remembered. I was too slow to pull it into thought.

I was too late. They had already passed judgment—harsh judgment—on me. The deep voice boomed with finality: "... convicted of practicing dark magic..."

The elder's staff slammed against its wooden base, echoing into the tumult of discord rising behind me. I reached out my hand to plead for mercy, to beg to be given a chance to explain, and he began to list my lineage for the records. I was flooded with fury at the injustice as I heard my mother's name. My outstretched hand became a fist.

The speaker's voice cut off. He grabbed his throat as the other council leaders rushed to him. His choking face stared directly at me, unquestionably an accusation, and I realized with a start that he was right. I was cutting off his windpipe as if it were there in my outstretched fist. I released my grip.

He was surrounded, and the room was filled with a roar of commotion and terror. My ears rang sharply. I had to look away from it all. When I turned, I caught my reflection in one of the larger mirrors, but it wasn't me. *No, it must be me, but I'm unrecognizable.*

Not unrecognizable, another voice inside me whispered. My hair was dark and windblown. The bell sleeve of the long white gown hung from my outstretched arm. It was the dream in the flesh. The pendant against my chest seemed to glow at my revelation.

I ran.

As I RACED from the chamber, I couldn't tell if anyone had even noticed. They all appeared to be staring at the speaker, but regardless, I concentrated furiously on not being followed. *Do not catch me. Do not find me. Let me go.* I was almost chanting in my thoughts. As I raced out the building and out of the village, running as fast as I could, I kept thinking it over and over and over. I didn't know where I would go. I just wanted away.

I found myself heading in the same direction I had the day before, but hiding in a briar patch wasn't going to work again—they would come for me. As I frantically tried to decide where to go, my previous conclusion snaked through my mind. They would find me if they wanted to. There was no stopping them. I had no magic, no tracking skills, and no clue.

I stopped running. My heart pounded, and the wind cut against the damp sweat on my skin. I wanted to understand what had just happened, but I couldn't process it. It was too painful. I was confused, drained to the point of exhaustion. I had no way out. When they found me, I would have to surrender. I could see no other option.

But no one came.

I wasn't foolish enough to go back voluntarily, but for some reason, they hadn't followed. I didn't know what to do with myself. I had nothing outside of home, outside of the village. I didn't know where I was or where to go. It was just another clearing outside of the only town I'd ever known, or at least the only town I remembered knowing.

I wandered toward the briar patch, finding it easily. It wasn't far, and despite my exhaustion, I crawled through the narrow path I'd made the previous time. It hadn't seemed such a tight fit in only pants. I settled in, jerking a length of skirt free from the thorns with a spray of colorless beads.

Brushing the loose dirt off the papers I had buried, I lay the soiled documents across my lap and untied the laces binding them together. I stared at the words on the ancient parchment, unable to believe that what I was reading was true. It had to be—it was signed with the official seal. The documents stared back at me from the smudged white fabric of my skirt, the letters on the page as real and words as patent as they could be.

They held the details of the trial and the punishment of Francine Katteryn Glaforia, who had been found guilty of practicing dark magic.

Her sentence included some sort of service to Council and a spell binding her from using any magic except practical magic. I was dumbfounded. It had never crossed my mind before, but as I considered it, searching for proof the documents were wrong, I realized my aunt had never used magic for anything but service. It hadn't seemed unusual to me because it was just the way it had always been. And besides, I could barely do anything aside from lighting candles.

Was this why Council was so quick to accuse me of practicing dark magic? It was rarely discussed and never tolerated. *What had Fannie done?*

I flipped through more pages, realizing something was

out of place. It didn't make sense that official documents about Fannie would be among those relating to the apparent extinction of the northern clans, and I couldn't figure out why all the documents I'd found about the tragedy were separated, mixed up, and missing pages. I tried to sort it out but found there were other council documents there too.

I kept reading, quickly scanning for something of interest. My eyes caught on his name a second before my mind recognized it: Chevelle Vattier. As I backed up to read, my shock turned to fury before I could even finish the page.

Chevelle Vattier had been a volunteer watcher, a council spy. He had volunteered to watch *me*.

Swift, white-hot anger flooded through me, and the pages I held burst into flames. The brush around me caught next, burning away as I stood to push free of the blazing patch of briars. *They had set a watcher on me. Why? Because Fannie had practiced dark magic? Were they afraid she'd teach me? I'll show them dark magic. I'll learn and go back... But how? How can I learn without a teacher?*

Chevelle.

The fire died as I thought of the concern he'd shown me in the clearing and the tender moment we'd shared. With one word, the flames caught again, burning with a vengeance through the field.

None of it had been real. He was a watcher. He'd volunteered to monitor me and to keep me in line.

So I decided to teach myself, to take the risk and learn the magic without guidance. I had nothing else to lose. I formed a plan: I would practice until I was strong enough to return to the village. There was nothing holding me back, nothing to do but that one thing.

I spotted a small toad as it leapt across the clearing in a

desperate attempt to escape the inferno. I concentrated on it, willing it to change. Its wide body started to swell, its sides bubbling out and puffing it into a tiny green balloon. It did not transform into that monarch butterfly I had imagined. It burst, spewing entrails across the hem of my dress.

My head fell into my hands as I groaned.

It took a while, but the anger eventually faded to a point where I realized I would need a new plan. I couldn't help but regret that the flames had consumed the documents that had caused everything in the first place. I should have fully read them first.

My heart tripped at the sound of cracking timber beneath boots across the clearing. The fire had burned out, but the ashes were plenty evidence that I'd been there. I ducked under the cover of a large spruce and watched. Chevelle walked through the tree line, and my jaw clenched tightly against a silent curse.

He was alone, carrying nothing but a small pack and wearing the same dark clothes and tall boots he'd had on during the trial. He kept walking as he looked in my direction, surveying the damage from the fire. I was convinced he would know it had been me, but he didn't stop or even slow. It made no sense why he hadn't investigated further. *Is he not here looking for me?*

He was my watcher, and I was missing. *So where else would he be going?*

Before I had torched the documents, I had seen Junnie noted as his contact. My pulse sped at the idea that he might be going to her, to get her help in finding me. If he was my watcher, I was his responsibility, and she was the only one who knew me at all, aside from Fannie.

He had gone a good fifty yards farther as I considered.

My feet were moving before I actually decided to follow him. My determination faltered. *How far should I go? What if he isn't even going to find Junnie?* And then I thought, *What else do you have to do, sit here and blow up frogs?* It was all the convincing I needed. Slinking out from the branches of the spruce, I crept along the trees and brush as I followed my watcher north.

5

Chevelle kept a quick pace, and I found myself struggling to keep up. Unlike me, he wasn't dodging between rocks and trees, bending out of sight, and watching the ground to keep from breaking twigs while he tried to keep from being spotted. I cursed the formal dress I'd been dragging as it snagged on a low-lying thicket, flinging another string of beads into the soft dirt. I considered dumping it, but didn't think it was the best idea to be sneaking around the forest unclothed. After crossing a few soggy patches of moss, the hem was damp and darkened. I might have ripped some of the excess material off, but Chevelle's quick movement wasn't leaving me time for that.

Finally, just before nightfall, he approached a small village, which didn't look like more than half a dozen structures scattered against the base of a large hill. He dropped his simple pack beside a tree and hunched down as he slowed his pace. His stance mirrored mine and gave me pause. He was sneaking into the village.

I watched as he crept around the back of a small hut,

knowing that if he was hiding, I definitely didn't want to get caught. He leapt into a rear window, and I followed as slowly and low to the ground as I could. When I reached the last tree I could use for cover, I darted up against the hut and peered through a gap in the twigs that patched it together. There was whispering.

"... mustn't let them find you... shouldn't have come..."

It was dim inside, but I caught a glimpse of a figure through the wall. *Junnie.*

Chevelle was whispering his reply to her, and though I couldn't quite hear, he must have given her a short account of the morning's events. I moved closer to the window, finding a larger gap there.

"Were you able to track her?" Junnie asked in a low voice.

"Not exactly. She's following me."

Heat flooded my face. I couldn't believe he'd fooled me again. I'd been trekking over rocks and through bramble half the day, he'd known all along, and Junnie knew everything.

I didn't care what else they had to say. I stood and marched away, fuming at the idea that both of them were in on it. They might have been council members, but it didn't stop the feeling of betrayal. They'd lied to me, acting as if they'd cared. I was done with them and with everyone. I wanted to get as far as possible from all of it.

But I didn't make it very far. Exhaustion caught up with me a few miles later, and I found an old oak tree then slid down its massive trunk to rest my aching legs. I'd never run so far in my life, and my head throbbed. I was seething with anger and frustration and the feeling of being ensnared. I didn't sleep. I just sat against the tree like a petulant child. I held a hand up and flipped a flame, tossing it up and down, rolling it above my palm. I was hungry, but I didn't eat. I was too stubborn and angry to go find food, too resentful I didn't have the magic to bring it to me. Yes, I was acting like a foolish, sulky child.

BRIGHT SUN and chirping birds tore into my still senses. I opened my eyes then squinted, resisting the urge to stop the birds. It was the first time I'd slept away from my bed, and disoriented, I glanced around. It didn't help. I'd never been far from home, and the new landscape was unsettling. When I looked away, I noticed a neatly stacked pile of fabric and a loaf of bread positioned beside me. I silently cursed the watchers who had apparently found me during the night.

I didn't see them anywhere, so I assumed they'd left me out there as punishment. Some part of me wanted to burn the pile for spite, but my stomach overruled the thought. Reaching out to grab the bread and then, since I had already defied my would-be belligerence, the stack of clothes, I stood to find a creek to clean up in, happy that I could finally get out of the ridiculous dress.

It took a moment to locate the trickle of water, but there was a creek only a short distance away. I walked down the softened earth to where the water had pooled then knelt, leaning over to splash my face.

Panic shot through me as someone stared back at me. I nearly bolted upright, planning to flee, but caught myself. The woman in the reflection was me. That was my dark hair and flushed skin. Cautiously leaning over the pool once more, I convinced myself it was only the dark water, a trick of light and shadow. My eyes were not that green, my hair not that dark. I straightened and held a lock of it forward to examine. It shimmered glossy black in the bright sunlight. My hand fell away.

Maybe I could just wash it out. Nauseous, I stepped into the pool, sinking beneath its surface. A thought that was darker than the rest said that maybe I should stay under, but the pressure to draw air stung my lungs. I could not drown the desire to breathe.

I pushed through the water, gasping and cold, struggling to climb from the muck as I stood and walked out. I was drenched, the material of the long gown soaked and heavy and more uncomfortable than ever. I loosened the wet corset ties and dropped the dress into a pile at my feet, shivering as I stepped free of it and onto a rock. I grabbed a shirt from the pile then the slim pants, aware of how nice the fabric felt and how good the cut was. A leather vest laced over the top. It seemed they were tailored for me. I'd never had such luck making my own clothes, but the new outfit was trim and made for traveling, not that I knew where I was going.

My desire to trail Chevelle had been smashed, but there was no way I could return to the village. I glanced around, still finding no sign of the watchers as I slid my shoes on. I should have kept running during the night, but I'd been too exhausted.

There was a pack in the pile as well, but I didn't have anything aside from a soaking wet dress. I stretched it over a low branch to dry, and the pouch I had hidden before the trial fell free.

I sat on the rock, picking up the small, weathered bag. I'd carried it for days now and still didn't know what was inside. I pulled the binding loose to dump the contents into my hand: a dark ruby, a silver medallion, and a tiny scroll. I held the stone up to the light. Aside from the depth of color, it didn't seem extraordinary. I also examined the medallion but didn't recognize the emblems. I dropped them back into the pouch then opened the scroll, reading aloud the first line of the tiny script: *"Fellon Strago Dreg."*

Electricity shot through my hands and I dropped the scroll. My palms felt as if they had been scorched. The unmistakable stench of charred flesh turned my stomach, and I twisted my hands to inspect the damage. There were curving lines and symbols burned into the skin of my palms. I gasped. I'd been around fire magic for as long as I could remember, and it had never burnt me or any other elf, as far as I knew—it would only burn what it was meant to burn.

I glanced back down at the scroll, realizing the fire magic *had* been meant to burn. I should never have read the words aloud. I carefully picked it up and rolled it back into place, certain I would never read from it again. Binding the pouch as I had found it, I tucked it into the pack. When I checked my hands to decipher the lines, I realized I was seeing a map like the ones I'd found in the council documents burned into my palms. I couldn't fathom why anyone would have cast a ridiculous spell like that, but it struck me that it had come from the vault, from my own family's things.

I bit down hard on my lip, fighting the impulsive urge that always got me into trouble. But I didn't want to go back to the village, not ever. And I only had one chance, one small moment before they came to retrieve me.

I grabbed the dress, the last evidence of me being there, off the tree branch and threw it into the pack. Swinging it around onto my back, I started to run. I didn't know where I was or where the map would take me, but I finally had a purpose. There were mountains burned into my palms, and there was only one place to find mountains: in the North.

I couldn't remember much of my life before going to live with my aunt Fannie. The village and surrounding meadows and forests were the only home I'd had, the only place I'd known. It wasn't exactly a comforting place, but there was something to be said for knowing where you were and where to find food, shelter, and water.

I'd been filled with determination when I started running, concentrating on north and nothing else. But as I made my way, I became aware of the sheltered life I'd been living.

The land started to roll, the trees a deeper green than what I was used to, their trunks too narrow. It didn't seem as if I'd gone that far, as it had only been half a day following Chevelle and then the time on my own. The changes in the landscape made me anxious to see the North.

I glanced at my palm once more. I thought I'd figured out most of the lines—creeks curving through the landscape, mountains a jagged ridge across the top—but there were still a lot of unanswered questions. I squeezed my hand into a nervous fist but kept moving.

I tried not to think about all that had happened—not Fannie or the trial, not Junnie, and especially not Chevelle. I just kept putting one foot in front of the other. I couldn't even imagine what lay in the mountains where I was heading, but there was no going back.

I wasn't tired anymore, at least not as I had been every day since I'd been using magic. I forced those thoughts away, counting steps as I ran. I was miles from a home I might never return to.

I pushed myself forward through the day, only stopping

when I found a patch of sweet berries and a small, babbling creek. The berries were wild, small, and much less palatable without the guiding hand of an elf, but the water I gathered from the stream was cool and refreshing. As evening approached, so grew my underlying discomfort with the idea of the coming darkness. I'd spent my share of time alone at home, just not alone in the middle of a strange forest outside. I might have run through the night and slept during the day, but it made little sense to struggle through the night out of fear.

It didn't stop me from seeking out a decent shelter before nightfall, though. Slowing my pace, I gave my surroundings more attention.

The strangeness of the sparse brush was a little shocking, and I had to surrender the idea of finding a proper tree. But a half mile or so later, I came upon a suitable hollow in a low embankment guarded by the curling roots of a sycamore. It wasn't bad, but I still gathered some shrubbery to cover the entryway, the bitter stench of its sharp green leaves giving me a little more security, or at least the feeling of it. The sun hadn't set when I'd finished lining the floor with vines, but I went ahead and settled in, sitting so I could see through an opening in the frond-covered entry.

It was quiet, harder to fight the thoughts that were trying to creep in. I began to run songs through my head for distraction, mangling the lyrics and humming through the parts I couldn't remember at all. My fingers tapped soundlessly into the dirt until a flicker of movement just outside stopped me. I held my breath for what I was sure was impending, painful death and saw it again.

I released the breath, which was not, in fact, my last. A soft white rabbit loped in front of the bushes I'd made into a doorway. My stomach was interested, but I'd never prepared meat. I'd only ever gathered berries and vegetables that someone else had grown. I didn't have the first idea how to make a bow, let alone shoot one, and I'd never killed anything except plants and a bird. I had no idea if an animal killed by magic was edible. I thought of the thistle, its black roots, and how it had turned to ash. The rabbit sniffed the air in my direction and continued on its way, answering the matter for me.

I was sitting in a hole, utterly alone, and it was beginning to get dark. Night bugs chittered, their high-pitched keens rising with the loss of light. I lit a thin flame to practice fire magic, leaning forward as I danced it back and forth above the ground. My control had progressed a good deal since my training had begun, and it seemed almost easy to navigate the small flame. I smoothed it out into a line and traced arcs then more intricate designs. The designs started to resemble portraits, and I had to concentrate hard to keep from seeing the faces of council members and the people I'd left behind, so I focused on landscapes, but those grew from tiny village houses and trees to rolling hills and curving creeks. Before long, the hills rose to mountains that melted into unidentifiable monsters. I snuffed the flame with a wave, and the den was black with night.

Eventually, the clouds broke, and the soft glow of moonlight filtered through the opening. I leaned onto an elbow to examine the glistening patches of light on the skin of my outstretched hand, twisting it from day to night, pale to dark. Weary and as if I was in a trance, I lowered my head, tucked my arm back as a pillow, and fell into a deep sleep.

6

The early morning sun streaked through every break in the makeshift door, lighting the entirety of the hollow. I considered covering my head with that damp dress and sleeping for the rest of the day, but my stomach ached for food, and Chevelle might not be far behind. I crawled out, rubbing my eyes and squinting, and was able to locate a few roots and greens that would have to be enough to tide me over until I could figure out a way to hunt.

After knocking the brush away from my shelter, I slung the pack over my shoulder and trudged north once more. There was an abundance of streams running through the hills and a few patches of fat, amethyst berries along the way, so I couldn't complain. The route was undemanding. The ground was smooth with nothing too overgrown to make passage difficult, and there were none of those nasty snarls that could form from a maze of thorn trees or a network of vines that could tangle around legs and cause falls. The grass was tall but soft, so it rolled over in the wind, hiding no more than the occasional field mouse or vole. Sporadic wildflowers dotted the hills in small sprays of pinks or spiky yellowbird. The sky was cloudless and blue, the sun a constant companion as I carried on through the days and hills.

Each new day was something unexpected, and the trip became less daunting than it might have otherwise been. I was moving during every moment of light, so exhaustion pulled me into sleep for every moment of darkness. I concentrated on each step, breathing in the new scents, counting trees, and doing anything I could to keep myself on task and the past out of my mind.

I was counting fallen catclaw seeds when I crested another hill and spotted a bridge in the valley. I hesitated before slowly making my way down. *A bridge might mean a village was nearby, and a village meant elves.* I didn't want to get caught, not after everything, so I was fully prepared to run by the time I reached the crossing. Its stacked gray stones were bulkier than those that had been appearing more frequently on my path. Water flowed beneath, smoothing the stones at the base. They were so worn that they must have been in place for centuries.

The leather soles of my shoes skimmed over ancient stone, the bridge curving gently before flattening out into a worn dirt path on the other side. It was more traveled than I would have liked, so I swung wide and moved through the trees instead. The wind shifted, and the scent of roasting meat assaulted me, dragging my attention and my feet its way. Despite my concerns about other elves, my stomach tightened, my mouth watering as I followed the smell through the trees.

I broke into a small clearing, and there in the center stood a cloaked figure, kneeling as he turned a meat-covered spit.

Pressed tightly behind an oak tree, I shuffled sideways to get a better view. I was sure from his size he was a male elf. The smell of real food consumed me, and I was watching the cooked meat roll over the flame as I moved again. A dry leaf crushed beneath my foot.

"Come, then. There's plenty for both of us," he called.

I cursed then walked cautiously out of the trees. He turned, tossing the cloak aside as he propped one leg on a rock as if posing. He scrutinized me, and I resisted the urge to straighten my hair and brush the dirt from my clothes.

"Don't be shy." The stranger beckoned, gesturing to an upturned log beside the fire. The meat sizzled and popped as I crossed to him and sat obediently. *It's too late to hide, so I might as well at least have something decent to eat.*

The smell was unfamiliar, but I didn't care. It smelled like food. He reached down, tore a hunk from the spit, and tossed it to me with a wink. When I blushed, he smiled a wicked smile. My mouth went dry. He was tall and broad with dark hair and eyes, like Chevelle. Handsome too, I supposed, though I could tell even from a few gestures that he was a bit cocky. He reminded me of Evelyn, always so proud of herself for finding me out.

The stranger watched me as I ate. After I devoured the first piece, he laughed and threw me another. I hoped I looked appropriately abashed. As I finished the second serving, he stepped closer to sit on the misshapen rock that rose through the earth beside me. He held his hand wide, and a canteen flew up from a pile of things on the other side of the fire. He passed it to me, and I tilted it back, expecting cool water. I almost choked when warm wine hit my throat. He leaned forward to get a better look at me as I lowered the container.

He looked as if he thought I might spook—otherwise, I guessed he had plenty to say hidden beneath that smirk. It didn't stop him from moving uncomfortably close, though, or eyeing me with what I was certain was the same look I'd just given my meal. I cleared my throat, thinking I'd made my sense of discomfort clear when he started to move, but he only stood, which brought him even closer. Well, parts of him.

I turned toward the fire, tugging the pack tightly against my shoulder as I prepared for a graceful exit, for departure from food and warmth.

I jumped a little when a tree uprooted across the clearing. It was only a sapling, but a second and third tree followed.

"You look like you'll need shelter, sunshine," he explained.

I stared in disbelief as the trees split to form a low lean-to. He shot me another wink, but I couldn't be sure he was kidding. The tearing and popping noises ceased, and I examined his creation, which was quite impressive, really. He didn't even seem to be watching, let alone concentrating, and he put no blessings on it, nor did he pause to show his gratitude. It seemed he was just enjoying himself, not being responsible to the magic.

It was magic that I needed and wanted. He was good enough—there was no question of that. *He would definitely be able to teach me.* I started to ask but fell short. I had no idea who he was, and I probably shouldn't let on who *I* was.

He noticed my expression and sat again, eyeing me questioningly, all humor gone.

"You seem to be very good at magic," I offered.

He chuckled. "Is that so?"

"Yes, and... Well, I need to learn."

"Learn?" The humor was gone again. "What do you mean learn?"

"I've never, well, except for fire, and I need someone to teach me... and you're..." I waved a hand in his direction to indicate his skill.

His brow rose. "I don't understand," he said, clearly concerned about my mental state. Maybe I was a few nuts short of a bushel.

"I've lost my mentor. Can you teach me magic? Help me, so I don't do something out of order, hurt myself?"

He knitted his brow, and as he began his reply, a fallen branch cracked at the edge of the clearing. His head snapped toward it. I sucked in a harsh breath as Chevelle strode our way. The elf who had been sitting with me moved into a fiercely protective stance in front of me. I leaned around him to see, placing my hand on his leg as I angled my head past it. That broke his stare, and he glanced down at me.

Chevelle still walked casually toward us as if there weren't two angry panthers preparing to pounce on him. I must have appeared about as threatening as a kitten, because the leg I was gripping shook with laughter. My angry gaze turned on my new acquaintance, and he raised his hands in surrender, still chuckling. "I take it you know him?" he asked.

"He's following me," I announced too loudly.

He gave me a concerned look, so I let down my guard, moving to stand behind him. Chevelle approached us, staring directly at me as if the tall form of the stranger wasn't between us. He let me see his irritation for one long moment before his features melted back into their standard sternness. For some reason, it infuriated me, and I nearly berated him right there. Then I remembered that I was on the run and that there was a strange elf in front of me. I decided to keep my mouth shut before I dug a deeper hole.

An arm wrapped around my shoulder and drew me forward. "Introduce us, buttercup."

I grimaced. My companion was certainly enjoying himself.

Chevelle held his hand out in a formal greeting, his entire posture making it clear he was not one to be trifled with. "Chevelle Vattier."

"Vattier, eh?" I thought I heard the stranger mutter under his breath, "Well, you can call me Bonnie Bell."

Chevelle seemed unmoved.

They stared at each other for one long moment, both tall and broad-shouldered, with dark hair and dark eyes. Their clothes were plain and well-fitted but trail-worn, but where the stranger wore brown, Chevelle donned black. There was something vaguely hostile about their silent exchange, but I could not pin down exactly what it was. The other elf finally held his hand out in return. "Steed. Steed Summit."

They shot me a glare as my giggle slipped out.

Steed stared down at me, not seeming to think it was funny. "Our lineage is long, and we breed the best stallions in the land."

Chevelle spoke up, clearly trying to draw back the man's attention. "Yes, I have heard much regarding the lines of Free Runner and Grand Spirit. Tell me, is that what brings you out this far?"

They carried on with the discussion, and Chevelle explained that we needed horses. I sat, defeated, knowing he was there to drag me back to the village to serve my sentence. I listened as plans were made for a trade. Steed agreed to bring in the herd so Chevelle would be able to choose, and they kept talking, settling into conversation. Steed offered Chevelle what was left of the roast, and they sat, Chevelle beside me and Steed across from us.

I picked up the canteen and choked down more wine.

The evening carried on, and though the conversation still held a formal tone, neither man talked of anything personal. In spite of their glaring lack of easy humor, they seemed to be getting along. I faded in and out of the various discussions, listening occasionally but never talking. There wasn't anything for me to say.

Steed seemed markedly aware of me, watching me in a way no one ever had. It must have been obvious, because when he excused himself to check the herd, Chevelle studied me, sliding a strand of my black hair through his fingers. "It suits you better."

It was a familiar gesture and it should have made me flinch. Maybe it was the wine, but as I looked at him, my anger faded. The way he'd reacted when Fannie had struck me and the caress against my cheek were not the actions of a council elder. As we sat so near, it was hard to believe the concern wasn't real. His eyes burned with intensity, even darker than before. *Dark... like mine.*

I looked away.

Steed broke through the trees, gesturing in the direction from which he'd come. "They aren't far. Ready and able for a morning adventure." As he approached, he glanced at me then Chevelle, who still sat close beside me. "We can get an early start." He lifted a pack from beside the fire. "Bluebell?"

I stood, following the stranger without question, not missing the irritation on Chevelle's face. Steed unclasped the pack to roll the blankets out with a flip, a twinkle in his dark-brown eyes as he nodded good evening before stepping away from my hastily constructed hut. I unlaced my vest and threw it down, kicked off my shoes, and fell into the blankets, stretching happily in something like an actual bed. The conversation outside quieted, and I slipped off to sleep, trying not to think about my capture and coming return to the village.

~

"Freya."

A low voice broke into my dreams of gently rolling hills and soft gray stone. I peered through slitted eyes to see Chevelle standing outside the entrance, his back to me as he watched the dull-red horizon. I sat up, laced the vest over the thin material of my blouse, and slid on my shoes to join him.

"It's dawn," I complained.

"And good morning, sunshine," Steed called from atop a large, black stallion. The beast's nostrils flared, its breath steaming in the cool morning air. Two more of the animals pawed in the distance behind him. Steed chirped a whistle, and they walked forward, the slim, muscular one moving to stand beside Chevelle as a mammoth crossed in front of me and knelt. I drew in a startled breath at the sheer size and nearness of it.

Steed shot me a mischievous wink. "Well?"

I was speechless, my mouth agape. Up close, the thing seemed as large and black as a starless night. Steed was clearly pleased with my reaction, but Chevelle's eyes rolled heavenward. He didn't comment, though. He simply held out a hand to help me mount before swinging onto his own horse.

"I will ride with you as far north as Naraguah then make

my way east to trade with the imps at Bray," Steed told Chevelle.

I swung a shocked look at my watcher, who simply nodded. Steed saw my confusion and gave a disapproving glance in Chevelle's direction. He sat straighter, leaving me alone with Chevelle as rider and horse shot past us, a long black tail whipping in their wake.

I stared at Chevelle. "North?"

He looked back at me, his calm a contradiction to the thundering beat of my heart.

"You aren't taking me back? You are going—*we* are going north?"

"I'm sorry, Freya," he said. "I let my guard down at the creek." His gaze fell to my hands, which closed instinctively into fists, protecting my newly-scarred palms. "I was distracted. I should have been paying closer attention. I should have prevented this." Regret was thick in his voice.

I could only stare at him, mystified.

"It's too late now. You'll never rest until you've followed the map."

He was wrong. I'd forgotten my plans and surrendered to my captor. I had thought it was over.

"Yes," I answered boldly, the word echoing with the thrum of my pulse. It made no sense, but I didn't take the time to think it through, didn't give him a chance to change his mind. I smiled, kicking my heels hard into the horse's sides.

The animal jolted forward, and I gripped the saddle with all my might as its hooves cut into the earth. I'd never ridden a horse. There weren't any near the village, and I'd only ever seen one from the occasional visitor. The beast was huge, and I could feel his power as the ground rushed beneath us. We were gaining on Steed. I glanced over my shoulder to find Chevelle's horse running too, but not with the same determination as mine. Wind whipped my hair as we caught up to Steed, who gave me a wide smile and edged beside us.

"Enjoying the beast?" he shouted over the thunder of hooves and the rush of wind.

I smiled in return, but as the horse kept up speed, we started to pass him, and I realized I didn't know how to slow down. I didn't know how to stop. For nuts' sake, I didn't know how to *ride*. My head jerked back to find Steed, my exhilaration replaced by fear.

Recognizing my panic, he let out a short, sharp whistle, and the horse slowed at once, falling in beside his. Our legs almost touched as the animals loped in tandem. "Never ridden?"

"No." My voice was shaky, along with my hands and legs.

"We only train them with commands for the imps. Just use your magic."

I tamped down an image of the horse bursting into flames. "I haven't learned animal magic."

His lip pursed, one brow dropping low, the same strange look he'd given the first time I'd mentioned learning magic. "Just feel it, Elfreda." I ignored the slight annoyance that Chevelle must have told him my full name.

"I don't understand."

"You don't *learn* magic," Steed said. "It's a part of you. Feel it. Think about what you want the horse to do."

My confusion must still have been evident.

He shook his head. "It's like a muscle. You didn't think about lifting your leg to get on the horse, you just knew you wanted to climb on, and your leg lifted."

Chevelle caught us then, riding up and cutting off Steed's

explanation. "This isn't the time for a magic lesson," he said in a clipped tone.

All three horses slowed to a walk as Chevelle shot Steed a glance. I could only think of our lessons, of the fire in the clearing. It had been so obvious once Chevelle had urged me to control a stronger flame, I guessed because I had been using the power in small doses for so long. "What about your hands?" I asked.

"What do you mean?" Steed said, ignoring Chevelle's warning glance.

"Why do you use your hands, if you just think it, I mean?"

He laughed. "A quirk, I guess. Habit. Like when you're playing flip ball and you want your piece to go in so badly that you lean hard to help it."

I remembered the game from when I'd first come to the village. The children would be bound from magic and have to throw an odd-shaped piece into the corresponding hole on a game board across from them. They would lean forward after they threw, sometimes bouncing and chanting, "Come on, come on," twisting as if wishing would somehow make the ball respond. The game had held no interest for me. I didn't have to be bound to not have magic. It wasn't a novelty. It was everyday life.

"We should stop for breakfast," Chevelle said.

We hadn't been riding long, but it wasn't a suggestion. I didn't mind because I'd eaten mostly berries for days and I wasn't quite sure about riding yet.

"I suppose you're right. Might as well enjoy the journey," Steed said, throwing me a private grin.

We stopped under the canopy of a red oak, and Steed grabbed me as I slid awkwardly from the horse. "You may ask him to kneel, Elfreda." He didn't appear to mind handling me about the waist to help me down.

Looking up at him, I pushed the hair away from my face. "Yes, well, I guess I should start practicing."

Heat brushed my skin as the fire Chevelle was building flared. It returned to its proper size, and Chevelle commanded, "Sit, Elfreda."

Steed followed as I walked to a fallen limb by the fire and settled atop the widest part, drawing my legs up from the ground. He sat as well, apparently not concerned about who was finding us breakfast.

Irritation rolled off Chevelle as he ran into the thick line of trees that bordered the clearing. In only a moment he was back, carrying three large, white birds.

"Where is your bow?" I asked.

Steed's laugh was loud. "She's a hoot!"

Chevelle looked as though he could be in danger of losing his temper. I didn't get the joke.

"You're serious?" Steed said, his humor vanishing as he gaped at Chevelle. "What, she's a bright lighter?"

Chevelle was across the gap and in his face almost before Steed could stand. I jerked back in response, but a screeching siren pierced my ears, and I doubled over, covering them. It was inside, a screaming, terrible howl coming from my ears.

I tried to force my eyes open, hoping someone would help me, but they were just standing there, chest to chest, arguing. *Do they not see me?* I ached to scream for help but couldn't get a sound out and couldn't breathe. They leaned toward each other, oblivious to anything else. My eyes closed as I curled into a ball. The seconds dragged on, and I began to wonder if I would die.

Then it stopped. I sucked in a ragged breath, then

another. I seemed fine, maybe a little dizzy, but otherwise, it was gone. Unclenching my body, I looked around, expecting someone to be leaning over me, attempting to help. But nothing appeared out of place. I pushed up on shaky limbs. Chevelle was by the fire, preparing to roast the birds. Steed stood beside his horse, adjusting the saddle's straps. Both had their backs turned to me as if they hadn't even noticed.

A wave of vertigo hit when I tried to speak, and I fell back against the tree limb to steady myself. It seemed only a moment, but when my eyes opened again, the scene had changed.

Steed reclined beside me, an elbow resting on a bent knee as he lazily wound a feather in his hand. Chevelle was across the fire. He looked up at me through his lashes, past his furrowed brow, and then brought me a piece of meat. It was cold.

I sat stunned. *Have they nothing to say? Do they actually not know?* I wanted to scream, but the words wouldn't come. I was too drained. And I was scared. I didn't know what had happened or what was wrong with me, but I was certain that whatever it was, Chevelle would take me straight back to the village, where I would be punished.

We stayed there for some time, a fact for which I was grateful. Even though whatever had happened seemed to have passed, neither man gave the impression he was in a hurry to go. Chevelle glanced at me occasionally but kept himself busy around the fire. Time seemed to be moving strangely.

Steed still played with his feather, entertaining me with it. It spun toward me and turned down, tickling my arm and then my nose as his magic made it dance. I giggled despite my wariness and reached up to rub my nose where the plume had brushed it. I noticed the map on my palms. "What about spells?"

He eyed my hands. "Been working spells?"

"Not on purpose."

His grin was automatic, and I had the feeling delight came easy to him. Steed was charming and warm, and there was a strange sort of magic to the way he looked at me—as if he truly saw me. And yet, I couldn't quite forget someone else's eyes were on me as well. "Yes, spells can be dangerous."

"Yes," I agreed, "but why do you need words for spells and not magic?"

"A spell can be left, set with a trigger, or larger than your magic. They are complicated and wicked things. And the ancient language is... tricky. Definitely something you should stay away from. Years of learning and practice, and you can still wreck a spell pretty good."

I thought about that for a moment.

Steed jumped up and held out a hand to me. "What do you say we water the horses?"

I didn't have to ask my horse to kneel because Steed grabbed my waist and threw me up there. He was mounted before I had settled into the saddle, and our horses took off, galloping north synchronously. I looked back for Chevelle. He was leaning forward, his legs nearly straight in the stirrups as his stallion raced to catch us, entirely displeased with the both of us, if I were to guess.

We were covering distance so quickly that I could barely take in the new surroundings, and it wasn't long before we came up on a wide creek. I assumed Steed had control of my horse—I was simply concentrating on staying in the saddle as we ran beside him. The horses edged closer to the creek, splashing along the muddy bank then in the shallows of the water. Silt and cold water sprayed my face as we ran, and I wondered if this was what it felt like to fly like the fey.

We followed the creek until it turned west, and we kept north, slowing to a walk. I tried to catch my breath. Steed was watching me, smiling appreciatively, and I realized I was wearing a huge grin along with about three pounds of mud.

The slower pace gave me time to take everything in. The ground had leveled out again, clearing to open meadows of low grass and a few scattered trees. Large gray rocks dotted the landscape. There was a haziness on the horizon, but as we rode, it began to clear, revealing a mammoth lake ahead. It was a hundred times bigger than the tiny forest ponds I was used to and as smooth as glass. Behind it, the haze thinned just enough that I could see the outline of mountains.

The image was like a punch in the chest. Chevelle rode up beside us. "The hills of Camber."

I looked at him, my watcher, and thought his features were peaceful for the first time. Junnie had said he was from the North, and I wondered if we had reached his home. Maybe that was why he'd brought me here, for a much-needed vacation from the duties of Council and the task of being a watcher. They would never know, as long as he got me back soon.

When we reached the lake, the horses stopped, and in the quiet shadow of the dreamlike setting, I forgot I was riding. The mountains and lake were almost too much to take in— none of it seemed real. Chevelle edged in next to me before Steed had the chance. As my horse knelt, he held out his hand, and I stepped down beside him. The three stallions followed Steed to a nearby tree, where he fed them small green-skinned apples from its branches.

I glanced back at Chevelle. He was watching me. I wanted

to ask if he was from there but was afraid to set off any conversation that might end with me being hauled back to Council that much quicker.

I looked over the lake to the mountains. If I was incarcerated for a thousand years in the village, I would want this memory. I breathed deeply. The air was cool and moist and smelled so unlike the harsh floral scents that saturated every part of the village. I could sense the deep-green moss covering the rocks at my feet and the fir trees that edged the east bank. Even the soil smelled richer. My eyes were closed as I took it in, and a soft touch brushed my cheek. *Chevelle.*

I opened my eyes and realized he had swept debris from my face. I wiped a hand across my forehead, and dried mud crumbled away. I looked down and realized it was caked on the fabric of my pants and splattered nearly everywhere.

Moving to the edge of the bank to walk in, clothes and all, I waded out until I was waist-deep then relaxed, falling back and gliding under the dark water before it lifted me to float at the surface. The water covered my ears, lapping at my mouth and chin, and I stared upward, marveling at the size of the mountains as they seemed to dissolve into the blue haze of the sky. I wondered if it would ever seem real.

Eventually, I made my way back, wrapping my arms around myself to control the shivers. I was surprised and more than a little grateful to find that a shelter had already been set up for me. The idea of being drenched hadn't mattered until the cool air cut across the lake. Chevelle nodded toward the hut as he prepared a fire, and I found my pack along with a pile of dry clothes on a bed of birch branches.

As I tugged off my soaked pants to exchange them for the new ones, I wondered if Chevelle had brought both sets or if they'd been packed by Junnie in that small, strange village. I couldn't fathom why I hadn't considered that he would so easily be able to follow me when I'd run from there or how I'd been oblivious to the dangers of being caught. It was not my aunt Francine I was dealing with. It was Council.

The shirt was fitted to my shape but of a heavier fabric, and a pair of boots was at the bottom of the stack. *It must be much colder in the mountains,* I thought. It reminded me of stepping out of the cold, wet gown on the bank of the creek then finding the scroll and the map. Chevelle's words echoed in my mind. *I'm sorry, Freya. I let my guard down at the creek. I was distracted... should have been paying closer attention... should have prevented this... too late now.*

The smell of cooked meat cut through my thoughts. I ran a hand through my wet hair and walked out to the fire. The scene wasn't any less impressive than it had been the first time, and I sat on one of the large, flat rocks facing the lake. Chevelle brought me a plate of food, settling in beside me. There were berries, roots, and a rich, savory meat that dripped onto my hands as I tore into it. It was a feast compared to what I'd been eating. And even though he was my watcher and my captor, I had to admit I felt less alone with Chevelle there.

Steed pulled his own ration from the spit and sat on my other side in companionable silence as we all watched the surface of the lake, and beyond it, mountains.

THE MOUNTAINS at dawn were much more intimidating, and I was hesitant to leave our camp. I felt as if I'd finally found some solace there, safe and far from my punishment by

Council. I'd been eager to follow the map on my palms and leave behind everything I'd ever known, but I was staring at the possibility of a strange new land, and the reality of what I was about to do came crashing in. I tried to distract myself as we rode east around the lake, attempting to name the species of plants as Junnie might have made me, but there were so many I had never seen that it started to remind me of the differences rather than distract me. I bantered with Steed about horses and imps and everything I could come up with to keep him talking. He didn't seem to mind. Chevelle rode quietly behind us, scanning our surroundings. I wasn't sure if he was enjoying the scenery or playing lookout. Maybe I wasn't the only renegade he was after.

We rode a few days into the base of the mountains. One night, we had stopped to camp when over dinner, Steed announced he would be leaving us the next morning to head east. His easy humor had become a reprieve to me during the long days, and our quiet evenings were a comforting pattern I knew I would miss. The disappointment must have shown on my face.

He reached a hand up and brushed my hair behind an ear. "Don't worry, sunshine. I will see you again."

I smiled a little, and he winked at me. Chevelle stiffened at my side, as he often did when Steed touched me so casually, and I couldn't help but think of being alone with him after that night. My stomach tightened, and suddenly in comparison, the mountains didn't seem like such a big deal.

The next morning, Steed said goodbye privately to Chevelle then came to where I stood with the horses, stroking one's neck. "You'll remember me, butterfly?"

I smiled in return. "Always."

"Yes, well, at least as long as he's yours." He patted the horse.

"Mine?"

He smiled and swung onto his horse, nodding farewell as he spun and galloped east.

My horse knelt, and Chevelle offered his hand to help me get seated. My grin widened as he mounted his horse, and he looked back at me questioningly.

"I'll name him Steed," I announced proudly.

Chevelle pressed his eyes closed, shaking his head as I patted the horse's neck once more.

7

We rode through the morning hours. Chevelle seemed content not to talk, but I was wound up in anguish, trying to decide whether I was brave enough to ask him questions. I had no idea how much he would put up with before he called it all off and hauled me back to the village for sentencing. *You're being paranoid*, I reminded myself. Chevelle had done nothing to cause me harm. Despite being a member of Council, he'd never treated me the way the elders had.

But there was something dark about him that sent warnings from deep within me, and I was alone with my watcher in a place that set me on edge, unable to stem the tension inside me. Our path became more defined, pushing us through trees and between rocks, trailing upward so minutely that I didn't even realize how far we'd gone until I glanced back and saw the base of the mountains beneath us. I appraised the narrow path ahead, snaking high through a vast, rock-strewn mountain, and turning back didn't seem so bad after all. Fists clenched, I pushed out the question I'd been most afraid to ask. I was so tied up, it twisted into something of an accusation. "Watcher."

My skin flushed when the word came out harsh. Regardless of how he'd treated me, Chevelle was still a member of Council. I was on dangerous ground. He spun on me, but I couldn't place the expression on his face.

Panicked, I tried to recover. "You're my watcher." It still sounded wrong, so I added, "Why?"

He hesitated. "Frey..." His voice was unexpectedly gentle, and I had the strangest feeling he was searching for an answer. But I had no right to question someone of his station, and his face turned hard, his tone formal. "The Council was concerned after you tried to choke Evelyn of Rothegarr."

I drew a sharp breath, caught off guard. "What are you talking about?" Then I was offended. *How could anyone believe I choked Evelyn?* I bit down against the reply I wanted to snap at him, mindful of the trouble I was already in with Council. But that brought on images of the speaker's discolored face as he struggled for air and the blackened thistle in the back room at Junnie's. Evelyn's expression as she'd run from our argument had been accusing, and it suddenly seemed right.

I swayed, my vision losing focus. I didn't even realize I was falling until Chevelle's arms were around me—he was quick, catching me before the rocks did.

He was kneeling, cradling me in one arm as my back rested against his leg. "I'm sorry, Freya. I thought... How could you not know?"

Humiliation flooded through me. He was right, and not only had I wished her to choke, I had been too much a fool to see I had caused it, just as I had caused the speaker to do the same. I squeezed my eyes closed in misery, rolling away from him to curl onto a rock. He let me, stepping away to unsaddle the horses and settle onto a seat of his own. I felt sick.

We were both still until nightfall, when he retrieved a blanket from the pack and laid it over me. I didn't thank him, fearing what would come out if I spoke.

THE NEXT MORNING was quiet as Chevelle saddled our horses. I had plenty to think about besides the questions that had seemed so important the previous day.

I'd been convicted of practicing dark magic. I had thought it was a mistake. But the images rolled through my mind as we continued up the mountain: the lifeless body of a small gray bird. A garden of weeds with roots as black as soot. The faces of Council as their speaker struggled to breathe. A thistle growing in Evelyn's throat, slowly choking off her airway. Chevelle's face when he had asked who had showed me to fuse the crystal with blood. His expression as he'd looked down at me the night before. *How could you not know?*

That image haunted me the most. It seemed familiar somehow. He'd let his guard down, and though strained with concern, there was something else there, sadness or maybe just plain pity.

"This is a good place to stop for the night," Chevelle said, breaking my trance. I'd barely noticed the day pass. A glance at the path behind us showed the lake far in the distance below. It shook me from my stupor.

I climbed down from my horse to stretch my legs, facing the mountain top instead of the view below, some part of me unable to accept the distance and height we had traveled. Chevelle led the horses to a thickset tree, its limbs stretching low and wide above the rocks. His hand spun to form a trough from the bark and tinder scattered beneath, and the horses drank as he used the same method to gather grasses from the sparse patches on the incline.

Movement up the mountain caught my eye, and I looked to Chevelle in alarm. Though he appeared calm, he was staring in the same direction. A dark, cloaked figure advanced in the dusk, the full cape covering every part of its owner, the drawn hood shielding their face.

Chevelle nodded in greeting as I scanned the area for others who might approach. The stranger seemed alone and reached Chevelle first, since he stood nearer to the horses than I did.

The newcomer whispered to him, and Chevelle's eyes flicked in my direction more than once. Curiosity burned through me. And then a delicate hand reached out to pass Chevelle a package. Her fingers lingered against his during the exchange, and my chest felt like it was blistering inside. They were whispering about me, my watcher and this woman. Chevelle's gaze brushed mine once more, and I hungered to hear what they were saying. I was fixated on it, my mind spinning, convinced that if I were as invisible as everyone thought, if they truly couldn't see me, at least I could get closer and finally know.

As I shook my head at the idea, my eyes fell downward. A small scream escaped. My arms were covered in tree bark, blending seamlessly with the stump on which I sat. I bolted upright, batting at them as if my shirt were on fire. Chevelle and the cloaked woman ran toward me, and I looked up in panic. When my eyes fell again to my arms, they were normal. *Had I imagined it? Am I losing my mind?*

When my head came up, the woman drew a sharp breath.

It was Junnie. Her cloak had fallen, and her golden curls were a welcome sight.

Relief flooded me, and I forgot all my previous resentment. "Junnie!"

"Frey," she murmured, reaching out to stroke a strand of my black hair.

The shock of seeing her disappeared at the reminder of my changed appearance. "Are you here for Council? To collect me?" My voice was colored with the shame of being a criminal, a bird-killer, an elf-strangler.

Surprised, she glanced at Chevelle then back to me, forcing a smile. "Are you all right, Frey?"

I stood there, baffled, then remembered screaming. I cleared my throat. "I was covered in bark."

Her eyebrows ticked up as she looked again at Chevelle, who was mirroring her concerned expression. "Maybe it's time to allow her a few small lessons."

Magic. I was ashamed by how long it took to realize I'd unwittingly camouflaged myself. That whole thing was going to take a while to get used to.

"Tomorrow," Chevelle answered. He glanced at the darkening sky. "Dinner?"

Junnie grinned as she reached an arm back, her cloak moving aside as she drew a bow from beneath. "I'll get my own, but thanks."

He nodded, a knowing smile stretched across his face—and not entirely the friendly sort. They turned in opposite directions, each disappearing behind the trees and rocks that were strewed across the mountain, as I stood alone and confused. I sat on a fallen tree, shaking my head as I stared down at its rough bark.

Chevelle returned quickly with two small, furry animals

slung over his back. As his gaze reached the log that lay in front of me, it burst into an orange flame, thin branches forming a spit as he skinned and attached the animals. The process was so smooth, I couldn't say exactly what had happened.

Chevelle was changing. Or, more likely, he was becoming more himself. He wasn't as formal. Away from the village and Council, he seemed relaxed, and apparently quick and powerful magic was intertwined into his every routine. He didn't need to do much by hand. I would have spent hours trying to build a spit and skin an animal.

As he wiped the blade of his skinning knife, his strong hands deft and clean, an old question came back to me. "How do you hunt?"

"Hmm?"

"You don't have a bow," I explained. "What do you use to hunt?"

He hesitated as if deciding what to tell me. "I use magic, Frey."

He looked like he was waiting for me to be upset. "Oh." I contemplated his answer. "I thought maybe you had a throwing knife."

He smirked. "Yes, well, that would have been easy enough."

"And Junnie prefers to hunt... for sport?"

He had that look again, and I wondered why he would be so cautious. *Because I'm dangerous? A practitioner of dark magic?* "No. Some prefer the meat not to be tainted by magic. They feel it is more... pure." He pronounced "tainted" with an edge.

"Is it? Tainted I, mean?"

"I have lived on it for—" His words caught midsentence.

"Well, it doesn't seem to be, but to each his own." He turned to the fire.

Junnie came back into view, a large animal slung over her shoulders, bow in hand. She dropped her burden on a smooth gray rock near the fire and whispered a short thanks before removing the arrow to skin the animal. My gaze moved between the sizeable carcass and her lithe form.

"I'll be traveling fast and far, and don't intend to stop and hunt. I will pack the extra with me."

I managed a sheepish smile. It seemed like I needed things explained a lot lately. "Where will you go?"

"Back to the village."

"To Council?" I breathed. "They sent you to find me?"

Her bright-blue eyes flicked to Chevelle and back. "No, Freya. They will not know I saw you."

"Are they looking for me?" Terror crept into my voice. I was Chevelle's captive, but he'd given me some sort of reprieve. The thought of Council brought the danger of my situation to the forefront.

"No. They will not risk it."

"They are afraid," Chevelle said from his spot by the fire. Junnie shot him a warning glance.

"Afraid?" I asked, doubtful. "Afraid of what?"

"The mountains." Junnie's answer was curt as she returned to her work on the gazelle.

THEY WERE quiet the rest of the evening, but as I dozed by the fire, their conversation restarted in hushed voices. I tried to listen, but exhaustion won out, and their words began to meld into dreams.

I could hear them as I was drifting, floating in a great shadowed lake. My white gown spread around me in the water, my dark hair swaying with the ripples on the surface. I rose above, peering down at myself, and the image turned into my mother before the dark water went black and the ripples transformed into wind. I recognized the scene as her pendant began to glow. The wind howled, and screams pierced my ears.

It was the same dream, but different. I glanced around to find a village I didn't know. Someone was coming toward me, an expression of concern on his handsome face. His familiar face. He reached out to me, and I stepped toward him, tears streaming down my cheeks.

He wrapped his arms around me as I turned again to see my mother. A howl of rage escaped her, and I started to go to her, but he held me. He was restraining me. I thrashed against him as I tried to scream, to tell him to let me go, but I had no voice. She reached her hand out, and I could not move, could not help her, though I knew she was dying. I was imprisoned there, unable to move, unable to scream, and unable to save her.

Then I couldn't see her anymore. Something was covering my eyes. I struggled yet again, but my body felt like lead, heavy and useless. Darkness enveloped me, and I was underwater, struggling to reach the surface, desperate for air.

"Frey." A husky voice woke me. It must have been early dawn. The faint light revealed concern on Chevelle's face as he stood over me. His *familiar* face. The memory smashed into my chest like a battering ram, stealing my breath.

"You," I hissed. He backed away as I sat up and glared at him with fire in my eyes. "You. You held me back as my mother died. You held me and made me watch her die." I could almost taste the acid in my voice. He was still backing away, holding his hands in front of him with his palms out. A wordless hiss escaped my throat as I felt the fire coursing through the light in my hands. He would burn for this. *Burn*.

I was standing, walking step for step toward him as he backed away. He said nothing, his face calm as the fire flared, and I raised my hands to strike.

Then everything went black.

I heard chanting. My ears had been roaring with anger, but all that was left was a soft recitation: *"Gian Zet Foria. Gian Zet Foria. Gian Zet Foria."* *Junnie*. Junnie was chanting something.

I was engulfed with an empty, lethargic feeling. My eyes batted open, and I was lying on the ground, looking up at my tutor and the watcher. Junnie's words ran together as Chevelle mumbled. "Gian Zet Foria Gian Zet Foria Gian Zet Foria." It seemed so familiar. Like *Georgiana, Suzetta, Glaforia*. They stopped simultaneously.

"Frey." Junnie was talking slowly. "Stay calm and lie still." I tried to convey my incredulity as I lay there, unable to move. "Explain to me what happened."

All the anger and excitement had turned into numbness. What came out sounded no more than a statement of fact. "Chevelle held me back and made me watch my mother die." Junnie didn't have the outraged look I expected. I sifted through the dream—the memory—searching for a way to explain so she would be as stunned and infuriated as I was.

They stared at me, and I was abruptly certain that they were the reason I was lying on the ground, incapacitated. They had control over me. My thoughts shifted, and I ran through it again, going backwards from where I was... Their faces, the chanting from behind me, Chevelle backing away, the dream. *The water.* I remembered being trapped under-water just before waking, but I hadn't been drowning. And it wasn't a dream.

I grew horrified as more of the memory returned. The cloaks who had surrounded and killed my mother had been circling me too. I knew they'd intended to destroy me, though I couldn't see why. Chevelle had held me, pulled me into the water. He had tried to keep them from finding me as they attacked, tried to keep me from calling out to her. His fear, his sympathy was clear. He'd held me back to save me.

Tears streamed down my face, and my body began to release from its prison, no longer dead weight. Chevelle had saved me from my mother's fate. *How long has he been my watcher?* In the memory, he'd fought to keep me from seeing and tried to cover my eyes. And later, he'd pulled me from the water and dragged me away as we fled.

I shook with sobs, and that same pair of strong arms wrapped around me, supporting me as my limbs became heavy, my body and mind spent from the stress or whatever trauma the spell had caused. I couldn't say which, because I was pulled from consciousness into a black, dreamless sleep.

CHEVELLE WAS STILL HOLDING me when I awoke, the sun high in the late morning sky. I wondered if he'd slept at all. Cradled in his arms, I reached up to rub my bleary eyes. As I glanced up at him, it struck me how close we were. His dark eyes were on me, a blue so strange and still, and yet something seemed to boil beneath them. Something dangerous, something I should not have felt drawn to. My hand dropped from my face to fall against his chest. That didn't help. Heat rose in my neck as I felt the corded muscle beneath his shirt.

I had to look away. He must have thought I was searching for Junnie.

"She left just after dawn, when she knew you were safe."

"Oh," I breathed. *Perfect. We're alone in the middle of nowhere, and I'm sitting in a council watcher's lap.* My flush deepened, and I hastily stood to straighten my clothes.

He watched me fidget.

"So I guess we should get going?" I stammered.

"No."

My breath caught, and I forced myself to look at him, still edgy from the closeness the moment before. I convinced myself I was just imagining the way he studied me as he sat against the downed tree, that he had no idea what I was thinking, that it was the furthest thing from his mind. "No?" I asked, unable to mask the tremor in my voice.

"Magic first."

That wasn't exactly a relief. It was obvious he saw my anxiety, but I couldn't be sure he wasn't enjoying it.

He just remained sitting there.

Practice it was, then. "What should I do?"

A sly grin crossed his face, and he rolled his hand out in front of him. "You are only limited by your imagination, Freya."

Great, so if I screwed up it was just a problem with my mind. I considered that, recalling what Steed had said about feeling it, thinking about what I wanted to happen. But I didn't know what I wanted to happen. I had to catch that line of thought before it spiraled out of control, so I concentrated on finding something small. A tiny pebble lay on the ground at my feet. I focused on it hard, willing it to rise. When nothing happened, I looked for Chevelle's reaction.

He watched me, his serene mask back in place. "Do you need motivation?"

I was afraid of the kind of motivation he would provide, remembering the fireballs flying at me in the meadow. "No." My answer was too quick, and he laughed. I knelt closer to the gray rock. I thought it moved a little, as if trembling in fright, and the notion had me shaking my head.

Chevelle stood. "You're trying too hard, Freya. Let us play a game." He held out his hand, and a stone flew from the ground to land in the center of his open palm. He closed his fist around it, and when he opened it a moment later, the stone was floating half an inch above his palm, slick, black, and shaped to form a tiny hawk sculpture.

"It's beautiful," I said, moving to touch it.

He held up his other hand up to stop me. "Take it."

I wanted to hold the trinket. I reached forward and concentrated on moving it from his palm to mine. It floated shakily across the space between us, which seemed so odd that at first, I thought Chevelle must have moved it. I squeezed my fingers around it, as if to verify that it was real, but when I opened my hand again, it was only the dull gray rock.

I didn't hide my disappointment as I looked back at him. He tilted his head toward the stone, and I understood I would have to make the sculpture myself. I closed my fist around it, mostly because I had seen him do the same, and instantly, I knew what I wanted. I opened my palm, grinning triumphantly, and exposed my creation for Chevelle to see. Balancing there was a slightly misshapen but undeniable sculpture of a small black horse. Chevelle rolled his eyes, apparently not impressed with my preoccupation with the horse I'd dubbed Steed.

Still smiling, I looked back to the stone, but it had returned to its uninteresting round shape. Chevelle answered my unspoken question. "Yes, it's... tricky." He smiled a little as he used Steed's word, the expression softening his face. I liked the tilt to his lips, the way it eased that constant strain he seemed to hold at the back of his jaw. "You can't change something's makeup, but you can change the way it appears. You can move it, but only if you're near. You can stop someone's heart, but you can't make them feel happy about it."

He hesitated after that last part then continued. "You can manipulate the elements, move water, draw it from the ground, but you cannot easily make it appear from nothing... though one can usually collect moisture from the air. Fire is easier. It spreads so fast. You can pull a small spark from anywhere to create a flame fueled by the air and..." He trailed off as I leaned closer to him, listening intently.

Chevelle looked into my eyes his explanation ceased. *How well does he know me? What else can I not remember?*

I didn't know what he saw in my gaze, but he blinked and shook his head. "Let's keep working." He stepped a few paces away as he spoke, as if there wasn't a tension between us, an odd sort of friction in a strange situation. "You'll need to think clearly and stay calm. The best fighters are the best thinkers."

"Fighters?" I asked, confused by the direction of the conversation.

He shook his head again as if clearing it. There was a long pause as I waited for his answer. "I'd like you to practice, just for protection."

"I have fire."

He picked up a fallen branch, long and jagged, and snapped the smaller twigs from its side. His knuckle was marked with a short scar, a thin white line clearly faded with time. "Yes, but you should learn to think more openly. It is an important resource that should be familiar to you. You should have years of experience by now."

He was my watcher. He knew things about me I didn't. "Why don't I?" I asked.

He stopped fiddling with the branch. I could tell by his expression that he hadn't meant to say so.

"Why can't I use magic?" I asked. "Why couldn't I use it before?"

There was another long pause before he spoke carefully. "You were bound."

Bound. The word was so foreign in that context. All I could think of was the young children in the village, binding themselves to play the games of fey children who were unmagical until coming of age. I recalled seeing it in the documents in the briar patch—*Francine Glaforia, bound against using all but practical magic.*

I had been bound.

They must have known not to trust me. They must have known. My knees gave out, and I crumpled to the ground. *How many times can the earth be pulled from beneath my feet?*

Chevelle took a step toward me, but I held up a hand to stop him. *Bound against using magic. Assigned a watcher.* My swift and unforgiving anger toward him returned. He had been a volunteer.

He stared at me, his outstretched hands curling into his palms. His thumb twitched, and he opened his mouth to speak. My glare cut him off.

Something flashed in his expression before it finally

settled to resignation. Whatever fellowship had been growing between us was gone. I had been lied to again.

"Let's just go," I said coldly, looking up the mountain.

WE RODE WORDLESSLY on as I stewed over the new knowledge. As my watcher, Chevelle probably would have been involved in the binding by Council. Maybe Fannie should have been punished for whatever she had done, but I couldn't figure how they could have assumed I would follow in her footsteps. So what—I'd killed a bird and stolen a few papers from the council library.

My argument faltered, so I went back to anger and betrayal that Chevelle and Junnie had kept this from me—and it hadn't been only them. The entire village must have known I was bound and that I couldn't perform magic, even as they sat and watched me try. They'd sent me to a special tutor for lessons, allowed Evelyn to taunt me without recourse, and pinned the blame on me for everything that happened, all because they expected me to turn, to resort to dark magic.

The horses slowed to a stop, irritating me further. I didn't even have control over that. If I'd wanted to run away immediately, the beast carrying me would have ignored my commands.

Chevelle stepped down and started a fire. When he walked away, I recalled what he had said earlier in the day, that one could stop someone's heart. It hadn't occurred to me then, but that might have been how he killed his prey. I'd not seen him speak over a weapon or even over his prey, and both he and Steed had seemed to use magic for whatever they did. *Are their clans so different?*

Chevelle made his way back over the scrubby brush with two small rabbits in hand. He dropped them and a branch covered in fat, blood-red berries by the fire, and I posted myself on the edge of an uneven rock to watch.

He didn't speak, but I couldn't tell if he intended to give me my space or was just indifferent. I had, after all, apparently been guilty of something. In his eyes, I was a criminal.

I'd choked a council elder right in front of him. Surely, there was no other way he could see me after that. But there must have been something before, some reason he'd given himself to be my watcher and that made him agree to bind me from reaching my magic.

I was too dangerous. Not to be trusted.

I felt sick. I blinked away hot tears before they could fall, silently wishing Steed was there to build me a shelter, so I could crawl in and hide until morning. I wasn't about to attempt to build one on my own, not when I'd barely been able to mold a tiny sculpture.

A gust of wind pushed the flames beneath the spit, causing them to writhe and jump. They formed shapes that pulled at my memories. I tried to follow them but couldn't seem to get my thoughts to cooperate. I could remember my dreams, the wind and fire surrounding my mother. But the memories that came back when I woke from those vivid nightmares were dull. The harder I clutched at them, the more they faded away.

When recognition dawned, I leapt from the rock, cursing Chevelle. He turned to me as I yelled, "Give it back!" He didn't appear to know what I was talking about, but I was so angry that I was having trouble forming the demand. "Give my memories—my *mind* back!"

Chevelle's confusion seemed to clear, but he didn't offer a response.

My hands trembled. The fire in me itched to burn. "Unbind my thoughts."

"Freya." His voice was smooth. "You don't understand."

I fumed. "Well, I'm sure that has nothing to do with you rummaging around in there."

He shook his head, and his complete lack of agitation caused me to pause. I supposed it was possible that he actually *couldn't* free my thoughts. If the council had bound me, it was likely that all of them would need to reverse it, and they wouldn't do that because they had convicted me. To make matters worse, I'd run away.

I might have asked how the process would work, but I was too furious to pursue conversation with any kind of composure. And it didn't matter, because they'd already counted me guilty. I was staying bound, and there was nothing in the realm that could change it. I let out a frustrated growl, clenching my jaw. He was one of them, and I had to remember that, even if being near him made it so hard.

It didn't matter if he wasn't the sole person responsible for my binding. It hurt worse, mattered more somehow that it was him. I might have run back to the village right then, just to get away from him. But Council would never release me. I had nothing. I glanced down the mountainside. I couldn't have found my way back even if I'd wanted to. I had no idea where I was.

I stared at my shaking palms and the spell-bought map carved into my skin and was hit full force with the knowledge that I didn't even know where I was going.

I was about as low on options as I could get. If not for Chevelle's desire to skip out on council business for a few days, or whatever we were doing here, I would already have been imprisoned. I could hope that with the dreams, the mountains, and wherever the spelled map from my family's vault was taking me, I could remember more and could break some part free. But as it stood, it was the mountains or nothing. I could see no other way.

It was days before I spoke to Chevelle again, though he didn't seem to mind the lack of conversation. He simply rode as he always did, with intermittent glances in each direction, as if I wasn't even there. In truth, he hadn't appeared to notice my behavior at all.

When I finally broke the silence, we were navigating a narrow pass. "How long will we be riding?"

I wasn't specific in my question, not wanting to reveal that I had no idea where we were headed. If he'd really been under the false impression that he had to take me where the map led, I wasn't about to mess that up only to be dragged back to the village, especially after everything that had happened. But I presumed he'd been doing it for other reasons, to delay his own return to the village.

My horse quickened his pace to ride alongside his, and I made a mental note to learn how to control him on my own. The constricted path forced us close together, our stirrups and legs brushing as we rode. Chevelle nodded at my hand, and I held it out, palm up.

Chevelle indicated a spot on one of the mountains. "We are here."

I tried not to let my disappointment show. The information would only have helped if I'd known where I'd started on the map or its end point. But at least I knew we were closer to... something.

When we came through the pass, our path widened, but the horses didn't separate as I had expected them to. I decided I'd had enough of that. "How do I control Steed?"

I could see the humor in his eyes at my phrasing, but he kept a straight face. "Think of where you want him to go and lead his head so."

I concentrated on turning left, and we were instantly spinning, the unexpected twirl throwing me half from my saddle.

Chevelle caught my arm and righted me on my horse. "Maybe not so severely next time."

My face heated, but I focused on the horse's head again, turning him back to our course as I gave a small nudge with my heels.

I was cautious after that, but it became easier to control his movement as we rode. I practiced guiding him, eventually even maneuvering him back and forth between the misshapen rocks and spiky brush on our way. I was still afraid to have him kneel when we stopped for the evening, though—I imagined him rolling on top of me if I tried. I slid down awkwardly and stretched my legs, glad for a rest after the hours of tensing every time the horse changed direction. The air was brisk, and I ran my hands over my arms to warm them.

I started as black swirled around me. Chevelle had thrown a cloak over my shoulders, and he moved in front of me to hook the clasp, his dark eyes piercing mine as he stood so close. My heart stuttered when he leaned in, our faces unbearably near. Just before he touched me, his cheek slid alongside mine, his mouth at my ear. I froze as he spoke low, his breath on my neck sending a shiver through me. "Stay. Still."

Then he was gone. He moved so fast that it took a moment to understand. The hood of the cloak was drawn over my head, and Chevelle stood a good distance away, facing the trees. I was watching him as two men drew near. I hadn't seen them—they must have been concealed or camouflaged by magic, as I had been days before. The tassels decorating their long robes identified them as members of Council, but I wasn't familiar with the two. They mustn't have been from the village.

As they approached Chevelle cautiously, I examined their insignia. Even if they weren't from the village, I still needed council members to unbind me, and I had a sudden urge to go to them. But I remembered Chevelle's warning that I be still.

"She's not going back." Chevelle's tone, level and uncompromising, caught my attention.

I pushed the hood back to better hear, and the taller figure glared at me as he hissed, "You're protecting her when you know what she's capable of?"

I flinched at his words, but something else had caught my eye. The robes were ornate, the tassels interwoven with color. He was Grand Council, the order above those who had convicted me.

I studied the other newcomer, who acted as if I wasn't present. He was incredulous, staring at Chevelle when he spoke. "Her mother slaughtered your clan, your family. Why release this terror—"

The man's words were cut short, his face contorted in

pain. Chevelle had gone rigid, and I could see that every muscle was tense. The councilman struggled, suffering from some unseen force. Blood poured from his nose, and I gasped. Chevelle's head jerked toward me, and I couldn't catch my breath—his eyes were as black as onyx. When his focus returned to the men, they eased away, the first supporting the other by an arm as both bowed slightly, stepping and stumbling in their retreat. Chevelle watched them until they spun to disappear then turned to me.

One look at his face, and I knew the cause of the devastation. I still couldn't remember, but I knew what I had heard was truth.

My mother had killed his family, his entire clan. He'd been there in the village in my dreams and memories. He had saved me. His family had been there as well—the people running and screaming and dying were his clan. I suddenly knew the cloaks in that vision too. They were Grand Council, just as the men had been. Council was circling my mother to stop her from killing the northern clans. I didn't know why. I didn't know how I knew, but I was certain I didn't want my memories back. What I had was already too much.

I couldn't fathom the pain Chevelle had suffered, which was surely a hundred times mine at the loss of my mother. *His mother... his father... each member of his family? How much loss had he endured?* Tears streamed down my face.

Chevelle took a step toward me, and I was struck by fear. *He must despise me.* That was why he'd become my watcher.

He gave a curt nod at my reaction, his head still dipped as he walked away. I wanted to speak, but the words choked me. I wrapped myself tighter into the cloak as Chevelle constructed a hasty shelter.

I was his responsibility, but surely, he loathed me—I

couldn't fathom how he could feel any other way. I thought back to the scenarios I had envisioned after the memories of my mother being killed came back to me. What I would do to those men if I were ever to find them.

But then I remembered the truth. They were saving the North.

I couldn't say I didn't still want revenge, though, and I contemplated what he must have felt about me for taking so much from him. My mind was reclassifying every look he'd ever given me, everything that had happened since I'd met him, why he hadn't looked at me as I'd lain under the tree in the meadow, explaining why Fannie had struck me, why I'd wanted to learn transfer magic... to get my mother's things. The look he'd given the pendant on my neck... my mother's pendant. Of course he'd volunteered to be my watcher. I had taken everything from him.

My thoughts began to muddle as my mother, my dreams, and my own life twisted together. I still couldn't retrieve my memories—I only had the last years, which suddenly seemed a haze. The only parts clear to me were the days since Chevelle had walked through Junnie's door.

I thought of how I had cursed him when I'd found he was my watcher and the hate in my voice when I'd demanded my memories— the memories of his family's murder—back.

My mind writhed with anguish through the night. As I emerged from the shelter late the next morning, I was resigned to continue my journey with him and let him return me to Council without resistance. It was all I could do.

I found him sitting near the shelter's entrance, distress apparent in his features.

"Thank you," I said, indicating the shelter.

He nodded, but his face didn't quite return to the serene mask he usually wore.

My stomach knotted. I hadn't eaten since our ride the day before.

"I'll get you some food," he said. A fire lit beside us as if of its own accord. He strode off in search of food, and I sat close, tucking my cheeks into the material of the cloak for warmth. A moment later, he was back and roasting our breakfast over the flames. We ate in silence then mounted the horses as we had each day before, but it was obvious that nothing was the same. It never could be.

I was racked with guilt as we made our way up the mountain. I purposefully rode behind him, glad to be able to control the horse on my own.

Small patches of snow had started to dot the landscape, and the vegetation had turned a darker, sharper green. Occasionally, the sun would break through the mist, making me squint, and I would appreciate the calmer, hazier atmosphere —gloom, as they called it at home, in the usually sunny village where I would spend my eternity. I wondered where I would be kept as a captive, if there would be windows, if I was unfit for public view.

Chevelle picked up speed after we passed through the more difficult part of the trail, and we rode fast for the rest of the day. I struggled to keep up. I was sure I knew the cause of his hurry. He'd decided he wanted to get the journey over with, end it, and return me to Council for punishment. He wanted to be done with me.

We rode long into the evening, well past sunset, and I began to wonder if he would stop at all. Maybe it was that torturous to be near me. I was contemplating possible ways to sleep on a horse when he finally stopped. We were riding through a small pass, the moonlight barely lighting our way, and Chevelle's horse disappeared. My head swiveled, searching for any sign of them, and then my own horse turned beneath an overhang and stopped in a cavern so dark I hadn't seen it until we were there.

Chevelle tossed out a small flame, giving us enough light to dismount. The horses walked to one end of the cavern, their hoofbeats echoing softly as we remained on the other end.

"Frey." Chevelle turned to me as he spoke. "Yesterday... the council trackers..."

Trackers? I tried to focus on what he was saying and not let my mind run wild with new information. "They will send someone for what I have done." I thought of the councilman's face, distorted in pain.

"We should continue your training."

"Training?" Even I could hear the dread in my question.

"Practice. You should be able to protect yourself."

I remembered his words from before the revelation that had ended my magic lessons. *Fighters.* A chill ran down my spine at the word, at the remembered violence in my watcher's gaze. I nodded my assent, biting back my questions. I'd skinned out of a few run-ins with Council, and it was no secret how they operated. I might be safe enough with Chevelle, but if the others retrieved me...

"We will work again at first light and possibly as we ride."

Part of me wanted to argue. *As we ride?* But I knew how serious it was. I was a fugitive, and it appeared that even Grand Council was looking for me. I had no idea what my punishment would be. We weren't in the village. It would be far worse than anything High Council could have planned. I'd heard the stories of prisoners thrown into holes dug deep into the earth and void of light and air, trapped in too-small cages while they awaited trials that never came, taken into the depths of the ancient council chamber system never to be seen again.

And that wasn't even counting what might happen before my captors delivered me. "What will they do if I can't protect myself?"

His face was grim. He didn't reply, and I suddenly didn't want him to.

We settled onto the floor of the small den, our backs against the wall, the rocky overhang blocking the light of the moon.

"That is my flame," Chevelle said. "Try to extinguish it."

My training began.

8

Early the next morning, even before first light, Chevelle woke me for training. Gone were the games we had played—the lessons were intense and stressful. I'd been unable to generate magic on demand, so he'd started lunging at me with weapons, sticks, and fire, forcing me to respond to protect myself. After each attack, he would come right back at me, and if I tried to repeat a tactic for defense, he would overpower my magic and push me to find a new maneuver.

I was beat, winded, drained.

"Mount up," he announced.

When I started to climb onto my horse, the horse shot off like an arrow, almost knocking me to the ground. I glared at Chevelle's back, but he was already galloping away.

I reached out with magic, drawing Steed's head around to press him back to me, climbed up, and clicked my heels hard to catch Chevelle. He was riding too fast again, and I was not looking forward to the day, sure it would be worse than the miserable morning. I rode up beside him, planning a snide remark about the trick, but I was distracted by a black stone in his hand. It was oddly shaped and just smaller than my balled fist. *Onyx,* I thought, though I'd never seen an onyx that big.

His gaze was intent. "Be prepared at all times. This will come at you from every direction. It is the only way you can learn to respond quickly. You need to get past that block and to use your instinct as defense."

I really didn't want to play anymore, but before I could protest, a black rock hurtled toward me. My hand jerked up automatically to swat it away, but my arm hit an invisible wall. The rock slammed into me. I was fairly certain there would be more than a minor bruise from the impact. I tried to slow my horse but no longer had control of him.

"Again," Chevelle said.

The rock came for me a second time. I tried to duck out of the way, but the wall was there once more, blocking me from moving. I cursed as the stone glanced off my arm.

"This isn't fair," I complained. It seemed he was holding me in place just to strike me.

"It's the only way, Freya. This is for your protection."

"I highly doubt they will pummel me with rocks," I spat out.

"No," he said, "they will bind you and burn you alive."

I felt sick. A vision of the Grand Council cloaks circling me was convincing enough.

But he continued. "You will not know their thoughts. You must be ready for any attack."

I nodded, even though part of me was certain there was a less painful way.

The rock came at me again. I couldn't respond quickly enough, couldn't counter and hold onto a galloping horse in the instant it took him to decide. It wasn't dangerous, but it was like being slapped—the irritation had me itching to burn something. The volley continued, and whenever my anger showed, the rock came harder and faster, so I tried to control the emotion or at least hide it. That was the hardest part. Eventually, I found the best defense was to block the attacks by deflecting them with other objects. His magic was too powerful to counter directly, and he'd prevented me from ducking.

When I was blocking about half the strikes successfully, he pocketed the stone and progressed with sticks, water, fire, and anything else he found on the trail. We were still riding too quickly, and I was exhausted from the mental and physical exertion when he switched to full-body attacks. By nightfall, I wasn't able to fend off anything that came at me, and he mercifully stopped the horses beneath another hollow in the mountain. I was practically asleep before I slid off my horse.

THE NEXT MORNING, I woke to the sound of rock against rock. There was no sign of Chevelle or his horse in the dim stone hollow. I sat up, rubbing my sore legs, unable to believe he'd left me. And then the rock wall struck me in the face.

I cursed, my voice hoarse from sleep. The wall came at me again. "Okay, okay!" I shouted. "Let me up."

Chevelle's camouflage dissipated, and he stared down at me, disappointed. His short hair was smooth, his face clean. He did not look nearly as bedraggled as I must have.

I frowned. "Where's your horse?"

He smirked as the beast nipped at the back of my head, yanking my hair. Grumbling, I swatted the horse away and ran my hand over my face, sure it was mottled with bruises and scratch marks.

"Drink this." Chevelle offered me a hide flagon.

I took it, swallowing a mouthful before the taste hit me. I gagged, losing half a mouthful onto the rock.

Chevelle chuckled. "It will help with the healing."

Why bother? I wondered. *It'll be another day of bombardment with mountain fixtures... maybe whole trees this time.* My face pinched with annoyance.

Chevelle threw me a piece of dried meat, barely holding back a smile as he jumped on his horse. "You'd better get started," he said, "it's going to be a long walk."

As he kicked his heels, I spun toward the corner where my horse had been. The beast was galloping up the mountain, just over a hundred yards away. I tried to think quickly and to keep the anger from slowing my response. Using magic to pull Chevelle's horse by the tail, I ran after him, hoping to leap on. A tree branch came from nowhere and smacked me flat across the face. Chevelle's horse grunted as they rode away.

"Why the face?" I yelled at his back.

I winced as a second branch, young and green and more like a lash, struck me from behind. A fierce growl escaped me, and I took off, running at full speed in the direction my horse had gone.

By midday, I was completely spent. I had eventually caught my horse, but the training hadn't let up. I was too exhausted for any anger to remain, but I had the sneaking suspicion that Chevelle was enjoying my lessons.

We stopped by a patch of snow that had gathered in a rock basin, warming it to water for the horses. Chevelle jumped down from his horse as I melted off the side of mine and onto a rock, my limbs like molasses.

He came to sit across from me, and I flinched, expecting another attack.

He smiled. "Well, at least you're anticipating assault."

I didn't have the energy for casual banter, but I did manage to glare at him.

He pointed northeast. "The village is a few hours' ride from here." He retrieved a fresh set of clothes from his pack and handed it across to me. "Go ahead and get cleaned up. I'll be back in a few moments."

I tried to pull myself together as he strode away, but I felt so drained. I stood, easing my clothes, soiled and tattered from the days of battering, off. The damage on my bare skin was minimal. I had imagined much worse, as I'd failed to block so many of the strikes. I satisfied my ego by giving that nasty elixir more credit than was probably due, but some part of me knew the training had not been hard because it was physical. It had been the use of magic that made it grueling.

I put the new shirt made of soft black leather and corseted tight around my waist, on. Slim, dark wool pants and tall boots went on next, and I wondered at the village we'd be entering, where black was appropriate. I could think of no one at home who had worn black—I envisioned the dainty blond elves dancing around in dark leather and giggled.

I glanced up to find Chevelle wearing an unfathomable expression. It was likely I looked as if I was having a breakdown. I hastily finished lacing the boots, throwing the cloak around my shoulders as he left more rations as Chevelle readied the horses.

I stretched out on the ground to eat, examining the carved medallion clasped to my boot. Chevelle stepped away again, disappearing behind the rocks that had become more jagged and taller along our way.

When he returned, the sight of him stole my breath. His worn traveling clothes were gone, exchanged for dark gray and black, a leather vest covering his shirt, the laces loose at his chest. A long, dark cloak was clasped at his shoulders, the material thick, coarse, and so unlike the soft robes the rest of Council wore. I knew I was gaping at him, but there was something so strange about it.

He caught my eye, and I let my gaze fall to his sword belt, struggling to gather my composure. I had to remind myself that he despised me.

By late afternoon, our path opened to look down on the village nestled in the rocks of a narrow valley ahead. Chevelle stopped on a ridge to allow us a better view, which made me rethink calling it a village—I couldn't count the structures from our vantage point, but it must have been ten times the size of home. The buildings were the dull stone of the mountain. None were made of trees. There was really no vegetation at all, no greens, no browns. The entire layout was made of dark, ashen stones and aged wood that seemed to melt into the bluish gray of the mountain. The cloudy mist filtered the sun, and I decided it was beautiful.

"Where are we?" I asked.

Chevelle nodded toward my hands as he started down the path.

The map on my palms was gone. My skin was unmarked, with no indication whatsoever it had even been burned. *Is this our destination?* My gaze shot up to find the village, then I hastily clicked my heels when I realized I was being left behind.

As we advanced, I could see movement among the elves. There was much activity, but it was nothing like home. There were no flags of quilts and rugs blowing in the breeze, no bright sunlight on a rainbow of colors, no dancing in the village center. A raucous sound traveled up to us, and Chevelle waved a hand, his magic bringing the hood of my cloak up to cover my head before he did the same with his own. At once, my stomach was a knot again.

We rode into town at a walk. Chevelle sat straight and tall in his saddle, but his arm hung casually, his hand resting on his leg. I was more comfortable watching him and looking for a reaction than I was with the passing elves.

Two men walked by in the opposite direction, their dark eyes on us. My cape blew back, exposing the shape of my leg, and they hissed indecent comments. I gasped, shocked, and my horse picked up its pace to ride beside Chevelle. Chevelle lifted two fingers slightly to silence me.

We hadn't ridden more than a quarter of the way into town when he turned the horses to a medium-sized structure, stopping before a water trough. He dismounted effortlessly and pulled me from my horse and into the building in a few quick steps, closing the door behind us.

It was dark inside, and his fingers lingered on my arm. I felt him shift as he waved a hand, and several lanterns around the main room lit, giving off a soft glow. He indicated a door on the rear wall. "Your room."

I drew back my hood, nodding.

"I have some business to take care of before we move on."

Move on? So this isn't our destination. Or does he mean back to the village?

He continued, apparently not noticing my perplexed expression as my mind ran through a list of possible scenarios. "The pouch from the vault. There was a stone in it."

It was clear he was asking for the ruby, but I wasn't sure why. I didn't think I had much choice in the matter, given that I was a criminal, but I could come up with no real reason to fight it. Standing in the center of that strange room, in the middle of a mountain, had me thinking through fog. I was going to be returned to the village for punishment or worse, since I was being tracked by Grand Council. I was completely ignorant of where I was. I had apparently lost part of my memories and magic because I had been bound—I was still bound.

I realized Chevelle was watching me, waiting for the stone. Shaking free of the thoughts, I removed the pouch from my pack to untie the lacing.

I reached inside, wondering momentarily what else might be written in the ancient language on the scroll. I handed the dark-red stone to Chevelle, who only nodded as he took it from me, not examining it before he slipped it into a pocket to hide it. There was a sound at the door, and his fingers slid over my lower back, urging me into my room. I was closed in just as the main door opened, giving me no more than a glimpse of someone's deep-red curls.

I tried not to be annoyed about being closed in a room—I

was a prisoner, after all. Chevelle's voice was barely audible as he spoke to his visitor in a formal tone. "Ruby."

Ruby? Before I could stop myself, I was at the door, peering through the frame. A tiny crack of light allowed me a partial view of Chevelle's back and all of his guest. Ruby looked to be a little shorter than me, a little smaller, but she seemed larger somehow. I thought I knew why. Around her petite face, by some means both wicked and charming, was a mane of deep crimson hair flowing in curls.

I considered her name, given that mass of hair, but any sympathy disappeared as she reached out a hand toward Chevelle. There was something sinful about the way her hand turned seductively in the simple task of retrieving the stone—my stone—from him.

Anger swelled in me. I wasn't sure if I had given it to Chevelle because I'd trusted him or because he was my captor, but I couldn't shake the feeling of betrayal. I couldn't fathom why he would be giving my family heirloom to that woman. The ruby had been in the vault with my mother's possessions along with the map that had taken us here, and he was giving that Ruby *my* ruby. I shook my head. There must have been a connection, some reason it would end here.

Ruby drew a package from her cape and handed it to Chevelle, smiling a temptress's smile. It was about two hands in size and wrapped in light-brown cloth. He slid it under his cloak, and it disappeared from my view. I couldn't imagine what she had given him, but it must have been in trade for my stone.

As I peered through the gap in the doorframe, the stranger's eyes flicked to mine, and I was sure she somehow saw me. I held my breath and jerked away from view, plastering myself against the wall. When she didn't speak up to expose me, my pulse began to slow, but I wasn't brave enough to look again.

I stared into the room and noticed that the space was relatively large and ornate compared to my bedroom at home. There was a stone-framed bed wide enough for two with dark-olive blankets in layers on top. A side table held a few trinkets and a decanter set, and there was a hickory wardrobe in the corner. A full mirror lined the east wall.

I took a few steps forward, staring in disbelief as my figure came into view. I had seen the reflection in the water and knew my hair was dark and my eyes a strange shade of green, but as I gazed at the woman in my reflection, I could not reconcile the two. The dark silhouette, her figure emphasized by fitted clothes, her black cape draped behind her—the woman was breathtaking. I moved closer to examine her, nearly reaching out to touch her windblown sable hair. Her eyes—my eyes—were dark. That muddy fog was gone, and under my black lashes waited deep emerald jewels, flecked with the darkest of browns. Chevelle had been right—it did suit me. The image in the mirror was stunning.

It felt odd to marvel over my own reflection, but I couldn't pretend I didn't like it. The changes were still unnerving, though, and I tried to remember what I looked like in my oldest memories and to see who I was before, to remember my mother's face.

The door opened behind me.

"Ah, yes," Ruby purred as she looked me over. "Lovely."

Her inflection left no doubt that the word was not a compliment, only that she found it lovely she'd discovered me. I could see Chevelle through the open door behind her, still in the main room and evidently annoyed.

"I, of course, am Ruby," she said. "I'm pleased you'll be staying with me during your visit."

Staying with her? This is her house? I was sure I was wearing the same irritated look as Chevelle. I was also certain, by the way she watched me, that Ruby had seen me spying. Her mouth was twisted in a smile, loaded with false honey. I noticed her eyes then, looking past the heavy paint they wore, to dark green jewels—emeralds. They were so like those I had just examined in the mirror that I had to look away.

"Frey," I replied softly. "Thank you for the room."

She seemed disappointed that I had no further comment. She flitted her hand in dismissal as she swirled out of the room and back to Chevelle, the metal bracelets around her wrists tinkling like chimes.

"I'm off to town, then. You *know*," she sang at him, "a handsome hunk of horsemeat was asking about you this morning."

My ears perked up. *Someone was asking about Chevelle? That must be why we're here.* And then I realized she had called someone a hunk of horsemeat, and I had to stifle a laugh.

Chevelle nodded but made no remark on the inquirer. Ruby winked at him on her way out, and the gesture lit a burn in my chest. I turned back to my room and climbed into bed, angry at myself more than anything else and determined not to let him see. I covered my head with a corner of the blanket, suffocating my fractured thoughts with the absence of light.

～

I WAS unsure how long I'd slept. The house was quiet when I slipped from bed, trying not to make a sound. I peeked into the main room, finding Chevelle sitting against the front wall, a small window above his head. He leaned over, working on something in the palm of his hand, a steady scratching accompanying the movement of his wrist. I started forward, and my boot scuffed the floor, alerting him to my presence. As he glanced up, he slid whatever he'd been working on into a pocket at his hip.

It dawned on me then that the main room had only the entrance and two other doors. If we were staying with Ruby, then the second room must be hers. I meant to offer Chevelle my room to sleep in, but the look on his face was so unnerving that I could not stop myself from offering something else. "You don't... You don't have to protect me." I hoped it was true. "I can turn myself in, take myself to the village, or —" I was trying to say Grand Council, but the words stuck in my throat.

No part of me wanted to surrender to my mother's killers, but I could not make Chevelle suffer more than he already had. My hands trembled, and I tightened them into fists. He was my watcher, and he must have felt he needed to fulfill his duties, to keep his honor. I knew he would finish our journey and return me to the village.

"Freya." He said my name as if it were tearing at him, and my chest ached. "You don't understand." His eyes closed for a long moment before they found me again. "You can't submit to Grand Council. You can *never* submit."

He was right, I didn't understand. *Does he intend to return me to the village, to High Council? Or will he keep me safe from the others?*

"You remember what they did to your mother?"

I felt my face pale. I'd known they were dangerous, but I wondered whether he meant that to submit was to accept her fate. The image of flames and a circle of cloaks surrounding her was there again, and I had to force it away before it turned to an image of me. "Protection," he'd kept saying as we worked on magic. *They're going to burn me.* "They would kill me because of the pendant, the library?"

"No, Frey. You have broken some of your bonds. They will not risk trying to bind you again."

I struggled with an intake of breath.

He stood and started toward me, about to speak again just as the door swung open. Chevelle's face flushed with anger.

"Elfreda!" Steed was through the door and to me in three long strides. He grabbed me at the waist, picking me up and spinning me so that my cloak swirled behind me.

The shock and exuberance of his greeting was too much, and I couldn't help but let out a breathless laugh.

He put me down but kept me close, his hands still at my waist. I stared up at him, taking in the clean version of someone I'd come to know as a bit dusty and wild. His short, dark hair was straight and clean, his clothes of a more casual sort.

"Steed," I said, very nearly winded. "What are you doing here?"

He glanced at Chevelle, who was still plainly annoyed, and his carefree smile dissolved. "I was heading to Bray and ran across some trackers."

Chevelle's eyes flicked to my face and then back to Steed.

Steed dropped his hands from my waist as he winked at me. "I saw the horses out front and couldn't resist. I knew you'd be missing me."

I tried to smile, but the thought of trackers had taken the

thrill out of the unexpected visit. The vision of flames was threatening again, and I swallowed hard.

Chevelle threw on his cloak and put his hood up. "Stay here," he ordered me. He gestured toward Steed, who turned to follow him outside.

I wasn't sure how long they'd be gone. I went to one of the narrow windows on the front wall and peered cautiously out. They were nowhere to be seen, but the sights of the village distracted me quickly enough.

It was so unlike home. Night gave the gray stones an even darker appearance, the firelight glinting off their ragged edges like polished onyx. Torches lit each walkway and building. It seemed late, but several villagers, loud and boisterous, were still outside. Nearly everyone was dressed in black, a few of the men bearing large silver breastplates or wrist cuffs. Most wore leather, laced tightly against thick, muscled frames. Few were as thin or petite as the elves I was used to seeing. These were strong like Chevelle and Steed. All but one had dark hair—*Ruby*.

I cursed. She was approaching the house, and I was alone. Part of me wondered if I was fast enough to get to my room before she came in. I hadn't made up my mind before the door opened beside me.

"Well, well. Alone, are we?" she purred, smiling wickedly as she neared, coming uncomfortably close. "Let's talk." She leaned in farther, and something glistened in the air between us.

I froze, unable to move away.

"Stop." Chevelle's voice was sharp as the redhead was whisked away from me, laughing. Her curls brushed my face on their way past, taking my head on a dizzying spin.

"Just having a little fun, Vattier," she said.

It sounded too far away or as if I were in a tunnel. Chevelle was reprimanding her, and then they were gone. My head swirled, and I felt off-balance. I started to stumble, but a strong hand caught my arm.

"Easy there, honeysuckle." Steed's voice beside me drew me from the stupor.

"What happened?" I asked. My mouth tingled.

"A little fairy dust. Breath of the siren."

"What?" My tongue was thick.

Steed chuckled. "Intoxicating, isn't it?" I could hear the smile in his voice. "It won't hurt you."

My nose tingled, and I scrunched it up, giggling at the feeling. I shook my head, trying to clear it. "Fairy breath?"

"Red. She's a half-breed. How do you feel?" Steed asked.

"Weird."

"Yes, that's normal."

"Hot," I said, unclasping my cloak and tossing it off behind me. I swayed.

"Maybe you should sit down."

That sounded like a good idea. "Half-breed?" I asked, unable to form full sentences.

"Half fey, half elf." He sat in a chair as he started to answer, and I kept moving past the bench where I intended to land and crawled onto his lap, curling my knees to my chest. His voice was mesmerizing as he continued. "Her mother was a fey from the West. Fiery one, her."

I wrapped my arms around my legs, holding my knees tightly, and placed my chin there to rest my head. "Tell me more." It was all I could do to pay attention to his words, but I was fascinated by their sound.

"Her father was a dark elf. When her mother died during childbirth, he left Ruby here in the village. I suppose it was for the best, really, since she can't fly. The fey would have tormented her. She's still a bit of an outcast, though." He was still talking as I struggled to catch up in my head.

I interrupted him, unable to stop myself. "My mother died." I had no idea why I was speaking. I batted my eyes and tried to shake it off, concentrating on Steed again.

He seemed to notice I was back and continued his story. I leaned my head on his chest, snuggling into his warmth. My face felt numb.

Somewhere in the distance, the door opened, and the vibration in Steed's chest quieted as his words stopped. Still in a daze, I turned my head toward the door, keeping it steady against Steed. Chevelle's furious gaze flicked to my cloak piled on the floor before returning to us. *Us.* I was curled in Steed's lap.

Chevelle stormed toward us. The arm wrapped around my back loosened, but Steed's body didn't seem to tense. *His body.* I giggled a little for no apparent reason then tried to straighten myself so I wasn't cuddling with him. Chevelle held his arm out, and I wondered foggily if he intended to strike one of us, which made me laugh again. He shook his head, plainly disapproving, and a flagon landed in his open palm. He knelt in front of us. "Drink."

I was so thirsty. I took a long pull then another. I couldn't seem to quench the thirst. He took the container from my hand. "Enough."

My stomach roiled, and I realized what I had drunk. "Ugh, blah." I thought I might vomit. *How much of that healing crap did I drink?* I heaved once, and Steed shook beneath me with laughter. I glanced up to find him looking at Chevelle. For some reason, it angered me, even though I knew Steed wasn't laughing at him.

I was talking again without regard to thought. "His mother died too. We killed her." It sounded so matter-of-fact, and my head bobbed along with the words. I couldn't seem to stop. My mouth opened to speak once more, but I was suddenly swept off of Steed's lap and into Chevelle's arms. I managed fear for half a second then lost the feeling to dizziness, followed quickly by only dull numbness.

Chevelle was lying me on my bed. "Stay here. It will pass." His words were gentle, the anger gone.

"I'm sorry," I whispered. He didn't respond. He leaned over me to straighten the bedding, his face close to mine. I stared at his mouth, wondering briefly what it might taste like.

I felt a sharp pain and realized I was biting my lip. The thought made me giggle again, but Chevelle's eyes shot to my face, and all amusement ceased.

The back of his hand brushed lightly over my cheek. "Sleep."

And I did.

My dreams were vivid. Crimson curls brushed my cheek and bounced as a slender fairy danced across the floor, flitting her painted fingers. Stone houses stood in the night, the glare of fire glinting off the rock. Massive stones rose high above. Dark leather was tight against my skin. Cloaks flowed in the wind, forming a circle and then massing together ominously. Black hair glistened with sweat in the moonlight and rolled in rhythm as the horse ran, its mane rocking hypnotically with the motion. Its heavy equine smell was unlike any other. I clung to Chevelle's strong back as we rode at full speed. The wind and rain cut at my face, and my eyes grew sore, my cheeks streaked with tears and ash.

~

I AWOKE STARTLED by the sound of laughter. It took several minutes to gather my thoughts enough to know where I was. *In bed... at Ruby's. Ruby, the half-breed.*

I was drenched in sweat. My head throbbed. Something had happened to me. Fey dust, Steed had said. Voices echoed through the open door. He was in the main room. Chevelle was there too. My mouth tasted sour. I tried to sit up, but my head spun. Before I'd moved an inch, I was back down. My pulse pounded in my temples as I struggled to recall what had happened during the evening. I hissed out a low oath when I remembered Ruby leaning toward me, blowing her glitter in my face.

My eyes opened again to find Chevelle offering me a glass. I winced, unsure of what I had said to him. I knew it was bad but couldn't quite piece it together. I glanced up at him timidly. "Thank you," I croaked as I took the cup, my hand trembling.

"Shouldn't have left you alone," he said quietly. There was a tinkling laugh in the front room, and I groaned. She was there too. The water helped. I was able to sit up with Chevelle's assistance.

Ruby swirled into the room, dressed in a red frock of sorts. The color hurt my eyes. "Here, a bath will help. Come with me, dear." Her hair was tied halfway back with a scarf, its tattered ends mingling with her crimson curls. I felt dizzy again. She hauled me off the bed, supporting me as I stood. She was much smaller than I thought and slipped easily under my arm. I kept my head down as we walked, mostly trying not to get ill but also unable to look Steed in the eyes. I watched Ruby's heeled boots as she led me through the main room and to the door of her bedroom.

"A bath?" I asked, confused.

She laughed. "Well, yes. A little cold for lake bathing here." She led me to a large basin in the corner of her room. Water streamed in to fill it halfway. "I've laid out some clothes for you, and there are some lovely soaps on the table." She spun and glided out of the room, closing the door behind her. *Lovely soaps.*

I examined the room as I undressed. A large bed, twice the size of the one I'd been using and topped with decorated pillows and colorful blankets was centered on the opposite wall. A tall rack in the corner was draped with material, deep-violet and emerald-green silks, dark wools, and a rainbow of patterned scarves. Shelves alongside were filled full with curiosities, and a few books lay on the bedside table near a lantern.

I stepped into the tub, sinking down as lavender-scented steam rose to dampen my face and hair. I breathed deeply. It seemed to be helping, so I closed my eyes and relaxed.

The water started to chill several times, but I was hesitant to get out. At the risk of boiling myself, I used magic to reheat the bath.

Finally, I felt well enough to stand. I picked up one of the soaps, washed quickly, then pulled the water from the tub to rinse the suds away. I'd not had much opportunity to practice with water, and I added it to the list of things to work on. It had been a long journey, and the bath was refreshing. The soap left a light fragrance in the air, smelling like morning and cold, and I wondered if the fairy dust was still affecting me.

I dried off and dressed in the clothes Ruby had put out for me. They were a little snug, but not enough to have been her castoffs. The room had its own full-length mirror, and I chuckled at my reflection. It was certainly not an outfit I would have chosen for myself, though I couldn't say it looked bad. I turned away, still painfully unaccustomed to my new appearance, and tugged down the hem of the short leather top.

Steed let out a whistle as I entered the main room. Ruby sat beside him, a warm smile on her face as if we were old friends. Chevelle was near a window on the front wall, leaning on one shoulder, his body turned toward me and his expression impossible to read.

"Better?" Ruby asked.

"Yes, thank you." I was polite, but it burned a little to thank her after what she'd done.

Steed smiled, shaking his head from side to side with exaggerated slowness. "Some night." He looked like he was trying to keep a secret. Heat crawled up my neck as I remembered climbing into his lap the first time and then again, the second time I'd gotten out of bed.

Ruby grinned at him conspiratorially. "Yes, so educational."

Had I talked in my sleep? Could this get any worse? Yes, it could. It came back to me then. I dropped into a chair, my head falling into my hands to cover my face.

Ruby started to say something, but Chevelle cut her off. "Won't you offer your guest breakfast?"

She sniffed. "Lunch, maybe." A plate of food landed on the table in front of me with a slap.

"Thank you," I managed. I was hungry despite the embarrassment. I grabbed the plate and started eating.

Ruby and Steed were sitting across from me. She was

reclined, her bare legs showing where the material of her skirt was pulled to the side. When I looked up, she resituated herself, leaning toward Steed and talking quietly about some nonsense. She walked her fingers up his chest as she talked, glancing at me for a reaction.

She was trying to make me jealous. I was suddenly furious. She'd poisoned me, and now this. I wanted to burn her right then and there. I caught Chevelle's expression as I glared at her. He had seen what she was doing and most likely knew her motives, but I could tell he thought it had worked. He thought I was jealous.

Perfect.

I smelled something odd and glanced down. The meat I was holding had burnt in my hand. I cursed, dropping it onto the plate.

When I looked back to them, Steed was watching me, smiling. I tossed the burned meat onto the table and considered going back to bed.

Ruby laughed, and it made my hair stand on end. *No, I'll stay.* She might have been our host now, but I knew I would get my chance. I would fix her. She shifted, and the markings on her leg caught my attention. A thin, painted vine trailed up to her thigh.

She noticed me looking. "Well, Frey, I feel like I know so much about you"—she smiled slyly at Chevelle—"but you know so little of me. Let me tell you a few things, since we will be traveling together."

I felt my head jerk to find Chevelle, not believing what I had just heard.

Ruby continued without pause, "I'm sure you've heard by now that I'm an amalgamation, a half-breed." She said the last part with distaste and glanced at Steed. "I will give you a short version of events, so when the subject comes up—and believe me, someone will ask—you are not overcome by curiosity and forced to seek less than honorable venues to discover the facts."

I chose to ignore the jab about my eavesdropping.

"My mother was a power-hungry wench seeking notoriety. She was an elemental fey and, like me, she sported a fine head of red hair." She ran a hand under the curls for emphasis. "She heard a story one day of a mixed-species birth and got it in her head that she could breed a more powerful magic. Apparently, she thought she could control her offspring and use the magic to her advantage... I suppose she thought she could rule the realm." Ruby smirked.

"She studied various species for a few moons and decided her best chance at conquest was a dark elf. She made her way to this very village and happened across my father, the poor, unsuspecting sap." Ruby flitted her fingers, and glasses of wine appeared before each of us as she continued. "So there he was, and she, just a wisp of a woman, flew up to him and blew a little fairy dust... You know about that."

I narrowed my eyes at her.

Ruby grinned. "He was putty in her hands. It was all over before he even knew her purpose. She kept him under her enchantments and lies as long as she could. She thought she was safe, hiding here in the village, but as you know, an elf birth is a hefty event. Upon the hour of my birth, the entire village had gathered to see the newcomer, at my father's request, of course. Can you imagine the shock when they found that my mother was his intended?"

She laughed, but her audience was quiet. Chevelle, wearing an uncomfortable expression, turned to look out the front window.

"Needless to say, it did not go as she had planned. At her death, my father was released from her bonds. He was horrified by what he had done, by what had been done to him. But he hadn't the heart to destroy his crop. He simply left."

I felt a tug in my chest at her story, but Ruby's eyes were dry and clear. I wondered how many times she'd told it.

"I hear he wanders the mountain, probably killing fey." Ruby laughed again. That time, it sounded like genuine humor. The tension in the room eased a bit.

"Ruby." Chevelle's tone was respectful as he turned from the window.

"They're here?" she asked.

He nodded, and she rose gracefully from her seat. "Well, looks like we have some gathering to do. We can finish this later." She smiled at me as she followed Chevelle out the door.

9

S teed sat quietly across from me, seemingly lost in thought.

"Seems so sad," I said. I was thinking of Chevelle's loss, of my own, and of Ruby's, wondering how we could all be without family. "Your mother..." I trailed off.

He sighed. "My mother died years ago with a large part of the northern clans."

I cringed. His mother had died because of my mother, same as Chevelle. I was almost afraid to ask. "And your father?"

His smile was arch. "My father wanders the mountain, killing fey."

My jaw dropped. "You mean Ruby is your sister?"

"Half-sister," he emphasized. He let me roll that around for a while before he spoke again. "You know, Ruby told me she'd had dealings with the infamous Chevelle Vattier, but I didn't believe her. One can never be too careful with the tales of a fairy."

Infamous?

"But imagine my surprise when he walked out of the trees, following a green-eyed beauty." Steed smiled at the memory before his mood turned serious. "When I ran into the trackers, I had hoped Ruby had told the truth and might know where to find you." He laughed. "She tried to hide you, but I recognized the horses out front."

"She tried to hide us?"

"Ah, yes. Fey are full of treacheries and wickedness. Always meddling in the affairs of others, causing trouble whenever possible. They have quite a time. At least Red's only half wicked."

His sister. I was having trouble wrapping my mind around it all.

"Don't worry. She's had her fun with you. She'll be helpful now." He grinned, and I wasn't sure if it was sarcastic. "Besides, it sounds like you're the biggest trouble going. She would do well to stick around you."

I frowned.

"I'll keep an eye on her," he promised.

"You?" I asked, remembering Ruby's announcement. "You're traveling with us?"

"You don't mind, do you?"

"No, of course not," I gushed. I was too eager. "Chevelle's been training me."

"Well, we can certainly help with that."

I grimaced at the thought of what Ruby's training methods might be.

"Don't fret. She's actually very talented." His smile warmed. "An asset, you'll see."

An asset?

Ruby came through the door in a movement that could nearly have been classified as whirling. "Come on, Steed. We need to set you up outside of town. Chevelle is afraid we're causing a scene in the village." She laughed lightly. It seemed as if she was enjoying herself. I wondered if that meant she was causing trouble. "Don't think he trusts you with the girl," Ruby added, smiling playfully.

"I prefer the outdoors anyway." Steed dipped toward me, his hand folding his waist in a bow as he stood to go. "Sunshine."

M y head was not up for this at all. *His sister. Traveling with us. An asset.* I rested my forehead against my knees.

"Are you ill?" Chevelle said from beside me. I hadn't even heard him come in. He was sitting forward on the bench next to me, and when I jerked up in surprise, it put us too close. I tottered, and he steadied me but didn't move away.

He leaned closer. "You smell... like morning."

I bit my lip, heat rising up my neck, but he lingered, breathing in the scent. "Ruby," I said.

He looked confused.

"Soap." I had been reduced to one-word sentences.

"Oh." He nodded, leaning back. "She does have a way with potions and such."

"I enjoy the mixing," Ruby said, startling me again as she entered the house. "But not to worry. I keep it contained to elements and minerals, no breeding. I leave that to Steed." She laughed at her own words as she passed us on the way to her room. I found myself reevaluating her as Steed's sister.

Chevelle noticed me watching her. "Do you mind staying with Ru—"

My expression cut him off.

"I have some business to take care of outside of town. She has given me her word she will behave." He eyed her with what looked like a warning as he spoke.

She replied from the open door of her room, "Yes, yes. No naughtiness." And then, under her breath: "On my part."

"No qualifications, Ruby."

"Just teasing. Now go. We have stuff to do."

My stomach knotted. *Stuff.*

Chevelle appeared reluctant to get up. For a moment, it seemed as if he might reach out to me, but then he stood and left without another word. It ached. I didn't want him to hate me.

Ruby whirled into the room and grabbed me around the waist from behind, spinning me up, over the back of the seat, and through her door before I could process what was happening. She plopped me down in the center of her bed and swung around to sit in front of me. My head was reeling from the spin as she grinned at me, waving her hands and bringing a plethora of bottles and canisters flying toward us to drop on the bed. I thought with disappointment that I hadn't responded to her attack as Chevelle had taught me and laughed at the image in my head.

Ruby gave me a genuine smile as she began twisting the lid on a small metal canister. "No mother to teach us the tricks of the trade," she said, sighing as she leaned in.

I jerked away from her, wanting to be angry about the comment, but Ruby had just told me her own story, which was no less tragic.

She mistook my reaction. "Oh, don't be silly. I wouldn't play the same design twice. No more dust."

I relaxed, but only a little.

"Besides, I will let you in on a little secret—fairy breath

isn't really breath. Can you imagine if it were? Why, everywhere we go, we'd cause a terrible ruckus. It's a blend, is all. We keep it in a tiny capsule in our cheek, and when we need it..." She chomped her teeth together with a click, the look surprisingly feral. Then she smiled, her face melting into something very near adorable as she held a finger to her lips, protecting the secret. "Old family recipe, you see. My mother left a diary." She was thoughtful for a moment. "Ah, what a thing, a mother's diary."

Ruby went silent for too long, and I wondered if she would be returning to this one-sided conversation any time soon.

Her eyes flicked back to me. "It was very fortunate for me that she'd kept a journal, you see, for I would have no fey knowledge without it."

I felt my brows draw together and tried to smooth my face.

"No, don't feel bad for me. With you in such a position..."

I didn't know what she meant, exactly.

"And my dear brother has been there for me all along, helping me with the elf parts."

She kept talking as she leaned forward, seemingly unaware I'd not spoken a word in response—not that she'd given me much opportunity. I contemplated whether it was her usual behavior toward strangers or if she felt we had a special motherless bond.

She ran a finger through the substance in the canister, and it came out coated in a deep, dark green. She smeared it across the base of my eyelid. She continued rambling as she coated various parts of my body with lotions and powders, smoothed my hair with a sweet-scented cream, and painted my lips with a soft balm that smelled of spice.

When she was finished, she opened a tall glass container with black liquid inside and dipped a cut braid of hair into the bottle. She drew it out, using the tip to brush an intricate design on the inside of my wrist. When she was finished, she leaned over and blew gently on the paint. *Or is it ink?* I was oddly anxious to see the finished work. I waited impatiently for her to raise her head again and hoped whatever it was wasn't permanent.

She finally glanced up at me, smiling easily. I looked nervously at my wrist, but it was magnificent. A simple outline of a bird with outstretched wings marked the delicate skin at the base of my palm. Unbelievably tiny runes surrounded the bottom of its wings, making a pattern appear.

I smiled as I praised her. "It's beautiful."

One eyebrow shot up, and she jumped from the bed, grabbing my wrist and pulling me with her. I hoped she hadn't smudged the design. I checked it as soon as she stopped in front of her mirror and let my arm go. "And this." It wasn't a question. She was proud of her work.

The eyes that stared back at me in the reflection grew large as they took in her mastery. Gone was the girl I'd been in the village. This woman, dressed in leather and dabbed with war paint, was striking, even imposing. Her dark gaze might have been fierce if it wasn't round with astonishment.

Ruby was thrilled by my response. She bounced twice and clapped her hands at her success. Then she was over it. "Let's eat. I'm famished." She fired a look back at me, her hair flipping in the process. "Hmm. I'm not supposed to take you outside. Not supposed to leave you."

I stood, waiting.

"Food," she said. She yanked two cloaks from the corner and tied them on, covering our heads, and led me to the wardrobe by her bed. I couldn't imagine how we could put any more clothes on as she opened the door and started to throw the clothes onto her bed. But she leaned out of the wardrobe door to whisper, "Come on." She stepped into the cabinet, dragging me with her.

We were standing outside the rear of her house. She slid the false wall back in place and grabbed my arm again, our heavy cloaks moving like shadows as we ran from the village.

We didn't go far before she stopped and jerked me to squat beside her. There was movement a brief distance ahead, a rabbit weaving from the cover of one rock to the next. As I watched, a stick shot from the ground and speared the animal through the chest, killing it instantly. I gasped, and Ruby giggled at me before she grabbed her quarry and rushed us back to the house.

We went to the main room, and she started a fire as she easily skinned and gutted the animal. The entrails went into an urn beside the fire, and I wondered what she used them for before remembering all the containers on her bedroom shelf with a shudder. She stretched the pelt to dry while the meat cooked then dipped her hands into an ornate basin to wash them clean.

She poured us wine and handed me half of her plunder. "It's not much, but game close to the village is sparse. Over-hunted. When we get to the peak, we can trade. It is the strangest thing—they herd the animals to town then corral them to eat at their leisure." She shook her head at the absurdity. "But you haven't eaten until you've tasted a fattened beast."

"The peak?"

She looked concerned. "You don't know where we're going?"

I drew a breath, uncertain how to answer. I never would have trusted her, but she was traveling with us. Still, it was probably best not to tell her, of all people, that I had no clue where I was or where I was going. I needed to stay on my path more than ever. Chevelle's warnings rolled through my mind, and I wondered whether he'd told Ruby and Steed that he'd protected me from Grand Council.

An idea nagged at me, but I couldn't quite drag it into form. Ruby waited while I searched for a response, but then Chevelle opened the door, and I was saved from at least that much.

When he saw me, he became still. I had forgotten Ruby's treatments until she squealed in delight at his response. He composed his face again, but she'd already marked him.

"Oh, you like it. She's fabulous, isn't she?" She was so proud of herself, but Chevelle only frowned at her. It might have pleased me too, except that I couldn't tell what had caught him off guard, how I had changed or the resemblance to my mother.

Ruby offered Chevelle a drink, and he sat in a chair beside mine. She prattled as she enjoyed the wine, and I tried to focus on her stories instead of the occasional glances he threw my way. Then he grabbed my arm. I flinched, afraid of the quickness and strength of the move, but he only trailed an index finger gently down the inside of my wrist, over the bird design, stopping in the center of my palm.

I relaxed into his grip. "You like it? Ruby did it. It's beautiful, isn't it?"

His finger stayed on my palm as he looked up at me. His eyes, piercing beneath dark lashes, lingered on my mouth for a moment then met mine. "A hawk?" It seemed like an accusation, but I had no idea why.

I sat staring back at him, blank-faced, and he turned to Ruby then gave her the strangest look. "A hawk?"

She appeared abashed for a moment then simply shrugged, smiling. "Seemed to fit." That apparently answered his accusation, and he released my hand, easing back into his chair.

"Well, now that you've returned..." She hopped off her own chair and bounded toward the door. "I can't wait to visit with our new guests." She frowned a little. "Too bad they can't stay inside with us. Frey can have my room—I'll be out all night—and you can take the spare." She took one last look at me before she rushed out, apparently satisfied with her project.

I was alone with Chevelle again. My pulse quickened, and I had to remind myself he was supposed to hate me. He was my watcher, and he was fulfilling a duty.

Then I realized what Ruby had said, and I wondered if my brain would ever be quick enough to keep up. "Guests?"

"We will be traveling with some friends," he said, hedging a bit.

He was so vague. A formless irritation started to crawl its way to the surface, but I had to remember I had no right to ask. They were my captors. My fingernails cut into the palm of my hand where the map had been. We would be traveling to the peak, Ruby had said. I couldn't guess what waited there, but that didn't stop the hope that it was something of my mother or my family. But even if it wasn't, at least I would be that much farther away from the village and Council.

The second bit of Ruby's parting comment registered, so I excused myself to her room with a yawn and a short good-night. I closed the door behind me, and though tired, I didn't think I could fall asleep after all that had happened. I walked to the back window and stared out into the night.

Moonlight glinted off Ruby's figure in the distance as she headed away from the village. I didn't think. I just pulled a cloak from the pile on her bed, put it on, then walked out the hidden door behind the wardrobe.

I ran in a crouch, praying no one spotted me as I gained on her. I only once glanced at the house in fear that I wouldn't be able to find my way back. If I wanted to catch Ruby, I wouldn't be able to take the time to mark my path. Her cloaked form leapt over a tall rock and disappeared. I hurried forward, sure I was about to lose both her and the route. When I topped the rock, I froze, taking a heartbeat too long to drop to my stomach. Just over that ridge stood a group of elves, though I didn't think they'd seen me before I'd fallen back. My pulse settled.

I wasn't quite close enough to hear, but I didn't see a better vantage point. I squinted, examining the figures. Ruby's red curls gave her away. She had tossed back the hood of her cloak and was laughing with a large elf. I was almost sure it was Steed because of his stance. I scanned the darkness and found two others. One was about the size of Steed, and the other was thinner and appeared restless, even in the darkness. They approached Ruby and Steed, and out of the shadows I could see their dark hair. The thinner one's hair was long, his bangs falling over sharp features.

I couldn't understand what they were doing out there or why the "guests" would be traveling with us. Chevelle had called them friends, but I didn't know if I trusted that assessment. They'd been secretive, and since we'd headed into the town, Chevelle had been wearing a sword. Weapons weren't uncommon, especially among council members, but he'd not taken it off, even inside Ruby's home.

I studied their gestures in the moonlight, occasionally catching a few words. It seemed as if they were planning something, but I couldn't be sure. There was movement again in the shadows as more figures approached. I inched forward, anticipating when they would come into view. One of the forms was a mass, low to the ground. I squinted to see better, and—I almost screamed as a hand wrapped around my left biceps with fierce strength, jerking me to my feet. I tried to see my attacker, to think of the magic to protect myself.

"What are you doing?" It would have been a yell it if wasn't hissed. The tone was harsh, and I recognized it at once.

"Oh," I managed. Part of me was saying *calm down,* but the other was screaming that I was still in danger. "Chevelle, I-I-I..." I didn't have an answer. *What am I doing?*

He released his grip just a fraction. "I went to your room, and you were gone." He shook his head. "I thought I had to come out here to get a search party."

"I... uh... You were in my room?"

He straightened, his expression making it clear he hadn't expected that response.

I took my chance and pressed. "Why?" I heard movement behind me, and the fear returned tenfold.

Chevelle didn't tense. He only let out an exasperated breath. "It's fine," he said. He released me, and I turned to see whom he'd addressed. Four figures stood in a line, almost formally, before they relaxed at his words.

My arm tingled as the blood returned to the limb, freed of his harsh grip. I flexed my fist, certain he despised me. There could be no other reason for him to have reacted so strongly.

"Ah, she escaped," Ruby purred. "And you didn't trust *me* with her."

The formation broke as Steed came to stand beside me, the corner of his mouth tipping into a grin. I stared at the group. I had no idea who they were, but from the way they spoke, it was apparently no secret that I was Chevelle's prisoner or his property.

"Frey," Chevelle said, "this is Anvil." He nodded toward a giant of a man who bowed his head respectfully. "And Grey." The wiry man bent and straightened, his movements quick.

I drew in a startled breath as two more figures came into view. A pair of slender elves stepped in sync then stopped just outside the group. They were tall and lean, dressed in robes the color of ash that only accentuated their shocking silver hair. I was convinced the moonlight must have been exaggerating it. And then I jumped again as, on either side of them, two beasts walked forward to stand just in front of the twinned elves.

Steed brushed an arm against mine, mumbling under his breath, "Yeah, they're not from around here."

I felt myself leaning on Chevelle for support. "Rider and Rhys Strong," he said from behind me.

They nodded, and I was surprised that the small gesture also seemed synchronized. A strange whine emanated from one of the beasts at the elves' sides as the animals shifted to sit on their haunches. By their size, I might have guessed they were wolves, but I'd never known a wolf to be tamed. Their fur matched the robes of their masters, down to the black trim. I couldn't be certain in the light, but I thought there was even some silver showing. Surely, they would have been less frightening in the light of day.

Ruby broke the tense atmosphere with a curtsey. "And Ruby Summit," she said.

I attempted a smile for her, not missing the silent exchange between Steed and Chevelle. They were trying to decide what to do with me.

"Since you're apparently not ready to retire for the evening, I suppose we will resume your training," Chevelle said.

I sighed.

"Ooh, let me!" Ruby shouted.

Chevelle gave her a doubtful look then glanced at me, apparently deciding I deserved it. He nodded once and walked toward the rock ledge. Ruby bounced from foot to foot, celebrating her victory.

As Chevelle moved past Anvil and Grey, they turned to follow him. The silver-haired elves and their dogs were nowhere in sight. My gaze caught Steed, who was watching me. I always forgot how striking he was until I looked right at him. He wore a thin, loose shirt, rolled at the sleeves and covered by a leather vest. It matched the long cuffs on his forearms, made of the same dark, worn leather of his saddles. He stepped closer, taking my chin in his hand to examine my face in the moonlight. He said something to Ruby about her decorations and gave me a wink as he walked off in the direction Chevelle had gone.

Then Ruby and I were alone, and I was sure it was going to hurt more than my other training. She untied her cloak and tossed it to land with a muffled clatter on the rocks, its hidden pockets apparently stuffed full. She was smiling a touch as she reached a hand across her waist, closing her fist around a black hoop I'd not seen before. She drew it out and around as a long black trail curved in its wake and came to rest at her side.

My mouth went dry. *A whip. Oh, this will hurt.* I loosened my cloak and pitched it aside then lowered myself into a defensive stance, my hands out and ready.

Crack!

Okay, I was *not* ready. "Ow! Mother Earth!" I yelled. Blood trickled from the strike point.

Ruby giggled. "All right, so we start slower." She paused for a moment. "Maybe we work on your attacks instead of defense."

I relaxed my stance. "I don't... actually... have any attacks."

"Well then, I suppose we had better focus on getting you some. How to begin?" She was talking to herself.

My mind started to wander as I listened for sounds from the men below, trying to decipher what they could be up to.

"I'm afraid we will have to use your anger," she said, a smile creeping into the corner of her lips. "It seemed to work with your lunch."

I remembered the meat I had burnt and flushed.

"Yes, this will do." She hummed with a sly grin. "Let me see... Yes, I've got it." She began stepping in a slow circle around me, talking as she moved, suddenly cat-like. "The dreams you had after the fairy dust—do you remember them?"

Oh.

"I have a few questions, you see. You had plenty to say about someone as you slept. You mentioned how his mouth tasted and something about muscles under his shirt. And, well, I was curious just who you meant."

No.

"It couldn't have been Chevelle—you should have seen his face. He was livid."

No.

"Steed was certainly enjoying it, but, my dear, he won't spill the secret to me. Whose strong back were you wrapped around, whose dark eyes—"

I was mortified. There was nowhere to go, it was too much, and it turned to fury as she continued. I snapped. The flames that had been coursing through me burst in my hands.

She laughed and tossed her head. "Oh, you should have heard it. You gave us such interesting details!"

The image of Chevelle hearing my dreams, the sound of their laughter when I woke... I knew what she wanted, and I gave it to her. Fire shot from my hands toward her, hotter than any I'd ever produced. The warmth hit my face, and Ruby's heeled boots sloshed as snow melted beneath her feet.

She batted away the flames and grinned. "Come now, you'll have to do better than that." She kept circling. "Let me try harder." She flicked her wrist, and the end of her whip caught my ankle before I even realized it was moving. She jerked, and my leg came out from under me, my hip slamming flat on the ground. The pain stole the heat from my anger, and I struggled to stand.

Crack! The whip struck out toward my head, forcing me back down. She circled me, cracking the whip every time I attempted to right myself. I couldn't get a foothold.

"Come now, Freya, you must defend yourself. Fight me. Stop me." *Snap! Snap! Snap!* She was going faster, cracking the whip above me and at each side, moving again and again, closer and closer.

I had to think of something, but my mind could only

concentrate on the snap of her whip. Her boots splashed in the melted snow again, and I sent the icy water racing up under the material of her skirt to her bare legs. Shock crossed her face, and I hoped it would buy the time I needed.

The cold water had thrown her for no more than a fraction of a second, but it was enough to right myself and execute one quick attack. I volleyed a nearby rock, which struck her in the back and threw her balance off for another instant. I knew I was larger than her, so I gritted my teeth and lunged, grabbing her as I tried to figure out my next move.

She raised her face, and when her eyes met mine, they narrowed. Part of me was aware that I should have been scared, but I was enjoying myself. Whatever pain I might have to endure didn't factor—I had wanted to hurt that wicked little redhead since the first time I'd seen her, since her hand had reached out seductively toward Chevelle and collected my ruby. My palms lit where they wrapped around her arms. I would finally burn her.

She cocked one eyebrow at me. "Half *fire* fey, silly."

I flew through the air to land with a heavy thump, yards away.

"Well, it was a little unconventional, but at least you're thinking on your feet," she mused, straightening the material of her skirt. Then she cackled as she realized I was, in fact, not on my feet.

My body ached as I stood. My best skill was useless. I desperately wanted to ask her to show me the way, but my ego stubbornly refused. Not her.

She must have picked up on my mood. "You see, most of us choose one particular favorite. We focus on that and practice constantly. That way, it becomes easier and uses less energy, you know."

I didn't know.

"Maybe we should see what your strong suit is," she said, motioning for me to follow her as she walked to the rock ridge and jumped over, hurrying down to the men.

"Sorry to interrupt, gentlemen," she announced. "I was wondering if you'd mind a little demonstration?"

They broke their circle to give her their attention.

"Frey here hasn't found her rhythm yet," she explained. They seemed to understand, and she bounded back over to me and drew me to sit beside her on a large rock facing the men before cueing them to begin.

The largest, boasting deep-brown hair and eyes, stepped forward. He wore plain clothing, but his broad shoulders and massive size made him seem regal. "They name me Anvil, but I am Reed of Keithar Peak." His voice was thick, though it was impossible to tell whether it was an accent or he had difficulty speaking. He was huge, frighteningly so, but something about him drew me in.

I wanted to be his friend for no reason I could rationalize. He walked to me and reached out his hand in greeting. As I took it in mine, a tingle ran up my arm, the fine hairs standing on end.

Anvil smiled. "Apologies. I will try to avoid touching you."

"It's fine, really," I said, though I didn't understand. It was like a static charge. Meanwhile, I had decided the thickness was a drawl. "I don't know your accent. Where is it from?"

"North Camber," he replied. A snicker slipped from Steed, and Anvil glanced at him before amending: "Well, that is where they cut out part of my tongue."

I recoiled, wrenching my hand from his. The tingle remained. He didn't seem offended—he simply took a few steps backward to start his demonstration. I brought my arm back to my side, and it brushed Ruby, shocking her just enough to make both of us flinch. She only smiled as she returned her attention to the start of the show.

The other men drew back, some sitting, some standing, but all giving him their full attention and space as he raised his hands and braced himself, taking one deep breath before shifting forward ever so slightly. There was a thunderous crack, and excruciatingly bright light flew from both of his outstretched hands, slammed into a tall pine, and snapped the top third of the tree off. Several limbs splintered and popped as it crashed its way down.

I stared in open-mouthed astonishment. Sweat glistened on the large man's forehead, and his breath was a little labored, but still, he stood. Understanding came slowly. He had shot lightning from his hands. The others nodded appreciatively, but I was having second thoughts about friendship with him, though not being his friend was probably more dangerous.

I was shaking my head in disbelief as he turned back to me and bowed.

He stepped back, taking a seat as the wiry man stepped inside the circle. He nodded to me. *Grey*. He was thoughtful for a moment, likely deciding the best way to display his skill, before finally approaching to offer his hand. I reached forward, placing my palm against his, and then he was gone. His entire body had vanished. I half expected to feel his touch—perhaps he'd merely camouflaged himself—but my hand was empty. I looked around, baffled. The makeshift audience wore easy, amused smiles. They watched me, not the vacant space from which Grey had evidently disappeared. And then I noticed someone beside me who hadn't been there before... it was him.

"How..." But he was gone again. I'd been staring right at him and still had no idea where he'd gone.

I was just beginning to doubt whether I'd seen him at all when I spotted him standing across the circle, grinning fiendishly while he dangled an object from his hands. It was the feather Ruby had tied in my hair. I'd forgotten about it. I reached up to feel for it, but it wasn't there. I started to get irritated, but then the feather was in my other hand, and he was back, his hands empty. And then, for no apparent reason, he did a few somersaults and landed in the center of the circle with his arms spread. I could only shake my head as Ruby clapped beside me, clearly thrilled with the show. I thought I must have missed something.

Grey bowed out of the circle and was replaced by the two tall, silver elves. I found myself unsettled again because I hadn't seen them sitting with the group or anywhere else. For some reason, it was much more eerie than the little wiry man who blinked in and out of my vision.

Chevelle leaned forward to speak low in my ear, startling me. I glanced up at him, and something in his expression made me feel as if the words should have meant something to me—maybe he was waiting for my response.

"Finn and Keaton," he'd said, "the names of the beasts with the twinned silver elves." Feeling as if I'd failed some test, I turned back to the show.

One of the men spoke in a formal tone. "We will not demonstrate their full power at this time, in fear of shorting our forces a man for mere display." I assumed he was probably joking. "As you can see, they can be frightening, however, without attacking."

At that, the dogs walked into the circle. They came forward to snarl, one regarding Ruby and one Steed, and I could only be glad it wasn't me as their muzzles pulled back to expose vicious sets of teeth, complete with meat-tearing fangs. The hair rose on their backs, and I was suddenly positive that they were larger than Ruby. A horrific growl ripped from their chests in unison, and I cringed. Then, at once, they settled back into relaxed seated positions as if they had never been angry.

"We also do not do *tricks*." There was humor there, and I was relieved to see that the intimidating pair might not be as strict as I'd imagined. "We will return to watch." They inclined their heads and walked out of the circle in unison, disappearing from view.

I twisted the feather in my hand. *How remarkable it must be to master a beast. I wouldn't have to be battered during training then,* I thought, and winced at the idea of Ruby cracking one of those wolf-dogs with her whip.

10

The next morning, Ruby was in the main room, waiting for me. She impatiently instructed me to bathe and change, explaining that we would be spending the day training. I followed her directions but couldn't decide whether to be grateful or worried when the clothes she'd laid out for me—utilitarian and unadorned with her usual baubles—were plainly meant for a hard day. It was still early as we stole out the back, cloaks covering our heads as we made our way to the ridge.

Steed, Chevelle, Grey, and Anvil were already there. I imagined the others—the silver twins, Rhys and Rider, and their dogs—were somewhere nearby, though I couldn't see them. *Watchdogs*, I thought, *all four*. It was comforting, but Ruby wasted no time in getting to training. She immediately trounced me repeatedly, cracking her whip, besting me with fire, and even overpowering me despite her slight frame. I felt defeated before we'd gone even an hour.

After watching us for a while, Steed stepped in to save me. "Frey"—he'd adopted the nickname the others used in place of the sunnier ones—"why don't you take a break for a while? Let us spar so you can watch. We'll give you a few pointers."

I didn't know if I liked the idea of the group sparring, whether it gave me a break from the torture or not, but Grey stepped forward, and my opinion no longer mattered.

"Just watch and learn," Steed said.

I backed away and sat cross-legged on the ground. Ruby joined me, and I could tell she was excited. It seemed everything excited Ruby—everything that made me nervous, anyway.

Steed and Grey stood opposite each other in the center of the clearing. Both were tall, and though Steed easily had him in breadth, I'd seen Grey move—he was fast. A cursory nod at one another signaled the onset of the bout, and both tensed and crouched slightly into a ready stance. I found myself leaning forward as we waited. Chevelle moved to stand beside me, also intent. Grey wagged his eyebrows at Steed, taunting him to make the first move.

"Come on, blossom," Steed teased back, "let's see what you've got."

At that, Grey disappeared, and then, in a flash, he was behind Steed, reaching up to smack him in the back of the head. The instant before he struck, Steed ducked into a squat and spun, taking Grey's legs out from under him. I flinched. Grey was gone again, that time reappearing midair in a flip above Steed's head, reaching down to tag him with a loud smack on the way by. I was sure it had stung. Steed stood still, focused on the spot where Grey had landed and was flickering in and out of view. I made an effort to consider possible responses in my head but was coming up blank.

The nerves were gone. I found myself wanting Steed to

win and leaned with his strikes, tensing as if they were my own. Grey bounded through the air once more, showing off, confident in his evident lead, and then a small rock rose at chest height in front of Steed. I was trying to figure out who had lifted it when Grey flashed back into view, hesitating only a moment as he considered the rock. At once, his face changed—he knew he'd been beaten. As he'd paused to study the floating rock, Steed had immobilized him and, just like that, the match was over.

Ruby leaned into me. "Steed is stronger than Grey," she said in a soft voice. "He only needed to catch him."

Grey conceded, his walk slower and his movements no longer restless as he made his way out of the makeshift ring. Steed threw me a quick wink.

Anvil approached next, stepping into the same starting position Grey had used, and Steed shifted several paces back before he readied himself and nodded toward his new opponent. I remembered the tree and was suddenly afraid for him, wondering whether Anvil would use the same method on a person.

A thunderous crack answered my unspoken question. The lightning bolt was faster than my eyes at such a close distance, but by the time I looked at Steed, there was nothing but a wall of water. He had constructed a barrier of sorts, caught the strike, and redirected it around himself by melting the snow that spotted the mountain. Anvil was winded, though the strike wasn't as severe as his previous show. Steed would unquestionably be the winner, and as he took aim to retaliate, his opponent raised his hands in surrender.

"Quick thinking, Mister Summit." The large man grinned, and I had no doubt that they were old friends.

Chevelle stepped forward eagerly. I had a feeling he'd

been itching to spar with Steed in the way I'd been itching to burn Ruby. Steed smiled in acceptance, but it wasn't the same smile he'd given his last opponent. They stood across from each other and readied themselves. Both tensed, but neither took the low, wide stance the others had used.

As their eyes fixed on one another, I felt myself, and Ruby beside me, lean forward in anticipation of the action. Both men went taut, their muscles corded and jaws clenched tight, wearing determined stares that focused only on each other. I saw nothing happen but knew there must have been something, some unseen force, causing them pain and draining them. I couldn't look away as I stammered to Ruby, "What's happening?"

"They are trying to overpower one another." I could hear the pleasure in her voice. "No silly games—just power."

The way she said it had some part of my mind wondering whether her statement about not having her mother's ambition was true, but I could only concentrate on the struggle in front of me. There was still no visible action, so I tried to judge who might be winning by appearance. Chevelle's jaw was set, his eyes dark. Steed flinched, but I had no idea if it was from pain or magic. The only thing I was sure of was that neither intended to lose. Their stances, right down to their gazes, were absolutely unwavering.

A sound behind me drew attention to how quiet and still the valley had grown as we watched that unanimated brawl. Steed and Chevelle broke their stare, turning to the noise— dogs, I thought—before the entire world shifted into action. The elves around me ran, swords drawn and weapons ready as I was whisked from my seat. Ruby was gone, vanished from beside me, and I only caught a glimpse of Steed and Chevelle as they darted past. I didn't know who had hold of me, but in less than a heartbeat, I was standing over the rocks in the opposite direction, Ruby before me, her red curls blocking my view and her arms outstretched in readiness. Steed and Chevelle were at opposite angles in front of us, both even more tense than they had been in their bout. I peered around Ruby's mane to see what they were focused on.

In front of our triangle, directly ahead of Ruby, stood a reedy, blond elf draped in the long white robe and tassels of Council. I felt sickened as I absorbed the idea that a council member—*is he a tracker?*—had been behind me as we were all engrossed in a trivial match. He was frozen, unmistakable agony distorting his features. I didn't know which of the group was restraining him, but Anvil and Grey flanked him, and Rhys and Rider were a short distance behind with their dogs.

The man seemed to be attempting to speak but couldn't get the words out. His hair was so pale, his robe so stark in the moonlight, that I became aware of how quickly I'd grown accustomed to the dark features of my new companions. Chevelle mumbled something, but I couldn't make it out. My ears had begun to buzz, not with the all-out siren that had crippled me before, but with a constant, crackling hum. I worked my jaw and tugged at the lobe of an ear. The stranger's lips moved—apparently, he was able to speak again—and Anvil approached him, dwarfing the captive with his mass.

Anvil exhibited remarkable menace when he addressed the frozen councilman, who mouthed another reply. I couldn't decipher their words through the ringing in my ears, but somehow, I did hear the breaking bones. A grotesque crunch accompanied the snapping of the councilman's thigh, and he dropped nearly to the ground. Anvil leaned over him, somehow even more intimidating as he spoke directly to the man as if they were the only two there, as if the councilman hadn't just suffered a traumatic injury. And, evidently, Anvil didn't like the answers he received, because the councilman's other leg snapped, dropping him to rest on the stumps of his broken, mangled thighs.

I should have turned at the sight, but I couldn't keep from wondering how it was possible that he remained upright at all. Anvil bent down to keep his stare close and threatening, and the broken man looked at me. His glare turned accusing, his mouth suddenly moving with heated, determined words, but my ears only rang more loudly, engulfing all other sound. I cringed but couldn't stop myself from watching the scene play out, even as my head turned down and I wanted to look away. *Why is he fixed on me? What are they saying?*

Ruby remained protectively in front of me, her posture lowered and her arms tensed tighter since the stranger turned his eyes on me. His face twisted in agony as his right arm was dislocated from its socket, leaving the limb hanging limply at the shoulder. I was glad I didn't hear that sound. He turned back to his questioner, his mouth a grimace as words, unmistakably a curse, came out, and his other arm was wrenched from its place as well. He winced, apparently not yet numb from the damages, and then his face went hard, his lips pressed together, his jaw clenched tightly. He wasn't going to scream or talk.

His back twisted, and he fell into a motionless heap on the ground. His body was bent out of recognition. It was over.

My ears had stopped ringing the moment he'd hit the ground. Ruby relaxed and stepped away from me. I wanted to catch up with what had happened, but no one was talking—

the mountain was silent. Rhys and Rider were gone from sight once again.

"Aren't you going to perform the death ceremony?" I asked as the other elves began walking away.

Anvil spat on the mangled body. *The corpse.* "It's done."

I stood staring at the crumpled mass as the others gathered, arguing.

A council member—

"It's time to move," someone said.

—came for me.

"No, not yet," someone else replied.

They killed him. I was glad.

"There could be more," Grey insisted.

That brought me back, no matter how disturbing my realization was. "More?"

Chevelle gave the bickering group an admonishing glare as he approached me.

I could hear the alarm in my own voice when I repeated, "There are more council members coming for me?"

He tried to calm me. "Frey—"

"I won't let you all pay for my crimes." Confusion passed over everyone's faces except Chevelle's.

"We aren't. You don't understand..." Something flickered in his eyes. "Besides, they are pursuing me for choking the tracker."

Grey shook his head.

"Because of me," I argued. "And now you've killed one." But I didn't know who had killed him. Anvil had stood before the man, but any one of them could have snapped his spine.

"Frey"—Chevelle's tone was solemn—"you know what they did to your mother."

I could hear what he didn't say: *You know what they'll do to you*. I didn't have a counter for that, and he had to have known it. He took advantage of the silence and gave orders to Ruby. "Take her to the house."

She had me at once, towing me beside her as she retrieved our cloaks.

Chevelle was still giving instructions. "Steed, watch the front. Stay inside. Grey, take the rear, out of sight. Anything, no matter how trivial, signal the wolves."

Wolves. They *had* been wolves, not dogs. I immediately had more respect for the tall, pale-haired elves. They were men who had tamed wild wolves.

We were back at the house in what seemed like a heartbeat. Steed watched the village from the front room, and Ruby sat with me on her bed with the door closed.

"This will calm you," she said. A sprinkle of glitter hit my face before I had the chance to protest. "Just a touch," she assured me.

It was too late. The dust had already taken effect. I relaxed onto the bed, just as Ruby did the same beside me. We stared at her ceiling, not speaking for an immeasurable amount of time. I rolled onto my side toward her, dimly irritated that she'd poisoned me again, though it was much less severe than the last time. I was simply enveloped in tranquility.

"Ruby..."

Her curls had tumbled back, and my complaint fell short as I was distracted by her ears. "Hmm?" she answered.

I reached up to feel my own ears as I considered hers. I had always hidden mine behind hair, never braiding it back or putting it up to expose them, not that I could have pulled off the intricate braiding and designs of the other elves. But my ears were clearly more rounded than everyone else's, almost blunt. Ruby's were different too. Hers were more angular, though, long and almost pointed at the tip. Neither of us matched the norm. Hers were one extreme, mine the other.

She turned to look at me. "Feeling okay?"

I remembered I was going to ask her something. I said, "Mm-hmm," and got lost in the hum of my reply. She smiled at my satisfied trance.

I faded off to blackness then, though my dreams were vivid and wild.

I was a hawk, flying high above the mountain. My wings stretched as I soared through an endless and open sky. Through keen eyes, I watched below, surveying a massive structure of dark stones.

Then I was a wolf, running through those stones, hunting, searching, protecting. My muscular shoulders tensed and released with each long stride.

I was myself again, though strong and confident. Two statuesque elves, twinned in white, glided past me. Lightning struck around me, cracking the dark stones of the walls. Reed of Keithar stood before me, and suddenly I was on a pedestal, looking down as he wagged his tongue at me. I scorned him, burning a chunk of it off, and he smiled.

I jolted awake, the smell of burning flesh still lingering in my senses, and stared at Ruby's ceiling. *Curse her*. I was alone in her bed but could hear an exchange of low whispers from the open door as she and Steed conversed in the front room. I wasn't about to announce that I had woken. My head didn't throb as before, and I had no sour mouth. Overall, it was overall a much better experience, but I wondered who could stand the dreams. I rolled onto my side, rubbing the sleep from my face.

There were a few books on the bedside table, and I reached over to draw the top one near. I flipped idly through the pages until I recognized that it was detailing different aspects of magic. I hurriedly scanned through, getting caught on a section marked Exchange. It claimed that using magic consumed a person's energy, and not just immediately available energy, but *life* energy.

I'd never known a book to lie, but I couldn't imagine its applications otherwise. *Ruby was giving part of her existence to draw me a bath? Chevelle and Steed forfeited time for a silly instructional match?* It couldn't have been right.

I tried to recall the magic I'd seen in the village, though it was still clouded with fog. The youngsters played carelessly, often until they collapsed from exhaustion. But the elders were reserved. I couldn't remember them using it for anything that could have been done with less physical energy. They hunted with weapons, wrote with their hands, and worked as if they took pleasure in it—maybe there was no energy left for magic, or maybe it was unimportant until one reached the close of one's years and realized it was almost gone. I remembered how long a thousand years had seemed to me before I planned on spending it in a prison.

Ruby walked in, and I snapped the book shut, positive I shouldn't have taken it from her table without permission. One glance at her stifled reaction told me that I would not be able to ask her about what I'd read.

"Sleep well?" she asked.

"Oh," I said with a start, my voice hoarse.

She handed me a glass of water, which she smoothly traded for the book.

"Dreams," I complained.

She smiled as she sat on the bed beside me. "Some seek out the breath. They say it is foresight."

"Foresight?"

She nodded. "What did you see?" She raised an eyebrow questioningly.

"Not the future."

She laughed. "Have a bath. You'll be good as new." The water was filling the basin again, and I wondered about what I had just read. Surely the dust and fog were meddling with my thoughts. "Chevelle will be swapping with us for the evening," she explained.***

The bath refreshed me, but unfortunately, it also cleared my mind. *No wonder Ruby drugged me.* I tried not to think about the tracker as I dressed. The smell of the cold morning hung in the air, and I felt a pang of guilt at using the fragrance again, knowing Chevelle would be there. I appraised myself in the mirror and smiled then shook my head, certain the dust was still influencing me.

When I walked into the main room, Chevelle was sitting on the bench seat, leaning over as he worked on something. He raised his head as I approached, closing his hand around whatever it was before sliding it into a pocket. He seemed mildly anxious.

I was still feeling peculiar, so I climbed into the seat beside him, curling my feet up close. He watched me, his eyes lingering even after I had settled. It felt as if he yearned to say something.

The tension became too much, and I broke. "Ruby drugged me."

He gave me a half smile. "She told me. She was worried about your sanity." The last word cracked. He appeared to regret saying it.

"Did she tell you"—I wasn't sure I should be admitting it—"I read her book?"

"Yes."

He wasn't offering any information. I would have to ask. The dust must have given me courage. "It talked about exchange." Still nothing. "About energy... life... for magic."

He cleared his throat. "Yes."

"Can you tell me about it?"

"Today, after Anvil sparred with Steed, you saw how the strike drained him. This is something you'll need to know for a group conflict. The tactics are different than one on one." He hadn't answered my question at all, but he was talking, and I would take it. I nodded for him to go on. "A single opponent allows you to use more energy and focus only on that and let yourself..."

My thoughts were wandering. *Cursed dust.*

"... but with a number of opponents, you have to conserve your energy so you don't leave yourself too weak..."

I was watching his mouth move as he spoke but lost the words. I couldn't focus.

"... tactics that do not drain your energy. Protect yourself..."

I was leaning toward him, my gaze tracing the lines of his face.

"... even hand-to-hand combat or choose a weapon. Ruby's whip, a staff..."

Cursed Ruby.

"Frey."

"Hm?"

He shook his head. "Never mind."

I was angled toward him and could feel myself moving. A voice in the back of my mind was screaming *stop,* but it was too late. I had closed in on his lips. I was close enough that my intent was unmistakable when he grabbed me, wrapping both arms around my biceps in a too-tight grip. "Freya—"

There was a howl. *A wolf.*

He let out a deep breath, and it tickled my nose. *Oh. Oh, no. No, no, no.* My head cleared, but Chevelle still held me around the arms. My neck flushed, my eyes shooting to my lap. I couldn't look at him. *What am I doing?*

The door opened, and Chevelle's hands dropped as he stood to face the newcomer.

"They are here." It was Steed's voice, but I didn't raise my head. The blood was still hot in my cheeks.

"Take her to the ridge. I will meet you after—" Chevelle stopped midsentence.

After what?

Steed must have been concerned, because Chevelle explained. "Ruby gave her a little dust to relax."

"Frey," Steed said from beside me.

I glanced at the door. Chevelle was already gone.

"Are you well?"

"Ugh."

He snickered. "Come on." He swept me up, clearly planning to carry me.

My head spun. "No. Please let me walk."

"You don't tolerate that stuff well. You're going to have to lay off the shimmer."

"It's not like I chose to take it," I complained.

He laughed.

THE COLD AIR HELPED A LITTLE. I was back in the circle—the group of us sat around a small fire. Ruby was telling stories. She related the tale of Bonnie Bell, a blue fairy from the East. "He hunts the human children, luring them in with glitter and lights, and eats them, beginning with their tiny little toes. Though he gives no choice in the matter, in exchange, he allows the mother one wish."

I scoffed. "Humans aren't real."

"Even so," she continued, smiling wickedly, "you'd be surprised by how many don't think to wish for their children back."

Raucous laughter floated up around the ring. *Fey tales, indeed.*

It felt good being there, surrounded by my new companions with a fire, stories, and laughter. It felt like more of a home than Fannie's had ever been. But I was also under the influence of a fey.

"Better yet?" Ruby asked.

I grimaced.

Grey approached. "Ruby, dear, won't you allow us to partake?"

"Speak for yourself," Anvil cracked from across the fire. "Last time, I lost a bit of tongue." I cringed and remembered my dream. I thought I could still smell burning flesh.

Ruby laughed. "Ah, well... I suppose just this once."

Grey sat, his rough brown boots resting among the stone, and she leaned over him as if for a kiss. Her lips stopped just short of his, and their eyes connected as a glint of firelight caught the shimmer. Grey breathed it in. As she pulled away, his fingers trailed slowly off her arm, and I felt I was intruding, so I averted my eyes.

Steed gave me a gentle smile beside me. *I like Steed. He's a good guy.* I shook my head to clear it. *Cursed dust.*

Ruby joined us.

"Do the effects last longer sometimes?" I asked.

"It depends."

"On what?" It seemed like an obvious follow-up.

"Your mood."

I was irritated all over again but got distracted when she licked the point of an arrow. "What are you doing?"

She grinned. "Look, Frey, I don't know if you're up for this story right now." I didn't think she was funny. She sighed. "All right, but you'll probably regret it."

"Just give her the short version, Ruby," Steed interrupted. "No gory details." His eyebrow cocked meaningfully.

"Oh well, yes, that would do." She smiled at me as she licked another arrow, her tongue sliding carefully along the blade. "You see, my dear, being a one of a kind—well, as far as I know—has its benefits. Though they weren't always benefits. In the beginning it was bad, but, well, that's the long version, isn't it? No gory details." She winked at Steed. "I am, how should I put it? Venomous."

I gasped.

It was obviously the response she expected. "Yes, yes. I know." She held her tongue out for me to examine. As she pressed another arrow against it, tiny slits opened up and released a translucent liquid. "Not really venom, per se. All fey have it, a chemical to help break down their food. It's just that mine is toxic to many. Not to worry, though. I have pretty good control of it now. Nasty, poisonous stuff." She laughed again. "You know, that's what Chevelle thought I intended the first time I dusted you."

I recalled the panic in his voice before he whisked her away. As disastrous a night as that had been, this one wasn't much better.

"Ruby, please take Frey back to the house." Chevelle was standing behind us. I was too exhausted to jump, but Ruby merely glanced back at him, not at all surprised he was there.

Her face crinkled. "Didn't go well?"

He didn't respond but was obviously frustrated. I couldn't tell if it was with Ruby or whatever hadn't gone well. *Or the idiotic offspring of his parents' murderer who tried to seduce him in a drunken stupor*. It didn't matter. I was being removed again.

Ruby rambled about all of the difficulties with and uses for venom on our way back. She'd gotten so involved in her stories that I thought she must have forgotten I was there. Her last words confirmed it. "No one knew to check. How would they? I mean, a new species. A new breed. And lethal. Poison to her mother. They couldn't even know that was what had happened until the others. Until the pattern became patent and they found the source."

I stared at Ruby, imagining the nameless others who'd been taken by her venom before they discovered its root.

But it was not the idea of those strangers that tightened my chest. *Poison. To her mother.*

11

My dreams were wicked that night, all venom and wolves, snakes and beasts, death and fire. I awoke in my bed, light filtering in through the window. The door was open a crack, and I could see Chevelle sitting in the front room. I was hesitant to face him.

I lay there, running back through the events of the night and the stories told. Embarrassment flooded me again, and I turned my head to bury it in the blankets, but something strange on the side table caught my attention. I picked it up and examined it—it was a small bird carved of stone. A hawk made of onyx.

I knew at once that it was what Chevelle had been carving. And then I recognized the stone, the large black stone that had pummeled my body for days, and I couldn't help but snicker. I remembered the tiny hawk he had made with magic and my disappointment when it had turned back into a dull gray rock. He had carved me the symbol with his own hands.

I was completely ashamed of my actions the previous night.

I closed my hand around it and noticed the painting on my wrist of a hawk. I knew I had to face him. The carving might have been a peace offering, and it might be my last chance. I stood and walked into the main room, clutching the figure in my fist for courage.

Chevelle was not alone.

A statuesque elf with pitch-black hair and eyes rose as I entered, not in the respectful a-guest-has-entered-the room way, but in a way that led me to believe he wasn't happy to have me, or anyone, find him there. He gripped a long staff so tightly that his knuckles whitened, and he was dressed in casual traveling clothes that didn't seem to fit his posture.

I found myself questioning whether it was a disguise, then I chastised myself for wandering around in ridiculous thoughts so often. They were watching me. *Cursed brain fog*.

I stood there for a moment, unsure if I should leave the room after I had so obviously interrupted or pretend I had a mission and make my way to Ruby's room. I clearly wasn't welcome there. Neither Chevelle nor his guest spoke, so I lowered my gaze to the floor and took the shortest route to Ruby's door, closing it hastily behind me.

Chevelle said something to his guest, and I groaned internally, wishing I'd heard their low voices earlier. Asher, as Chevelle had called the man, was apparently leaving. It sounded as if Chevelle was trying to persuade him in some way, but the man was short and cold in his responses. Quiet, too. I imagined he didn't want me to hear them. My mind accused me of paranoia.

I heard the front door close as I flopped onto the bed only

to jolt upright when Ruby's door opened a few seconds later. It was Chevelle.

My courage was gone again. He seemed to be waiting for me to speak. I tried. "I'm sorry I interrupted…"

He nodded, but I didn't know if he was acknowledging my interruption or pardoning it.

He walked slowly toward the bed, glancing at Ruby's things on the shelves and walls, then sat on the bed beside me. I forced myself to continue breathing and kept my gaze down, knowing a flush was coming.

He reached out and placed a hand under my chin, bringing my face to meet his. The flush that followed was not from embarrassment. Heat flooded my neck, and I felt it might engulf me as he spoke my name.

"Frey."

"Yes." It was all I could manage.

His eyes held mine, and I could swear he was searching for something. He opened his mouth to speak, but the door of the wardrobe flew open.

"Oh." Ruby giggled a tiny bit. "Excuse me. I didn't mean to interrupt." She seemed pleased that she had.

Chevelle's hand dropped, and his face was hard.

Ruby continued, "Steed said you had a guest, so I just used the back…" She trailed off when his stare didn't soften, but she smiled. "You know, you do have your own room."

He stiffened and stood, not at all amused by her implication.

Ruby began gathering things as she spoke, pretending she hadn't noticed his attitude. "So how did it go?"

He relaxed a little, but his mood didn't seem to rise in the least. "We shall see."

"Indeed," she purred. "Indeed."

He didn't look back at me as he left the room, simply directing Ruby to take me with her when she'd finished. She seemed more than happy to comply, and didn't doubt that we would be training again. I slid the hawk sculpture into my pocket.

She hummed as she gathered her things, throwing a cloak at me in the process.

I tied it on and drew the hood up. "Want me to carry anything?"

She eyed me as if I was being entirely absurd. "Well, if you would like to, I can find something for you." I glared at her back, and she turned to grab my arm beneath the cloak, yanking me behind her as we left the house through her closet. She replaced the cover that hid the entrance and snatched a quiver of arrows from the ground before pulling me forward again.

"What are those for?" I asked, afraid they would somehow be used in my training.

"They are arrows, Frey." She was really on a roll, in a delightful mood. I shook my head, certain that it didn't bode well for me, and she laughed. "We are leaving them for Rhys and Rider to find."

"Are they poisoned?"

"Yes."

I considered that. "Did they use all the ones you prepared last night?"

"You're silly, Freya. It's fun." The way she pronounced my name, like it was dear to her, made it harder to be angry with her.

But I made the effort. "It's not entirely my fault." I huffed. But then I was sorry I'd said anything. I didn't need to defend myself to her.

"I know," she said, "but it's still fun."

I wondered if she did know, as everyone before had. I pushed the thought from my head and stepped over a pile of loose rocks. "I thought the dogs were their weapons of choice," I said, cringing a bit as I remembered their demonstration.

"Wolves, Frey. And they aren't weapons."

"They don't use them to attack?"

She spoke like she was explaining something simple to a child. "Yes, the wolves attack, but not as weapons and not by command of the elves. The wolves attack who they want. Protect who they want."

"They don't control them?"

"No, silly. No one can control animals." She cocked an eyebrow at me speculatively.

"But—"

"All right, well, sure, you can lead an animal. You can turn your horse and guide him on the path, but that is simply pushing their heads and encouraging them with the click of your heels. You can't make them choose to take you—it just doesn't work that way. You can't get into an animal's mind and make them behave the way you want them to."

"But the dogs—wolves—follow them. They had them do a demonstration, and—"

"No, Frey. The wolves do not follow the elves. The wolves protect them by choice."

"By choice?"

"Yes. And I have seen them tear an elf apart as quickly as defend them."

I shivered.

"Rhys and Rider were saved by the wolves once. They think the animals understand. They follow the wolves, you see. That is why they are here." We topped the ridge. Jagged rock and loose dirt shifted beneath our feet, and Ruby dropped the quiver by the edge before climbing down with a deftness I had yet to master.

Steed, Anvil, and Grey greeted us before we resumed training. I tried to keep my mind off the wolves, off the reason I was learning magic, off the encounter with Chevelle, and off all of the terrible things it kept returning to, and I was grateful for the fog that clouded my thoughts.

Though I wasn't exactly winning matches, I was getting better. I'd learned to use my fire with more precision, and I'd improved immensely moving objects, mostly in defense and to shield strikes. The battering continued, and long days of constant fighting were making me tired. We took a break, and I leaned back on a rock, staring at the sky as I rested.

CHEVELLE WALKED me to the edge of a tall peak. The rock mountain ended in a sheer cliff, straight down into haze. He looked into my eyes as if he saw something there, as if he really knew me. We gazed out over the cliff at the endless horizon. I felt his hand on my back and closed my eyes, relaxing into the comfortable, familiar feel of it.

He pushed me with full force. I flew off the cliff, falling straight down. I stared back at him as he stood, watching me fall, with nothing but open sky above and below. I couldn't imagine why he'd throw me from the cliff, couldn't think of the magic to stop myself, and couldn't see when I would crash into the rocks below.

My arms flailed as I jerked awake. The group stared at me.

"Frey?" Ruby asked.

I grappled for breath. "Just a dream." A few chuckles moved through the crowd.

Ruby was more interested. "What about?"

I glanced at Chevelle, a few paces away. He had the same concerned expression as they waited for my answer. I only shook my head.

My chest still ached from panic. I sat up and took a drink of wine from the flagon, wondering whether anyone drank water anymore.

When Grey sat beside me, I tried to mask my surprise. "Ruby a little hard on you?" he teased. I smiled. "She's only trying to help, you know." He spoke with tenderness, and I recalled how they'd touched each other nights before.

I made an effort not to be too obvious about my real curiosity. "You've known her long?"

"Forever." The way he gazed at her when he spoke left no doubt.

She noticed us watching her. "Ready to get back to it, then?"

I grimaced, struggling to my feet. "Ruby, how long will the effects of the dust last?"

"Depends." It was the same answer she'd given me before.

I couldn't decide if I was truly that out of it or if everyone thought it was funny to make me drag answers from them. "On?"

She laughed. "Don't worry. The dreams will get better."

"They will get better or they will go away?"

She laughed again. "Depends."

We were facing each other once more, ready to begin another round. "Want to try a weapon?"

I was pretty sure I didn't, give how much the weaponless training hurt. I opted for a delaying tactic. "Why use arrows if you have magic?"

She had that Frey-you're-an-imbecile look again. "Magic uses more energy the farther away you are when you try to focus it. And it is less accurate. And you are more visible. And—"

I held up a hand. "All right, I have it."

She smiled. "Any more questions, or can we begin?"

"Fine. What sort of weapon did you have in mind?"

Her smile widened. Her hand stretched out to the side, and a long, silver sword came from the pile of gear to land in her palm. She righted it, twisting the blade for me to see.

My stomach dropped.

"There are a few things you need to remember when using a blade," she instructed. "First of all, always go for the fatal attack. If you merely wound someone, well, someone with magic will use the last of their power to stop you. Cut off their head or puncture the lungs and heart. Never mess around."

I imagined myself decapitating someone. I laughed as I realized my mind placed Fannie on the other side of my blade.

Ruby didn't look like she could think of anything funny about what she'd said, but she continued. "Secondly, don't cut yourself. These things are sharp."

She moved to toss the sword to me but reconsidered and handed it over, making sure I had a good grip. There were intricate designs carved on the handle and runes etched in the blade. It wasn't as heavy as it appeared. I moved it around a bit, slashing wide arcs though the chilly air. It was pleasant, nicely balanced in my hand. That didn't mean I could actually cut through someone's neck, though. "Ruby, how do you intend to teach me with this? I mean if there's no messing around, just lop your head off and all?"

She laughed. "Don't worry, Frey. I think I can handle you."

"I'll do it." Chevelle's voice startled me. I'd been absorbed in our conversation, unaware that anyone was listening. I glanced around and realized *everyone* had been listening.

It dawned on me what Chevelle had said as they all circled around to watch. Ruby smiled at him, making me instantly suspicious that she had set it up. A long sword was already in his hand as he approached. He raised it, expertly gripping the hilt with both hands. My mouth went dry, a vague part of my brain only managing a weak *uh-oh.*

Fear rushed through me, and I wrapped my fists around the grip of my own sword, praying I could protect myself. A smile was the only warning Chevelle gave before his blade cut the air. Instinct took over, and I flung my arms up to block his swing with my own. The metal clashed, and I felt the shock vibrate through me even as the peal pulsed in my ears. He struck again, and I pulled the sword back, twisting to block another shot. I straightened and raised it again, surprised at how powerful I felt the moment before releasing my blow. I smiled as I swung at him, sure he would stop me but reveling in being attacker instead of victim.

He wound his blade around mine, a metallic screech filling my ears as he knocked my strike aside before coming back at me. We continued, blow after blow, the repetitive clank forming a pattern in my head. Chevelle seemed to be enjoying himself as the exercise increased in intensity. I found I was as well. I'd taken no direct beatings like my other training, and I wasn't getting exhausted the way I did when I tried to use magic. I could see why they all carried weapons.

Chevelle pushed harder, assaulting me with faster and stronger swings. I was able to defend myself if I focused. Murmurs of approval floated in from our audience, and I enjoyed that more than I probably should have. I concentrated hard and began throwing a few good hits of my own in with the blocks. Our swords clashed repeatedly, neither of us hitting the mark. Certainly, he could have, but I felt confident that I was blocking well.

We continued until I became winded, then Chevelle lowered his blade, smiling with approval. Our audience commented on the show, and I glanced around to see that it was evening already—the sun had begun to set. I wondered how long we'd sparred. I could suddenly feel the ache in my arms, the sword hanging limp at my side.

Ruby took it from my hand. "We'll get you fitted with a sheath."

I stood there, facing Chevelle, breathless but grinning. He was smiling appreciatively. I realized we were still being watched and sheepishly turned from him to join the group as they prepared a fire for dinner. The evening was filled with stories and laughter. Chevelle's eyes fell on me often, and he seemed in better spirits in general, which made me wonder again about his morning guest.

Rhys and Rider approached, and most of the group went to meet them. Steed moved to sit beside me. "Very nice today, Frey," he observed. "You seem to be a natural."

I snorted.

Across the fire, Grey leaned over to speak in Ruby's ear. Steed noticed me scrutinize them, so I asked, "Are they...

together?" I was confident in Grey's affection, but they didn't act like a traditional pair.

Steed sighed as we watched them. "No."

There seemed to be more to his answer. "But he..." I wasn't sure how to phrase it.

"Yes." Steed glanced back at me when he spoke. "But you can't always have the one you want, Frey." His voice was soft, yearning.

I could never tell if he was teasing. "I heard once you could die from grief."

He smiled at my subject change. "It's true. I've seen it myself."

"Tell me about it."

"No, too sad." He was thoughtful for a moment. "I worried... about my father." His eyes returned to me. "After my mother died. Sometimes, I'm grateful for the fire witch's seduction. He was grieving so hard..." His expression lost all trace of its usual cockiness as he brought back the memory. "Her enchantments numbed him. Then, when he woke from them, the tragedy gave him purpose." A shadow of his smile returned as he looked away. "The irony is that her tragedy gained roots from the idea—"

"Frey." Chevelle was suddenly standing between us.

I gaped up at him, the trance of Steed's words broken. "Huh?"

"Time to go." There was anger in his voice. I didn't know what I had done, but I stood obediently. Chevelle pulled me away from Steed.

"I'll take her," Ruby offered.

"No. I'll do it myself."

I sensed a lot of anger.

"We'll both go," she pushed, biting the words out. The

rest of the group was quiet, watching us, and Ruby eyed Steed as we turned and headed toward the house.

As soon as we were out of earshot, though I was still being dragged by the arm, I asked Chevelle, "Did something happen with the twins?"

Ruby laughed. We both stared at her. "Twins," she said with a scoff.

"Right, well, you know what I mean," I said, embarrassed.

Chevelle's tone softened. "No. Everything is fine."

Ruby chimed in with, "It *is* fine." And I knew it was intended for him. He relaxed his grip on my arm and slowed our pace as he directed an almost imperceptible nod at Ruby. I relaxed, too—*fine* was better than anything I'd thought in a long while.

Chevelle stayed in the front room that night, watching through the small windows. When I closed my eyes, I could see the glint of swords making patterns as they crossed again and again. Ruby's hummed tune was sad, the sound drifting through the walls between us as I fell into an easy sleep.

CHEVELLE AND RUBY'S VOICES, low and confrontational, woke me. I rubbed my tired arms as I rose to join them in the front room.

"What's going on?" I asked, though I could tell they'd been arguing.

Ruby grinned at me. "Just planning for the trip."

"Trip?"

"Yes, you know, to the peak." She was scheming.

"Oh." I decided I'd let them work it out, heading instead to Ruby's room. "I'm going to take a bath."

As I closed the door, Ruby said, "It's time to tell her."

I didn't hear a response. I was soaking in hot water, my eyes closed, not even considering getting out, when there was a knock on the door.

"What, Ruby?"

She giggled. "How did you know it was me?" She didn't wait for me to explain that no one else was that annoying before asking, "Can I come in?"

"No."

The water streamed from the tub, and I swore. "Fine, I'm getting dressed." I dried off, gathering clothes from a pile I assumed was for me, as they were too large for Ruby's petite frame.

I opened the door and knew right away that I would regret learning whatever they were about to tell me. Ruby commanded me to sit.

Chevelle straightened, clearing his throat. "Frey, we need to talk with you about something." I waited uneasily, and he proceeded carefully. "You know you are partially bound."

"Yes," I agreed, even though I wasn't clear how that worked. I could use some magic, and I had lost some memories. I couldn't really remember anything from before the village except the dreams.

"And you're sure you want to be unbound?"

Why is that even a question? "Of course."

He nodded as if he were going down a checklist. "We know Council has bound you."

I waited for the next detail, my fingers curling into my palms.

"And we know they must be the one or ones to unbind you."

Some part of me realized the seriousness of the conversation, but all I could do was listen.

"They are obviously... unwilling."

The breath I drew was too sharp.

"I know some about the binding. I've studied it."

When he stopped, I said, "All right." I didn't know what he was getting at.

"The problem is... meddling with the bindings, meddling with your mind is... well, it's dangerous."

And there it was. "Dangerous," I repeated.

They let me consider that for a moment. They were being careful with me, obviously not wanting to upset me. I tried to put them at ease. "So we go back to the village and..."

They shared an uncomfortable glance. "Not High Council, Freya. *Grand* Council."

Oh, right. The ones who are trying to capture me. The ones who want to burn me.

Their cautious demeanor made more sense all of a sudden. Council had sent trackers—the pair Chevelle had choked and released and the other, the broken, limp corpse in the clearing by the ridge. We had killed him. *And they're worried about my stupid binding?*

The circling cloaks from my dreams were back, filling my head. My thoughts were twisting out of control. They would be hunting us all down. They would kill us. That was why I needed training, to protect myself, because they intended to kill me, not capture me. They intended to kill us all. And without magic, bound as I was, I didn't stand a chance.

My anxiety must have shown. Ruby shifted her jaw.

"No." I held up a hand up to stop her. "No more dust." I stood. "Let's just get back to training."

They didn't argue, though they were plainly concerned.

We went to the ridge with the others, but we didn't train. In fact, I was fairly certain Ruby and Chevelle were avoiding me. I waited through the morning, and finally, around midday, I gave up and relaxed onto the ground, staring up at the sky. The earth beneath me was warm, the sun shining brightly. I watched as a bird flew high overhead. It was gliding slowly and steadily on the wind.

As I shielded my eyes with a hand, I noticed the ink on my wrist and smiled. I suddenly knew the soaring creature above was a hawk. I closed my eyes and relaxed my arm at my side, imagining flying. I breathed deeply and conjured the image the hawk would see, looking down on us.

The picture was sharp, even at that distance, but the colors weren't as clear, the outlying shapes not as defined. I laughed at myself for adding that detail to my daydream, imagining a bird seeing differently.

My vision sailed over us, past the ridge, south. I imagined seeing the twins, perched in two trees, watching. Hardwood bows rested high on their backs. The wolves were mostly concealed on the ground, vigilant. One glanced up at me, at the bird. Someone approached, robe and tassels blowing in the cool breeze. The second wolf looked forward. He saw it too and abruptly the wolf pointed, calling out.

But the howl echoed in my ears, not in my imagination, and I jolted upright. The field was in motion, rushing in response to the warning. In seconds, they were set again in the same protective positions they had taken the last time a tracker had found us.

It was all I could do to steady myself as the councilman was brought forward, because he was the same one from my vision. I was in shock as he knelt, not under his own power, and was frozen there before us. *How could I have seen him?*

Chevelle mumbled something, and my ears began to ring, distracting me from my bewilderment. After only a few stuttered heartbeats, recognition came.

"Stop!" I hissed. All eyes turned to me, but I glared at Chevelle. "Stop," I repeated.

He understood. My ears ceased ringing, and my hearing cleared. I stepped forward, the rage still fuming. I felt like a fool for not realizing before. He had been the cause of my hearing issues, and he was the one holding the tracker there. Chevelle had bound the man from magic for questioning. He had studied it and said he knew something about it.

I was so furious that I forgot my own situation. It felt untethered, as if I was outside myself, watching as I approached the kneeling tracker and daring anyone to stop me. "Tell me what you know about binding."

He didn't answer, his jaw tight in defiance. The sword sat in my newly acquired sheath, and I drew it out, taking a peculiar sort of delight in the *ssshk* that sounded when the steel passed through. The others watched me, silent and wary, but the tracker only smirked. He wasn't afraid of a sword. The last tracker hadn't given at broken bones, not even before the threat of certain death. I would need something dreadful, a new tactic to convince him.

A tiny snake sunning on a nearby rock caught my attention, and I smiled. Even in my denial, some part of me knew what had happened before. I had felt it and knew I could do it again.

I slipped the tip of the sword down to the tracker's leg, just above where his knee met the ground, and sliced his trousers up to the thigh to reveal bare skin. Drawing the snake close with magic, I took it in my hand, its thin green body writhing over my left palm, the sword grasped in my right. The prisoner watched me, almost smug.

It was a small snake, its white belly confirming it was nonvenomous, its frame no thicker than my pinkie, but it would do. I slid the tip of the sword across the skin above the man's knee, making a narrow incision. His expression did change then, giving way to uncertainty. I smiled at him as the sword tip rested against his leg. In measured movements, I placed the snake on the base of the blade, letting it slide toward its mark. I closed my eyes to relax and settle into the snake, as I had the bird.

My knees buckled as I released too much, and I had to back off, giving myself just enough to control it. As it entered the wound, the tracker gasped, and my smile stretched wickedly. I wormed my way blindly up his leg, intent on getting the information I needed.

They're getting closer. They've found us a third time now. They'll kill us. I wanted to free my mind, free my bonds. *They won't take me.*

Something about that last thought didn't seem right, as though it wasn't mine, but I couldn't follow it. The tracker screamed—it had reached his thigh. My eyes flicked open. The body of the snake made a lump under the skin of the tracker's leg. His face was contorted in agony, but that wasn't what had made him shout. It was the fear. He had cracked. Chevelle released the tracker's hand long enough for the man to scribble a few words of a spell but didn't allow him to speak or cast magic.

He slumped after his surrender, clearly confident the worst was over. I reached the sword tip back to his leg and made another incision to release the snake. It jerked and coiled free of the wound, flicking blood over the tracker's pristine white robe. Behind me, a low voice ordered, "Kill him."

I glanced down at the sword, still in my hand, the sword I was supposed to take someone's head off with. I didn't know who the order had been intended for, but it wasn't me. The man was going to die. I knew he didn't have more than a moment before their magic broke him. They would take his life because he was after us, after me.

I didn't hesitate. I pulled my arm up and swung hard, backhand. The blade cut cleanly, and his head rolled backward, hitting the ground with a sickening thud.

I looked away.

The others stared at me, stunned. I couldn't blame them.

Steed's voice was low and wary. "He didn't mean you, Frey."

I turned, unable to stand the blood in my peripheral vision. The tracker's words waited in Chevelle's hand. "All right," I said, feeling detached from myself. "Let's try it."

Chevelle's disbelief was more than evident as he shot back, "No."

Ruby spoke up. "It could be a trick. He'll need to try it on someone else first."

Someone else? Who else was bound?

She could see I was prepared to argue. "It isn't safe."

"And if it doesn't work?"

She didn't answer. I remembered the story of her father then, and how he'd been released after the fey woman's death.

I faced Chevelle. "If the council member who bound me dies, then will I be released?"

He plainly regretted what he'd divulged that morning,

but something else rested just below his reluctance, something hopeful that burned beneath my skin. "Yes."

"Then we kill them," I said. *And if we don't know which ones?* "We kill them all."

I glanced around the clearing as the others watched me. The atmosphere had changed, and I realized only then that it wasn't the uncertainty I'd grown to expect from them. It was different. It was reverence.

Anvil smiled. Something had happened that I didn't understand, a wave of sentiment at my actions, and it was far from condemnation.

A movement at the tree line caught everyone's attention, and I turned to find Chevelle's onetime guest, Asher. He stood in the shadows, his staff in hand, as if allowing us to see. The air was still as he inclined his head toward Chevelle then turned, a long, dark braid whipping behind him as he disappeared into the brush. It seemed to mean something to the group—they seemed relieved.

I stared after him, but Anvil stepped forward, thumping his balled fist against his chest in a gesture I didn't understand. Grey followed, repeating the action and adding a single nod, and Ruby clasped her hands, bouncing excitedly from heel to toe. I felt myself drawing back together, tied by the knots in my stomach and mind. A tandem wolf howl sounded in the distance.

My stomach swam in unease.

12

The councilman's body was disposed of, and the group bustled around the clearing. I slid my sword into its sheath, careful not to touch the blade. I hadn't comprehended what the flourish of activity meant until Ruby grabbed my arm to conduct me. "Come on. We have to pack."

She dragged me along as she rushed back to her house. She threw things around her room, sorting and gathering. I didn't have anything to assemble. There was only the pack I'd acquired months ago with nothing in it but that stupid white dress and the pouch... *The pouch.*

I hurried from the room, explaining to Ruby that I would be getting ready for the trip.

"I already put your pack in the front room for Chevelle."

"I'll just check it," I said. "Thanks."

I found the pack with some of Chevelle's things in it. As I started to open it, I knocked one of his bags over then went to pick it up. The flap was loose, and a piece of familiar fabric hung out. I glanced over my shoulder to be sure Ruby wasn't watching and opened the bag to find the fabric-wrapped package she'd handed to Chevelle our first day there, the package he'd traded my stone for. I pulled the material back to reveal a leather-bound book. Afraid Ruby would catch me, I slid the book into my own pack and took it to my room.

I'd already been in trouble for stealing one book, but this was technically mine. It had been swapped for my ruby. I was careful anyway, pretending to lie down and placing the book where I could quickly cover it if I were caught. I ran my fingers over the dark leather cover, tracing the scripted V etched there. *Vattier?* The first pages had been torn from the bindings, so I flipped through, finding several more damaged sections, some torn, some by water. I sighed. It wasn't any more than I expected. It felt like everything I touched was destroyed.

I returned to the first page and began reading.

TODAY WAS the solstice celebration for the fey. They are such fools. They got hopped up on dust and raided the castle. We had to kill at least six of them before they sobered up enough to reason with. That was before Father killed two more just for fun. He said he had to prove a point, but I could tell he enjoyed it.

I STRAIGHTENED AND BLINKED. *What* is *this?* I shook my head and continued.

MY STUPID SISTER was mad because he didn't let her help. She started to throw a tantrum, and he stiffened her tongue. It was stuck like that for hours. I laughed so hard I kept having to wipe

*the tears from my eyes. She tried to yell at me, and it came out,
"Thut uhp! Thop iht!" Which made me laugh harder, and she got
so mad she screamed and busted a bunch of glass.*

I KEPT READING, enthralled. It seemed to be a journal written
by a girl, but I had no idea who. It could have been someone
in Chevelle's family, but I couldn't figure out why he would
have a young girl's diary. It was filled with pointless stories as
far as I could tell, but after a few pages, it seemed to jump
several years, and the writing matured. I wished it had been
dated.

*I TIRE SO EASILY of the formalities here. The only thing I have to
look forward to are the few breaks I get to go out on my own into
the pines. Father has increased my work periods to every other
day. Combined with my other duties, I am stationed in the castle
almost all week. The magic practice exhausts me, or I would sneak
out at night, the way I enjoyed as a child. It doesn't seem fair. My
sister is practically ignored. Father clearly prefers me, but sometimes I wonder if that is really better. She wanders idly around the
castle, no practice, no duties, no formal gatherings.*

MAGIC PRACTICE, castles—*who is this girl?* I read the entries
for hours while Ruby gathered supplies and made her
arrangements. I had no idea what in this journal could have
been of interest to Chevelle unless he knew the woman, and
that kept me reading. For as much time as I'd spent with him,
it still felt as if I knew very little, as if a part of him was missing. It continued with her father's rigorous schedule and their

distaste for her sister, and then the entries got more detailed and frequent.

MOTHER HAS BEEN TOO ILL LATELY *for guests. I have not been able to see her. The tedium of my duties is getting to me, and Father has been relentless with my studies, pushing me harder and harder to strengthen my control.*

My sister has been exploring the mountains. I see her bring in all sorts of interesting finds, but she refuses to tell me where she got them. I wish there were a way to sneak out. I would follow her or force her to show me, but Father is keeping a close eye on me, making certain I stick to a strict schedule.

This morning, he brought in a detailed list for Rune, giving him direction through a series of tasks. Rune is supposed to grade me on them and see which I excel most at so they can pick a specific field to concentrate on. I don't know how extensive it was, but I saw "wind," "water," "growth," "transfer," "fire," and "foresight" written as it passed between them.

We have already done months of fire. Pass it through water, see how large a flame I can create, see how hot I can go, test me on this, test me on that. And now, he asks Rune to test me in the impossible, to see the future.

He expects too much. Merely because I am different. My sister is different too. But she never has to practice. He doesn't expect her to stay in the castle, not even when we have guests. No doubt he prefers her not be seen, embarrassed by her light hair and features. It is infuriating! I wish I were as strong as he hoped. I could do what I wanted, then.

THERE WAS a clank of metal in the front room and talk of

horses. Ruby complained of a delay—apparently, they were waiting on a meeting before we could leave, and from that meeting came some sort of guarantee. Ruby did not seem to have the patience for it. I yawned and rolled over, flipping another page of the book.

I ATTEMPTED SLIPPING in to see Mother this morning, but the doors were protected. Father found me trying to break through and sent me directly to Rune for practice. At least I got out of my duties in the throne room. We started with water. I was so exhausted that I had to sleep through most of the afternoon before they brought me back to work again in the evening. Every muscle in my body throbs. I think I hate Rune.

A SERVANT BROUGHT a letter to my room this morning. It was from my father, informing me I'm to prepare for a banquet. I've put on my formal attire. I wonder what sort of tricks he'll want me to perform for our guests. How will he display my talents this time?

I understand he needs to show strength in his position, but it seems as if he's being a bit obvious. "Look at my aberration. See what she can do?" I'll be too tired for anything but sleep tonight, or I'd try sneaking out when he's occupied with visitors. Maybe he'll give me a break from training tomorrow.

FATHER HASN'T LEFT his room this morning. No one has seen him since the conclusion of the festivities. My sister has sealed herself in her room. No one will tell me what has occurred.

～

Late last night, a servant brought a note from my father. It was four words long... "Your mother has passed."

I am still in my room. I guess I am waiting. I don't know what will happen.

I heard a noise in the front room and slid the book under a pillow, dropped my head, and pretended to sleep. I'd been so absorbed in the book that I had no idea how long I'd been reading. There was a light rap on my door.

My voice was hoarse. "Yes?"

"Frey, I'm on my way to the ridge. We will be leaving in the morning." Ruby's words confused me. I must have read well into the night.

"All right."

"Steed is here. You can stay with him or go with me."

"I'll stay." I listened to her footsteps recede. When I was sure she was gone, I slipped the book into my pack and hid it inside the material of the white gown. We would be leaving soon, traveling to the peak. I laughed to myself—no matter how many times I said it, I had no clue what it meant, but I suddenly felt a sense of urgency. No matter if it held safety, no matter if it held my family secrets, it held my escape from the bonds. It held my only chance.

I hadn't slept, and I knew I would have to sneak a nap in at some point, but I had priorities. It might be my last opportunity for a real bath. *And lovely soaps.*

～

I sat with Steed for a while after I'd bathed. He was reclined on the bench, his feet propped on a low table. He didn't seem as excited as Ruby had been about our coming trip, so I asked him about it.

"I'm just riding the wind, Frey."

"Oh, so you don't know where we're going either?"

He laughed. "No, I know where we are going. It's only that I don't know where we'll end up."

I didn't know what was going to happen, either. I thought of the tracker and realized what a good distraction the book had been. "Steed?"

"Frey?"

I smiled but it fell away quickly. "How will we get to Council? I mean, how do we find them?"

His smile dropped too. "Well, there's a good chance they'll be looking for us."

Of course, and they'll all come together. It was clear we were too strong for one or two—they would need to attack as a group or pick us off one by one. I wondered how large their force was.

"Frey?"

"Steed?" It wasn't as funny this time.

"How did you do it?"

I raised my brow, unsure what he was asking.

"The snake," he clarified.

"Oh. I-I don't know."

"Was it transfer magic? Did you simply push it there?"

I didn't know how I'd controlled it, but it wasn't from the outside. *Should I tell him?* "How else?" I asked innocently.

He nodded. "Some of the others, well, they seem to think you encouraged the snake to go under its own power. Silly, I know." He was watching my response.

I tried sidetracking him. "Ruby says no one can control animals."

"You've been talking to Ruby about it?"

I had never been great at lying. "Well, Ruby just talks."

"Mm-hm."

"So, some of the others... Who, exactly?"

He smirked. I'd given too much away. "You couldn't tell by the way they looked at you in the clearing?"

I *had* noticed Anvil and Grey. It brought back a memory. "Who was the old guy with the stick?"

"Staff."

"Staff." I waited.

"Shouldn't you be preparing for the trip?"

"Shouldn't you?" I countered.

"*I* am minding you."

I stuck my tongue out at him. Tired, I settled back into my seat. "Steed, tell me about breeding horses."

He sighed. "How much detail do you want?"

I giggled, and he smiled as he started into the subject, explaining what he'd been taught about breeding techniques and dominant traits when he was young. His father had imparted to him all he had learned in his lifetime and all their ancestors had passed down before him. They bred the animals methodically, striving to combine certain traits and bring them together in a single horse. With each generation, they strengthened the line, even bringing in new breeds from other lands to add to the list of desired attributes, such as smoother gaits, better endurance, stronger health, and longer lives.

I faded off somewhere during the part about bloodlines.

～

I WOKE in the early morning when Ruby switched places with Steed. She had brought some meat back with her, and we shared a strange pre-morning meal together before I headed off to bed. Ruby didn't question why I seemed to be sleeping so much. She was busy being excited about her upcoming trip.

I didn't share her enthusiasm, so I retired to my room to read more of the journal. There were many sad passages after the passing of the writer's mother, though their bond didn't seem traditional. It seemed more... formal. And there were several complaints about the additional workload, both with the castle duties—which were described in more detail—and her training. I couldn't be sure how much time had passed without the entries being dated, but her mood had definitely shifted.

FATHER HAS BEEN merciless in my practice and testing with Rune. Unrelenting sessions are wearing on me. I can barely concentrate. I don't have the energy for the simplest tasks, let alone the new and wild trials he's created. He thinks he has to test every possible idea he has, or else he won't know what I might be capable of.

He's gone much more often lately, but Rune doesn't let up in his absence. I wish there was a way to handle him, some way he'd give me a break when Father was away. I can think of nothing short of begging, and that would only result in punishment.

Sometimes, when Father's away, I remember my mother. I try to see her room, but it is sealed. I am sorry that I destroyed the only thing I had of her, this insignificant journal—tore her pages out and tossed them away to make it my own, like a silly child.

I remember most of it, though I can't recall the tone of her writings, whether she was happy in the beginning. My father's indiscretion was no secret. The entire kingdom knew of his noto-rious action, of stealing a light elf for his bride, though the stories vary. Some insist he was overtaken by love, and that she came willingly. Others say that he raided her village and took her in the night. A servant once told me that my father heard of her extraordinary powers and beauty and sought her out, bargaining with her parents. I scoffed at that. What kind of person would trade their child? But now that I am older, I see. I see what power and greed can become. My doubts about the more outlandish stories, those about the obsession with power and ideas of breeding a stronger line, are gone.

But maybe they were in love. Maybe she was impressed by his station, maybe she had her own ambitions. Or maybe she lived a nightmare and only hung on so long for her children.

I WAS able to piece together some things about her life. She didn't go into much detail about the magic, which I would have found useful, beyond the fact that she practiced often and was apparently unusually talented. But she did describe her duties in the castle. Her father must have ruled a vast kingdom, and she was his second.

I heard someone in the front room and hurriedly slipped the book into my pack and pretended to sleep. Ruby woke me minutes later to head out to the ridge.

13

The group was waiting for us when we crossed over the ridge and went down to the site where we had spent so many days and nights. If I hadn't been so exhausted from lack of sleep, I would have probably been nervous. As it was, I blindly followed Ruby as we gathered and eventually mounted to leave.

Chevelle, Steed, and I were back on our mounts from the earlier leg of the journey. Ruby, Grey, and Anvil each rode their own black horses, though Anvil's was larger—I assumed to accommodate his massive frame—and Ruby's was decorated with tendrils of red and gold in his mane. Though it wasn't unusual, I didn't see Rhys and Rider or the wolves. I wondered if they had their own horses and preferred to stay out of sight or if they ran with the wolves. I felt slightly comforted either way.

Once we were on our way, I didn't mind so much. I was enjoying being back in the rhythm of the ride, not to mention the break from training. Conversation flowed easily as we made our way farther up the mountain. I had been thinking about my discussion with Steed but hadn't decided how to respond if I were asked again about the incident in the clearing when I controlled the snake. No one knew about the hawk, and I wasn't sure how I had done it to begin with, so I couldn't exactly explain it. Like Steed had said, "you just do it." But it had been easy for me, much easier even than fire.

I drew my cloak tighter around my shoulders and yawned as I considered my horse. I'd had so much trouble learning to control him, trying to push him from the outside. Falling back from the group only enough not to gain notice, I tried to settle into his mind as I had with the snake and the hawk. I closed my eyes, trusting him to avoid running into anything, though a low limb was the more likely problem. It was more difficult and... different. I was there, though, leading him and seeing what he saw. It felt odd and uncomfortable, not like the hawk.

The feeling reminded me of something, and I drew back, opening my eyes to focus on remembering the small gray bird on the lip of the library window. For a fraction of a second, I had been there inside that bird before I dropped it. I hadn't realized. The moment had seemed insignificant in the course of things. I shook my head at myself as it dawned on me that I probably simply could have made it stop singing. And the frog that had exploded on my white gown—I had been there for a mere instant. Their minds were so small, so simple, it was like nothing. The horse was different. It was watching for predators, concentrating on the path and its steps, carrying a load.

I tried to find another animal to experiment on. Our group wasn't exactly small or quiet, so I was sure we'd frightened most of the larger animals off. I wondered if I could figure out a way to locate them without seeing where they were first. I thought of the wolves. If I had an animal trained, I could call it to me to use at my leisure. I had no idea where they were now. Besides, the thought of entering those massive, vicious-looking animals made me uneasy. Maybe I could get in on the hunt later and find something away from the clatter of rocks under horse hooves.

At the lack of options, I closed my eyes again to fall into Steed's horse. It felt similar to my own, though I could tell he had more power, a more confident stride. I pulled back and experimented with each of the other horses. Anvil's seemed slower, fatigued. The others were about the same, though I noticed Chevelle's horse was skittish. I was sure Steed had done that on purpose.

"Frey?" Ruby was talking to me.

I pretended I'd been alert. "Yeah?"

I hadn't fooled her. "Doing all right?"

"Uh-huh." I decided to take the opportunity—I had a dozen questions since reading the diary. "Hey, Ruby, are there any castles around here?"

The caravan stopped as everyone turned to stare at me. I had no idea what I'd said wrong. I must have given away the fact that I had no clue where I was. It wasn't my fault. I'd never left the village. I didn't know anything about anything.

She glanced to the watching eyes and again to me. I was sure they were waiting for something.

"Well, it's just that I remember reading in the village about castles in the North." *Was I supposed to have read that? Had that been in the documents I had pilfered from the library?* It was probably well past time I stopped talking.

They seemed to relax a bit as Chevelle shook his head and brought his horse back to pace. I thought I knew what they were thinking. *Imbecile.*

Ruby answered, "Hmm," with a cocked eyebrow as she turned to follow the group.

They were mostly silent the rest of the day, until we stopped to make camp. The group split after dinner as Anvil and Grey positioned themselves on rocks at the perimeter of our site. Ruby hung out by Grey, and Steed busied himself as Chevelle paced stiffly around the camp. I was bored again, with everyone entertaining themselves, so I leaned back against a rock and pulled my pack to my lap. I wrapped my cloak loosely around me and positioned my legs so I could place the book there and hopefully not be found out. I wondered how many more days of traveling we had. I didn't see a peak and didn't even know if we were going to the peak of the mountain we were on, but I was too cowardly to ask, to think about what had happened, so I distracted myself with the journal.

My sister hasn't spoken to me since our mother passed. I wish she was... different. Not merely a different personality, but different altogether. I can remember the stories in my mother's journal about her own sister. They were so close. That was, of course, until my father. But I suppose my sister might be different as well, if not for him. He's taking a journey, they tell me. He'll be gone a long time. I'll be here alone, except for Rune. He's to continue my practice.

Chevelle approached during his pacing, and I slid the book into my pack, pretending to examine the beading on the material of the dress, which seemed to disturb him. He avoided pacing near me for the rest of the evening but threw me odd glances now and again. I shrugged it off and went back to reading.

FATHER HAS BEEN GONE for weeks. Rumor is he's searching for a new mate. Someone unique, someone powerful, I'm sure. I can't stand it anymore. He thinks I'll sit here and exhaust myself practicing while he's out running around. All the servants are gossiping, and I know nothing.

I have had it. Mother's room remains sealed, but I was able to obtain some of her things from Father's study. I am only to use them under Rune's supervision, so I took the books out and returned to my room with them in secret last night. I have scoured through them, and though I don't know all the words of the spell exactly, I think I've found a way to escape. I'll have to practice on a servant first.

"PRACTICE ON A SERVANT" brought back something Ruby had said. Chevelle would have to practice the unbinding spell on someone else first. I wondered whether he would use one of our group and what would happen if the spell went wrong.

I glanced at the others as they stood at intervals around the camp. Gone were such usual habits as sharpening a blade or casual banter. Their eyes were on the surrounding landscape, their postures giving the impression they were more worried about staying alert. I could only imagine they were waiting for trackers, and the thought made my stomach turn. I swallowed hard, going back to the book.

I TESTED the spell on Rain last night. I'm not sure what went amiss, but she convulsed for hours before she fell into a sleep. She finally rose late this morning, but she couldn't remember who she was, and she kept scratching at her face until it bled. At least she'll not be able to tell anyone I did it. I'll have to catch another servant tonight.

No, I had a feeling he would not be using one of our group. I was starting to get sleepy but didn't want to put the book down. The others didn't seem to notice, though they never slept as much as I did.

I'd positioned myself near the light of the fire, and across from me, Ruby sat watching the darkness, occasionally tossing some bit of dust onto the flames that turned their glow from orange to blue. I could see the outline of Chevelle's form near a large rock, the jut of his shoulder and his hand on the pommel of his sword. I wondered where he had studied the binding spells and how many other spells he might have learned.

THIS ONE WORKED. Dree's nose bled for the first few minutes but after that she slept soundly and woke just before noon not knowing she had missed anything. Tomorrow, I try it on my watcher.

WATCHER. I tucked the book into my pack and fell asleep with her words in my thoughts. My imagination had filled in all the blanks and let the fear I'd been suppressing creep in and take over. It turned her words into my nightmares. Watchers and trackers, tassels and robes, Chevelle's furious gaze as he pushed me from the cliff again. *Chevelle. My watcher.*

~

"FREY." Ruby woke me at dawn, urging me to stand for a few moments before we were back on the horses.

I was exhausted again, so I hung back from the group as we rode. Steed slowed to ride with me as I watched Ruby and Grey banter ahead. "Steed, why *aren't* they together?"

He sighed. I didn't think he enjoyed discussing his sister's personal life. "Ruby doesn't believe she can get close to anyone... that way."

I considered the way she was with me, as if she wanted us to be friends, the way she touched Steed, sat near him. "Why?"

"Past experiences."

She'd killed her mother, and I wondered how many others. *What had she said, "until a pattern became noticeable?"* I shivered at the thought. "Poison."

He nodded in silent acknowledgement.

"In the village, some of the elves never paired up." I thought of Junnie's family. "But I guess most of those had received the calling."

Grey scoffed ahead of us.

I hadn't realized he could hear us. I was embarrassed but couldn't stop myself. "What?"

His horse slowed to fall in with ours as he spoke. "The calling?"

I didn't understand. It had been a thing of honor, but he spoke of it as if it was a joke.

"Do you really believe such nonsense?"

"What nonsense? It isn't real?"

He let out a harsh laugh, and I flinched. "Oh, I suppose it's real. The service is real. Honestly, Freya, don't you see?"

"See what?" I cursed my bound brain.

"Grand Council."

I drew a sharp breath at the words.

"The calling is simply service to Grand Council. A hundred years of servitude under the guise of duty and honor. What is honorable about doing their bidding?"

"So you don't... answer the call?" I stumbled, searching for words.

His laughter was a roar. "No. We do not answer." It settled, and he added, "They do not call." At that, Steed joined in, chuckling.

It didn't make sense. I knew I had been assigned a watcher from the North. "No one?" I asked.

"No. Council does not attempt to rule the North."

I considered that and considered my watcher. He was a volunteer. I seethed for a moment, but flashes of my mother and council cloaks flooded my thoughts, and I had to block them.

"So the North has no Council at all?"

Grey's answer was uncomfortable. "No. No Council." He paused while he formed the rest of his reply. Steed watched him intently. "We are... unruled."

"Unruly," Steed added with a half laugh.

"You've never had a Council?"

Grey shook his head.

"No rulers?"

He gave Steed a sidelong glance. "Not anymore." I could tell he intended to end the conversation with that, but it only made me more curious.

I was tired of having to make everyone spell things out for me. "No Council ever. No rulers anymore? So what, then?"

Steed flinched at my tone but didn't answer.

"Frey," Chevelle called from the front of the line.

I glared at him.

"Time to resume your training."

They had me work with Anvil, trying to anticipate when he was preparing to send a small current of electricity toward me, which meant I spent the day getting shocked. I was grateful when we finally stopped to make camp.

I was afraid they would resume training after dinner, so I found a place off by myself and pretended to rest as I went back to reading the diary.

TODAY WAS EXHILARATING. For the first time in I don't know how long, I was out of the castle and free from practice, free from duties, free from walls.

Though tricky to set up, the spell worked on Rune. I showed up at practice early and whispered the words in case something went wrong and he heard. I can't imagine what my punishment would have been, though it might have been worth it. He fell asleep quickly, and I ran as fast as I could, my pulse pounding with excitement.

I spent the entire day away from the castle. Without the drain of practice, I was thrilling with energy. I could feel the trees, the mountain. I hope Father never comes back! I am sure I will try again tomorrow and every day I can spare after that.

AN OWL HOOTED from far away, echoing off the jagged stones. I'd not heard much in the way of wildlife the farther north we'd gone, and I had assumed it was owing to the size of our group. But the elves of the North were not like those I'd grown accustomed to, and I wondered if more than a few of my assumptions had been wrong. The answering call came, another owl in some far away tree, and I glanced at Steed where he spoke quietly with Grey. He winked at me before falling back into his conversation, and I returned to reading.

RUNE WAS COMPLETELY unaware of any foul play yesterday, so I had full confidence in the spell this morning. Not that I wouldn't have attempted it again anyway, but at least I know I'm safer now. No worries when I'm out of the castle.

My sister is out every day, but I can never seem to find her. She keeps bringing back the strangest treasures. I have run for two days now. I think tomorrow, I will follow her. She refuses to tell me where she goes, neither under threat nor for a bribe, so I'll have to use stealth.

GREY WALKED into the darkness outside of our fire, and in the shifting shadows, I saw the broad form of Anvil. He carried a sword at his hip, like most of the others, but I'd rarely seen him draw it. I supposed since he had lightning, he didn't always need steel. I glanced at Steed, his back to me, and then Ruby, who only offered me an encouraging smile. I wasn't certain what it meant, but she busied herself with tying a thin braid into her curls, so I carefully turned the page where the diary was tucked against my cloak.

TODAY WAS BRILLIANT. I left a sleeping Rune just in time to find my sister sneaking from the castle. I followed her all the way to her secret spot. It took us half the day to get there, but it was worth it.

It's so far away from any kind of traffic, I have no idea how she even discovered it.

Nestled in a patch of trees outside the forest was some sort of camp. I watched her at first. She scoured the area, searching through the things she found there. But I couldn't observe for long. I revealed myself and inquired about her previous finds and all the questions that were plaguing me. She was furious! She screamed and cursed and fumed. She was no help with my queries, so I was forced to look around myself.

Whatever had been there lived a little like the imps. And there were imp tracks there, but it appeared only one. A massive number of bowls and jars littered the camp. I have no idea who would need so many. The fey like containers, but not of this crude sort—the craftsmanship was almost that of a troll. I tried to stay on the opposite side of the camp from my sister's wrath, but I found tracks and had to follow them near her, stirring up another fit of rage. The prints were shoed, about the size of elves, but the treads were irregular. Whatever stayed here, there were a lot of them.

Near the center of the camp, the ground was beat down with tracks circling a ring of stones. I found remnants inside, and ashes. A crude fire pit. Around that, several feet out, were various logs, I assumed for sitting around the pit for warmth. A few huts were situated about the camp, but their construction was unlike anything I'd seen before, very poorly built. I ducked inside one and was shocked to see it was full of possessions. Clothing, bedding, so much left behind. I had thought they'd departed suddenly, but I was confident then that it was not of their choosing.

I went back outside and examined the tracks again. I followed the imp's this time and found my answer. Outside of the camp, I uncovered blood and drag marks. The imp had killed what appeared to be three of the camp's inhabitants and dragged them off, likely by stringer and tow. Whatever was there had run away because of the attack, and recently.

I questioned my sister again—she'd had some time to cool down—but she was no help. I immediately knew she had not even considered that whatever she had been so interested in was still out here, probably close. I didn't clue her in. After a little more time there, I acted as if I'd lost interest and headed home.

Tomorrow, I will follow the tracks. I will find whoever was there and solve the mystery of their rudimentary tools and strange huts.

I YAWNED. After a quick glance around, I slid the book back into my pack. I rolled over and fell asleep listening to Ruby's quiet tune.

THE NEXT MORNING, the group seemed in unusually high spirits. I had no idea why the mood had shifted, but I enjoyed the laughter and joking anyway.

We rode past a waterfall, the roar of water making me curious. I figured Ruby was my best bet. Chevelle gave me no answers, and though hers were sometimes cryptic, I knew she'd been reading books on magic.

"Ruby, is there a way to harness the power of things like that waterfall?"

Grey glanced at me. The look of concern for my intelligence was not exactly uncommon, but it was something I'd yet to get used to.

"Not that I know of," she said. She got her mischievous

grin. "Though I did read once that there was a way to steal life force and use it for yourself."

Chevelle shot her a stern rebuke from the front of the pack.

She continued as if excusing herself. "But it was merely a fey tale and probably not entirely accurate." Then, in a lower voice: "It is fun to speculate, though."

I wiped at my cheek to clear the dampness from the mist, mirroring her low tone as I questioned her. "How would you steal life force?"

"Well, like I said, probably not accurate... But you would have to take the other's life in order to gain their power. Take it in a specific manner." She noticed Chevelle glaring at her and clamped her mouth shut.

I waited until he turned back around before I whispered, "Ruby, did you bring the magic book with you?"

She smiled.

"Can I read it?"

She winked at me.

I started to share her grin, but before I could, Chevelle was in front of us, his horse blocking my way. I was almost thrown from my saddle when we stopped to avoid running into him. He was angry again. "Frey."

"What?"

"Do you remember the last time you used a spell?"

I recalled the smell of burning flesh as the maps cut into my palms. "Yes," I muttered, defeated.

The look he gave Ruby was clear. There would be no magic study for me.

But I did know she had it. Maybe I would be able to steal it...

Lost in thought, I began to fall behind the group. The higher we rose up the mountain, the more treacherous the jagged rock became. I felt every step, holding the reins tightly as the horse's hooves slipped and jumped. The haze thickened, keeping the view both ahead and behind close. It gathered in my hair, leaving it a matted mess with the single braid—Ruby's handiwork—dripping condensation over the shoulder of my cloak.

I decided to practice as we rode, closing my eyes to sink partially into my horse, still alert to my own self and the outside world.

It was there, leading my horse and seeing through his eyes, that the pain struck. It came on instantaneously, hitting me like a blade, cutting, shearing. It was accompanied by sharpness of sound as well. My ears were in excruciating pain. The horse dropped, and his head smacked to the ground. I watched through his eyes as he hit. The animal's senses stilled, not panicked as my own. I didn't understand what was happening and couldn't quite form a thought.

I yearned to retreat into the horse, run from the agony, but the severity of it tore me back and kept me there in my own head. It felt and sounded like metal bands inside my mind, screeching in my ears. I hadn't opened my eyes again, and I found that I couldn't. I couldn't find my body. I wanted to bring my hands to my head, cover my ears, but I couldn't feel anything aside from the pain in my mind.

I focused all of my energy on unearthing feeling somewhere, and finally, though the terror was unrelenting, I felt my body again and knew it was there. It still didn't respond, but I knew I hadn't fallen with the horse. Something had caught me. Not the ground, not a rock. Someone was carrying me. The horror must have stretched time, making the few seconds seem like minutes.

I struggled to bring myself back. I could hear nothing but a piercing squall. I willed my eyes open, though only a fraction. I was looking at the back of a horse from my position slung over someone's shoulder. My eyes closed once more as the pain doubled, and I lost my body again for a moment. I concentrated until I got it back then realized I was bouncing. I worked my eyes again, using every ounce of control I had left. I was on a horse, running. Not my own. Chevelle was holding me in front of him, my body limp and useless. I fought to focus on more but was overtaken by pain. *Are were running away?*

I could control nothing but my mind, and that just barely. As my eyes closed again, I reached out and found my horse as he lay motionless on the ground, my steed. He wasn't dead. I asked him to stand and tried to impress upon him to follow. I hoped it had worked as I faded into blackness.

14

I regained consciousness very slowly. I was hit with blurry images first, sights and scenes that melded into hazy dreams. Eventually, they became clearer, though they didn't make much sense. After a time, it occurred to me that the problem was that the images were mixing with the wrong sounds... real sounds. Panicked sounds.

I thought I recognized Chevelle's voice and tried to focus on it, to understand the agony. "Frey," he said, and something brushed my cheek, warm and feather light.

The distant impression that it might have been the brush of lips had me drawing in a sharp breath, and I coughed, gasping to fill my lungs. The air shifted as those surrounding me moved in response. I forced my eyes open and found Ruby, Steed, and Chevelle. They looked for a moment as if they were suffering my pain... and then I realized the pain was gone, and the siren was silenced. My breathing steadied, the fear abating, and their faces relaxed. Relief washed over their expressions, but their postures remained stiff and alert.

I pushed up to find the source of the danger, and dizziness incapacitated me.

They rushed to kneel beside me, and I could see that was how they had been before my gasp had moved them to standing. My throat was too raw to speak, so Chevelle gave me a canteen. I would have taken anything, but I was glad it was water, not hot wine or that foul-tasting elixir.

"What happened?" I finally choked out, but they were tight-lipped.

"How do you feel?" Chevelle asked. His tone was off, a little shaky. I couldn't tell if he was cross or something else. There was something so familiar about the way he leaned over me, but my thoughts weren't working right yet.

I tried to clear my head before answering. "I don't know." It was the best I could do.

"Are you hurt?"

"No."

He glanced at my hands wrapped tightly around the neck of the container then back at me. "Do you know who I am?"

Something about that was funny, and I laughed, but it came out hoarse.

He looked torn and tentative as he posed the next question. "Can you tell me your name?"

I wondered how badly I was messed up for him to approach me with such a line of questioning. "Frey."

"Your *full* name?"

I rolled my eyes then wished I hadn't as the room spun. I pressed a hand to my temple. "Elfreda Georgiana Suzetta Glaforia."

They all drew in a deep breath.

"What?"

Chevelle's sigh seemed to have let the air out of him. His

fingers rested on the edge of the cloak beneath me. "Are you in pain?"

"No. Not anymore."

He nodded. "What do you remember?"

"I was—" I faltered. I didn't know why, but I felt protective of my secret. I didn't want to tell anyone I was in my horse's mind. I started again, aware of my annoyed tone. "I don't know. I was following all of you and suddenly"—I threw my hands up in a vague gesture indicating the attack. It was the best description I could give—"just pain and screeching."

Ruby and Steed bolted to their feet as someone came in, but it was only Grey. "What is it?" Chevelle said, still kneeling over me.

Grey hesitated, rubbed a palm awkwardly over the woven material of his shirt. "A horse is at the door."

Chevelle glanced at me, and I hoped he didn't see my smile. I knew it was my steed.

Grey waited. "Well, should I let him in?"

Chevelle nodded once, and Grey left as quickly as he'd entered.

I realized he'd walked through a door. I glanced around, confused about where I was. Gray stone walls surrounded us, but I'd been staring at an open sky, nothing but the cloak between my prone form and the cold earth. "Where are we?"

"Fort Stone," Steed answered.

I snickered, and Chevelle's irritation resurfaced. I didn't know if it was for me or Steed. "Fort Stone?" I asked anyway.

"Named for Lord Stone," Steed explained.

Chevelle's gaze caught the other man, leaving no question as to the source of his crossness.

"A lord?" I tried not to sound too impressed as I took

another look around, reassessing the walls. I wondered how old it was.

Chevelle stood, directing Ruby to stay with me until he returned. Steed followed him without another word.

Ruby must have known I was curious. Or she just wanted to talk. It was hard to tell with Ruby. "It's been abandoned for centuries," she offered, making me a bed as she recounted ancient stories.

She helped me move onto the blankets, and the dizziness improved, but my muscles were weak and drained. I asked, "Why are we here?"

Her mouth twisted to the side as she considered her answer. "We were in need of shelter after your... episode. It was close enough to work. Are you cold?" she asked, tucking me under a blanket.

"I'll get it," I said, waving my hand to form a fire beside us. Nothing happened.

The vertigo was almost gone, and I was feeling close to normal, just a bit fuzzy. I tried once more, but it would not light. I pressed down the panic as I concentrated on pulling the burn together.

But nothing happened.

I sat up, holding both hands in front of me palms up, as I focused on lighting a flame, any flame.

Nothing.

I reached out to move a rock from the floor. It didn't budge. I concentrated on a pebble beside me. It didn't shift in the least.

"Ruby? It doesn't work." I held my hands in front of me helplessly.

Panic was taking me when she laid a hand on my shoulder and leaned forward. I expected her to calm me, explain it would come back, it would all be all right. Glitter was in the air before I could stop her.

By the time Chevelle returned, I was loopy with it. He and Ruby sat facing me. She must have filled him in on my problem.

I resisted the urge to touch him. I always wanted to touch him.

"Frey," Chevelle began in a measured tone.

I cut him off, trying to sound calm. "What happened?"

"It would seem that Council has attacked us."

I was too numb to draw in the quick breath I expected. My cheeks tingled. I didn't think I could feel my hands.

"Attacked *you*," he clarified.

Something came out of my chest that sounded like a moan. I blinked too slowly. "Attacked?"

"They must have tried to strengthen your bonds."

I knew I should have been shocked, but I couldn't produce the feeling. "They succeeded," I complained.

He nodded. "It seems they may have taken your magic completely this time."

This time. I concentrated on keeping my head straight and looking like I was listening properly, acting properly. My attempt at concentration must have come across as anxiety.

"You found a way to break their bonds before. You will again."

I nodded. My nose was itchy. I wiggled it.

"Rest now," he said. "We have time."

I reached forward, ready to ask him to stay, but he wasn't leaving. He only settled in. Both he and Ruby were staying with me. I was happy... downright blissful. *Stupid dust.*

I watched Chevelle's face as my eyes fluttered closed with exhaustion. My dreams brought him close in a much-too-vivid kiss on the cheek that burned like fire. My skin was blistering—I could feel the color. It swirled around me and shocked me awake again.

I lay on the floor with wide eyes and an unmoving body. I was weak, tired, and still under the influence, but I heard voices. I didn't move as I listened to discern if they were real.

They seemed to be close but were muffled—maybe in the next room or down a corridor—as they echoed off the stones. I thought I'd picked out Anvil's deep voice. "Trapped here like rats... cowards..." He sounded outraged.

Someone else, Grey maybe, worry coloring his tone: "We can't just leave them out there."

I knew Chevelle's voice, interlaced between the other comments. "She's not ready... we can't... too soon."

And a voice I couldn't place: "...another setback..."

They seemed to be in disagreement, but I couldn't find the interest to stay with them. I faded back into sleep.

These dreams took me further. My sight was off, not as clear, distorted. But as I lingered there, I knew the cause. I was seeing from a horse.

We were outside the stone walls of the fortress, finding sparse greens to eat, which bored me even in a dream. I encouraged the horse to run, and he responded immediately, taking flight down the mountainside. The rocks streaked past us as we ran faster and faster, the wind whipping his mane. A great bird perched on the dead limb of an ironwood tree, and I jumped to it just as it dropped from the branch and flared its wings out to catch the wind. We flew still farther as I watched the mountain pass below. There was a scrubby patch of trees ahead, and I could see movement there, inside. I tried to focus on it, the familiar silver and white.

~

COMMOTION BROUGHT ME BACK, and I sat up, startled. My head spun. Ruby caught my arm to steady me. Her smile was strained as she handed me a drink of water.

Chevelle was near the entrance of the stone room with Anvil and Grey. They appeared to be preparing to leave. "What's going on?" I asked.

"Nothing to worry about," Ruby assured me. "Just a hunting trip."

I was still muddled, but I knew it wouldn't take three of them to hunt. Then I remembered the bits of conversation I'd heard when I woke. "Someone's missing?" I took stock. I'd seen everyone but Rhys and Rider and the silver-and-white wolves. "The wolves are out there."

Each person in the room turned to me. Ruby finally spoke. "What do you know about the wolves, Frey?"

"Are they hurt?"

"We don't know. They did not return."

"Rhys and Rider?"

"They are attempting to locate them. They will not rejoin us until they do."

I started to draw a map for them with magic then cursed when I realized I was no longer able. *Bound.* Ruby had been right to drug me—I couldn't have handled it otherwise. They were watching me, unsure what I was doing as I sat helpless and swearing. "I need something to draw with."

Ruby pulled a piece of charcoal and scrap of paper from her bag. I rushed to sketch the path I remembered from my dream, focusing on the ring of trees with the most detail. "They are there."

The men stood motionless and staring until Anvil crossed

the room to retrieve the map. He bowed a little as he took the paper from my hands then hurried out. Grey followed. Chevelle stayed.

Ruby turned to him and breathed a deep sigh, but he didn't respond.

My head throbbed, and I groaned as I pressed the bridge of my nose. He was beside me in a flash, unspeaking. Ruby handed me another drink.

It helped, but I was still irritated about the binding. "Does this mean we'll have to train again?"

Ruby snickered.

Chevelle answered slowly. "There has to be a way. You broke them before."

I tried to remember how. The first magic I could recall were the thistle and thorns. It seemed so far away.

Ruby was speaking to him. "Maybe it was just the length of time..."

What does she know about how long I was bound?

"If we can find a way to test without endangering—" He stopped. "Don't worry about it, Frey." I wondered if I'd looked frightened. "We will figure it out."

How reassuring. I meant to smile at him but only succeeded in pressing my lips into a flat line.

"Rest now. There is plenty of time for tr"—he thought better of saying *training* again—"to test the bindings." He smiled, and again, I had the feeling he wanted to reach out to me. But he did not. He simply stood and walked from the room.

Ruby saw me watching. "He's right, Freya. Rest now. Plenty of time to get you straightened back out." She stood and walked to the front wall. I hadn't noticed the narrow window before, which was no wider than the flat of a hand.

Ruby positioned herself in front of it, watching whatever was outside.

I sighed. *Plenty of time.* I fiddled with the blankets for a while, tried a couple of times—futilely—to move tiny specks of loose rock on the floor, then gave up and decided to read the journal again. I rolled away from Ruby and pulled my pack into the curve of my body, settling the book open but able to be quickly hidden.

THIS MORNING, I extended my spell, giving Rune an extra day of sleep. It was a good thing too. I found the camp right off and followed the tracks easily. The occupants must have run in panic initially but then gathered back together and walked in a line, some two by two, some dragging sleds. They made temporary shelter in a cave, likely for just one night, and continued again. They must have moved slowly, and I could see they stopped often to rest. It didn't take long before I'd found their new camp. I slipped into a tall tree to watch them.

To my shock, I found something I had never seen before. I watched for hours before I was sure, too stunned to believe it possible. I had heard stories—the fey were always puffing dust about it—but I'd never believed it. Was I really watching humans?

I WAS PULLED FROM READING, confused. Humans weren't real. *What kind of book is this?* She had mentioned fey stories. I wondered if it was fiction, a fey ruse, given to Chevelle by Ruby. Or maybe the dust was still playing havoc on me. I glanced over my shoulder at Ruby still watching anxiously out the front window. I shook my head and found the line again.

. . .

But I couldn't deny it. Their size was about that of an elf, but all were different. The men were thicker. Not necessarily with muscle, some more bulbous. The women were varied as well, some thin and wiry, some stout like the males. Their hair was in all shades— light blond like the sun, brown as a fall tree... One even had rusty red, his plump cheeks peppered with light-brown spots. And there were so many children! They were loud and ran round the camp all afternoon. And they were just as varied as the adults. I examined their wide noses, rounded ears, and stubby fingers. Those who wore no shoes had short, thick toes like trolls. The men had patches of hair curled on their chests and forearms, and some even grew it around their chins like goats. Their clothes were tattered and ill-fitting rags.

They moved about the camp slowly. Clearly, they had no magic, and they definitely were the owners of the crude tools we had found. They spoke to each other often, their voices like the protest of an old hound. I watched until nightfall, when they settled into tents and lean-tos. They seemed to assign a watchman, wielding only a torch lit from the central fire. I slipped down from the tree and returned to the castle. I am dying to see what I can find of them in the books of Father's study.

Laughter broke my concentration. Anvil and Grey were back. I looked to the front wall, but Ruby was gone, having moved to the entrance of our room. She seemed to be waiting there excitedly for something. I slid the book into the pack and sat up to watch.

Chevelle came in, and Ruby greeted him.

"It's fantastic," she breathed. He smiled at her.

Steed was following. "Almost unbelievable," he added, shooting me a speculative look.

They turned to me as Rhys and Rider entered. They didn't approach but stopped just inside the room and dipped into a bow. "Our gratitude, Elfreda."

I blushed. I had forgotten the wolves. They must have found them. "Were they hurt?"

"No. And our thanks to you for that as well."

I wasn't exactly sure how that was due to me, but I smiled, glad they had found them and everyone was safe. They turned to leave, and Grey entered with two spits of meat and wine. It almost seemed like a celebration. Almost. Their high spirits from before hadn't quite returned.

I wondered how long I had been out. I wondered where the councilmen who'd attacked us were now.

The wine flowed. Steed took some food to Anvil, Grey and Ruby made their way to the front window, and I found myself sitting alone with Chevelle.

"How do you feel?" he asked.

"Better. And worse." Better because the dust was clearing. Worse because I was fuzzy and bound again.

He nodded. He was closer than before, sitting opposite me, and I had the disconcerting feeling that I'd lost the bit of time when he'd moved there. He reached out and took my hand in his, his fingers gentle as he turned it palm up to place a pebble there. "Can you do anything with this?"

"No." Frustration was clear in my voice. I had already tried.

"And no fire?"

"No."

"So nothing works?" The implication was there, but I didn't know what it meant right away. And then it occurred to me: the horse. I had thought he had shown up because I'd impressed upon him to follow before I blacked out, but I had already been bound again at that point.

I wanted to tell him, but I didn't. I didn't know why I felt so protective of the secret.

Chevelle drew a section of moss from one of the stones on the wall and it replaced the pebble. "Try this. They shouldn't have bothered binding you from growing."

I concentrated on it. Nothing. But I was never good at that, anyway. I shook my head.

He nodded, giving up, but our hands still lay together, connecting us.

"Where are they?" I asked.

He'd been looking at our hands, but his eyes returned to my face at the question.

"Council," I explained.

"They have retreated. They were able to briefly incapacitate the wolves, giving Rhys and Rider less warning of their approach before you were attacked." He hesitated. "When we heard the alert, I turned. Your eyes were closed." I didn't comment, so he continued, "I was able to catch you just before your horse dropped. I've no idea why they attacked him. They should have been focused on you."

I wasn't sure they *had* attacked the horse. Maybe it was because I'd been there, in his mind, controlling him. "What happened to Rhys and Rider?"

"They broke to keep from fighting such a sizeable force alone. They circled back to meet us. In the disorder, they lost track of the wolves."

"But the wolves weren't hurt?"

"They had been strung up by vine among the trees, but alive."

I winced at the idea. "Why?"

A wry smile crossed his lips and I couldn't help but focus on them for a moment. "Because the wolves would have fought to the death, and Grand Council does not kill animals with magic."

I remembered my mother. "Only elves?"

His mocking smile widened. "Only elves."

They thought killing an animal with magic was evil and dark, but they were hunting us down to burn us. I considered the alternative—pierced through with arrows, blessed with a prayer—and laughed.

His eyes were intense as he reached to cup my neck, his fingers resting gently at my spine. His thumb grazed the base of my ear as I felt him urge me forward. My breath caught, heart stuttering into a broken lope.

And then Ruby was beside us from out of nowhere, her words startling me back to the cold, dull room. "They're coming in."

Chevelle leaned back, his fingers brushing my collarbone when he pulled away. I bit my lip at the tingle that ran through me, and the corner of his mouth turned into a different kind of smile.

He stood to walk from the room, and I stared at the stone entry, struggling to keep my thoughts from spinning out of control. Too much had happened. Too much was wrong. My life had flipped, twisted into some strange reflection of itself, and I couldn't reconcile the fragments. It caused me physical pain to think about Chevelle's touch, about Council, and about what was happening, and I knew it was the bonds.

When Grey walked out, my trance broke, and I noticed Ruby by the front window, wearing an odd smile. I flushed and turned from her, rolling into a ball on my blankets, remembering no more than the feel of his skin on my neck, the quirk of his lips.

I had to keep distracted, and there was nothing for it but the book.

I WASN'T able to find much regarding humans in the study's library. But I had been right. Illustrations and descriptions matched what I had seen.

I know I took a risk extending Rune's spell further, but I did not want to get caught, definitely not followed. I wondered if my sister was still at the original camp. Surely, she wasn't bright enough to figure it out. And apparently, she wasn't willing to tell anyone.

I was returning to the spot where I had found the humans the previous day when I ran across one of them alone. I hid myself behind a patch of brush to watch him. He had a lovely complexion with a hint of bronze and cropped dark-brown hair with a few tiny streaks of blond just around his face. He looked less like the others I had been watching. He was built like the elves, strong and muscled, but still lean. He wore plain pants and tall boots. His light cloth shirt was unlaced, moving around him as he walked. He carried a small blade in his hand, but I couldn't imagine what he was doing there unaccompanied.

There was a rustle from the brush several yards in the opposite direction from where I was hiding. He rushed toward it, and I followed, unsure why he was running. The noise was made by a small boar, and the human was chasing it. He ran after it, gasping for air, and I followed close behind, thrilling at the clumsy spectacle. The boar approached a ridge of rock and turned, giving the human the advantage. He leaped after it, blade held wide, and landed, slicing into its side and twisting the blade back out. He was *leaning over its small, motionless body, heaving for breath, covered in blood. I laughed, shocked at myself but filled with excitement and amusement.*

He stood, whirling to face me, bloody blade held out. I had to stifle another laugh. I managed to keep my reaction calm, with only a smile.

He seemed disoriented for a moment, and then his breathing slowed, and his arms relaxed. He stared at me as if I were a delusion, a dream looking back at him. He was speechless, and it occurred to me that perhaps elves were not a part of this human's knowledge. I wondered if he would recover soon. I considered abandoning him and returning to watch the others, but his face was so interesting, the emotions so plain and readable there. But he wasn't afraid. It was awe.

I decided to have a little fun with him. He couldn't possibly be dangerous. "Hello." I spoke to him slowly, but it appeared he didn't comprehend. He merely stood gawking at me. I tried again. "Do you wish to speak with me?"

"Yes," he finally stuttered. "Uh... hello."

"I am..." I hesitated, unsure if I should tell him my name—I was on the run, after all. I decided on a replacement. "Lizzy."

He seemed to like that. "I'm Noble."

I was confused. "You are noble?"

He shook his head. "Noble is my name. Noble Grand."

"That is a large name. You are a ruler among your people?"

He laughed. "No, no. Noble is my given name, passed down for generations. Grand is the family name."

Generations? I was surprised again. I stepped closer, enthralled. "What are you doing here?"

"We are searching for a good place to start over," he explained. I was scrutinizing his blade. "Oh—well, I'm hunting."

He wasn't as slow as I had thought, quite capable of conversa-

tion. I couldn't help but wonder. "You were a bit... stunned before?"

He flushed a pleasing shade of red. "Yes."

"Why?"

"Well, it's only that you are quite beautiful. Surely the loveliest thing I have ever seen." I smiled in spite of myself, and he continued the flattery. "And then when you spoke, your voice... it's like a melody."

"And you are seeking a new camp?"

"A more permanent settlement, actually."

"You have found it here?"

"We are undecided. Days ago, we were attacked." Pain washed over his features. "A horrid creature took several of our men."

I nodded. "An imp."

"I'd never have believed it to be true if I hadn't seen it myself." He was clearly lost in thought as he continued. "We may move again. The risk seems too great."

Suddenly, I didn't want them to relocate. I wanted them to stay right there, where I could watch them. I tried to make him feel safe. "You know, I could protect you."

He was incredulous. I decided to show him.

I stepped forward, noting his unease at my movement, and faced the boar that lay on the ground behind him. He turned to see what I was focusing on. I was afraid to scare him too much, so I decided on a small gesture. I held my hand out in front of me, emphasizing the action as I twisted my wrist in the air, the boar's head spinning, the sound of its neck cracking in tandem with my movement.

He gasped and stepped back from me. I was afraid for a moment that I'd shown him too much. He looked at my face, searching, and finally let out a breathless, "Magic."

His expression was filled with wonder. I had seen many impressed with my talents but never with such an effortless show.

I laughed to myself. It was refreshing to have someone so genuinely awed. He didn't ask to see what else I could do. He wasn't sizing me up for battle. I smiled at him, and he seemed to think that alone a reward.

He was still speechless.

"Well, shall you stay, then?"

"Forever," he gushed. It was a curious response, but I had begun to think he wasn't that different from me, aside from the obvious lack of magic, skill, and grace. Moreover, where many of the others lacked beauty, he did not. Unconventional, yes, but nonetheless... interesting.

I led him to a set of stones to sit, wanting to get answers to all the questions that had been burning in my mind since I had spotted them. He had forgotten his prey, so I offered to help him with it. This befuddled him, so I simply skinned and spitted the animal while he sat, staring in amazement. It was as if he'd never seen fire before. It made the magic fun again. Like when we were children, before Father's ridiculous schedule. I shook off the memory of practice and focused on the human.

"So, how old are you?"

"Twenty-two," he said, almost shamefacedly.

At first, I was shocked at the number and thought maybe I'd misunderstood. But I remembered reading the human lifespan was very brief. By his manner, I'd have guessed twice that number, were he an elf. "Why the hint of embarrassment?"

"They tell me I should have a family by now."

"You have none?"

"A mother and father but none of my own. No wife, no children."

"You are expected to have a wife and child after just two decades of life?"

He laughed for some reason I could not see. "Then you have no family of your own?"

"I am not expected to pair for quite some time, if ever. And chil-dren? Ha!" He was visibly perplexed, so I kept talking. "I have a family as well, though my mother died recently."

Sadness washed his features. "I'm sorry. Was it an imp?"

"No." I laughed at the strange idea. And for no apparent reason, I told him the truth. "She died of sorrow."

His brow furrowed.

We shared the boar and talked further, casually, as if we were old friends. He resituated himself on the rock, coming closer to me, and his shirt moved to expose a different color skin where it opened at the chest. I reached out to pull it aside and his eyes grew wild at the touch.

"Your flesh is a different tone here."

He smiled, as if I were being coy. "Yes."

"Why?"

"Sometimes I work with my shirt on, to avoid the burn of the sun."

"The sun?"

He laughed but then realized I was earnest. "It is a tan... from the sun." He pulled the laces and lifted his shirt over his head, throwing it aside to show me his bare chest. The bronzed color of his face extended there but was a lighter shade. I examined him closer, taking his hand and turning his arm. The inside of his wrist was lighter still, close to the shade of my own skin.

I was still studying him when he spoke softly. "May I kiss you?"

His breath hit my face. I hadn't realized how close I had gotten. It surprised me, as did his request. I had a perverted desire to let him. I smiled thinking of it. He took that as an invitation, leaning closer, his hand raised to touch my face. His thumb caressed the line of my jaw as he reached for me, fingers tangling in my braids as he drew me to him. He started gently, teasing, then crushed our lips together, his strong hand holding me there, his breathing ragged.

At some point, I became aware of what I was doing and drew back. "I have to go now."

He looked devastated.

"Goodbye, young Noble."

"Can I see you again?"

I smiled. I couldn't seem to help it. "I will return."

He took a deep breath, satisfied. "I'll be waiting."

As I turned to go, I realized I hadn't asked any of the important questions that had been nagging me. I'd have to try harder tomorrow, stay on task. I ran back to the castle at full speed.

RUBY CLEARED HER THROAT, and I shoved the book into my pack. I glanced over at her, but she was still facing out the window. A moment later, Chevelle walked in, and she threw him a wicked grin. I brushed the length of my hair forward, hoping to cover the heat that had risen in my neck and ears.

"Ready to resume training?" he asked.

That cooled the flush, and I grimaced, moving to stand. I hadn't done so since the incident, and my head spun. I wobbled, and Chevelle was suddenly there, steadying me. I shook off his look of concern. "I'm fine. Really."

He shifted closer, and I became wholly aware of his hands at my waist. The grip he'd used to steady me became softer and yet, at the same time, his fingers tightened around me. My breath hitched as he pulled me against him, the length of our bodies touching.

My throat went dry, and black spots swirled in my vision. I fought to stay focused on his face, which was so close. His eyes grew troubled, and then he blurred out of vision as I went limp in his arms.

~

"Frey…"

I opened my eyes to the darkening sky. "What happened?"

"You seem to have blacked out," Chevelle said, a hint of some emotion under his reassurance.

I blushed. He must have seen that coming and held me because of it, simply to prevent me from falling on my face. I was a fool.

He helped me up, holding me only by one arm. I took a deep breath. "I'm all right now."

His lips twisted again, but I couldn't make out the expression. I could barely look him in the eyes.

I attempted every type of magic he could come up with, to no avail. I was beyond frustrated. Worse, I could tell he was being gentle on purpose, afraid I would break. I thought of what he'd said before about the dangers of messing with the bindings.

He must have read it on my face. "That's enough for now. Rest, Freya."

I didn't argue.

Ruby came in as if on cue, and Chevelle excused himself. I lay down, but irritation kept me from sleep, so I returned to the book.

I spent the next several weeks visiting him. I had forgotten about the rest of the camp. He had become infatuated with me, and I couldn't keep myself from indulging him. I was thoroughly enjoying it—reveling in it, if I was honest with myself.

He persisted in trying to touch and kiss me anytime I was close enough to allow, and I let him sometimes.

He surprised me one evening, when he knew it was time for me to leave, grabbing my wrist and holding me there. I was stronger than him, but I didn't resist his pull as he spoke. "Don't go."

"I will return tomorrow," I promised. "Early."

"No," he said, flush with emotion. "I don't ever want you to go." I laughed and he drew me closer. "Stay with me."

I started to pull away and he reached up, placing his hands on either side of my face, feverish now. "Marry me, Lizzy." I had long since gotten used to the name, but I wasn't sure he was talking to me at first. It seemed ridiculous.

I stopped myself from laughing, knowing from previous experience it would hurt him. I had come to realize he didn't know what I was. He knew I was different, of course, knew of the magic, though I'd shown him nothing of my real power. But he didn't understand I was an elf. I hadn't explained, knowing it would do nothing but perplex his simple mind. He merely thought I was something special, extraordinary. But did he actually think I was human, someone he could wed? I was incredulous.

But he was obsessed. The moment it slipped from his lips, he became more focused on that than anything else. Making me his bride. I couldn't understand.

He tried to explain. "I want you forever. I need you, Lizzy." The yearning in his voice was clear, and I was surprised that I ached for him a little, felt his pain and need. He touched me then, and I thought I understood when he continued, "We could be together..."

Marriage. He wanted to join us. I bit my lip, undecided. Curiosity was there too. And I couldn't help but imagine. He was *unmagical. He had no idea what I could do to him, for him, in such an intimate setting. What could it hurt, really? Sure, I could marry him. It wouldn't be real. But the other part, well, I could do that without the marriage, couldn't I? Harmless fun...*

I smiled as I leaned closer to him. This was the first time I had initiated a kiss, and he was grateful—more than grateful, he seemed overwhelmed with pleasure. I laughed to myself at what was to come, if this small, insignificant gesture brought him so much happiness. Our lips touched, and he gasped, and then the breath turned to a low moan.

I RUBBED the back of my hand over a cheek, trying to clear away the blush of color. The encounter was very *descriptive*. I threw a wary glance over my shoulder, making sure Ruby was still at the window as I continued.

THE DAYS we had spent coupling had done nothing to diminish his desire. If anything, they had enflamed it. And his obsession with marriage increased tenfold.

I had not met his family, but one morning when I arrived at the patch of forest where we met, he proudly presented his mother's wedding gown, a gift for me. He wanted me to wear it in our cere-mony. I had never agreed to the union, but I avoided telling him it was not possible. It would only be valid in his mind. But then again, what would that hurt?

I accepted the dress from him and looked it over. It was poorly made and ill-fitting but had potential as a design. I sat, using magic to work on the seaming and to arrange the scant pearls and beading in a more pleasant pattern while deciding how best to deal with him.

He was watching me intently. "We will have such prosperity. Think of it, with your magic, we will be able to conquer anything. Whatever we need, whatever we want, it will be nothing but a flick of your wrist."

I froze. It was irrational, I knew, but anger seethed inside me. I couldn't stop myself from thinking he was just like everyone else, interested only in my powers, my magic, and how it would benefit him. I turned to him, glaring, and he drew back, startled. "Is that what you want, why you are so intent on marrying me? For my power?"

He shook his head, mystified. The rage had overtaken me, though. The weeks of drugging Rune, sneaking out, my father being missing while he searched for a new wife, I was sure—all of it was too much. I slipped. A small crack in my stability let out enough magic to hurt him. I didn't hit him, but the surrounding trees and rocks were pulverized, and I knew I had done too much. He stared back at me... afraid.

I turned and ran, without another word, straight back to the castle. In these few short weeks, I had started to think of it less as a home and more as a prison. My limited freedom made me ache for more. My time with this human had felt like living.

It was wrong. I will return to him tomorrow, set things right. As I ran, I realized I was still carrying the dress with me. I couldn't understand why I had bothered dragging it along, but my grip on it was tight. I rolled it up, tucking it under my arm as I approached the castle. My prison.

PRISON. I pushed the book into my pack and finally slept.

～

When I woke, I felt better, stronger. I was hopeful that would apply to my magic as well. Chevelle sat against the dark stone wall, watching me. He seemed to recognize the change in my mood.

"Feeling well?"

I nodded. "I think I'd like to train again."

"That is probably a good idea. We'll be leaving soon."

I didn't know if I was *that* much better.

"Don't worry. It is safe. They will not attack again so soon."

"When?" I could hear the worry in my tone, despite his assurance.

"We will protect you, Frey."

Sure. I might have rolled my eyes.

"We knew they were following before. Our mistake was in assuming they meant a physical attack. We will not allow them so close again."

"So they're still following?" Panic set in.

"No. Not now." He paused. "They have accomplished what they came for. Now, they will regroup and return, which is why we need to move."

"Why would we leave a fort?"

He chuckled. "Trust me, Frey. We have a more secure location." I must not have appeared convinced. "Please," he added.

I sighed. I didn't have much of a choice. Then I laughed because I couldn't even trust myself.

I expected him to look at me like I was mad. Instead, he looked as though my behavior was... endearing. He stood and walked over to me, taking my hand to help me up. When he touched me, I tried to fight the heat that ran up my neck. I couldn't, and embarrassment caused my cheeks to color as well. I peered up at him through my dark bangs and could have sworn it amused him. I laughed at myself. The silly romance I'd been reading in the diary must have been affecting me.

I tried to stop my thoughts from returning there as we practiced, but it was near impossible. He kept working closely with me, touching me. I knew I should have been focusing on the magic, but it was useless. Each day ended with nothing but frustration and exhaustion, with naught to look forward to but leaving the safety of the fort. Only the book provided escape.

THE MOMENT *I entered the castle, I knew something was wrong. I had gone in through the servants' quarters, desiring to keep a low profile. When they saw me, fear crossed their faces, and they disappeared from sight. My heart sped. I wondered if something had gone wrong with Rune's spell this time. I decided to go check on him. I realized I was running.*

As I rounded a corner heading to the practice rooms, I ran into something hard. The impact didn't knock me down, but the shock almost did. It was one of Father's guards... one of the guards he'd taken with him.

He had me by the arm, dragging me along before I could think. I couldn't decide whether to run or fight. And then we were in the throne room. My father's face was indescribable, his fury almost tangible. I couldn't bring myself to look away from him, but I saw Rune standing in my peripheral vision. I was caught. I frantically searched for some explanation. But he didn't speak. He flipped his arm, dismissing me.

The tension showed in that small movement, and I blanched. I started to pull away from the guard, but he didn't release me. I realized then I hadn't been dismissed. It had been a direction for the guard. He wrenched me beside him, jerking unnecessarily, then shoved me through the door to my room. I listened, but his steps did not recede. I tried the door, but it was already bound.

I threw myself onto the bed. I felt absolutely wretched. Actually, I felt worse than that. I felt as if I'd been poisoned. The room turned, and I heaved over the edge of the mattress.

When I woke late the next morning, I was covered in sweat. My head spun as I stood, but I steadied myself and moved to the basin to splash my face. As I looked in the mirror at my pallid complexion, my features twisted in horror.

Understanding came suddenly and would not be denied. I scoffed at myself humorlessly as my words taunted me—just harmless fun... what could it hurt? For half a second, I wanted to scream. And then my hands found their way to my stomach and rested there.

I drew in a sharp breath. I hadn't noticed I had gotten so deeply involved in the story. I needed to rest, finish my recovery, and break the bonds. But I couldn't seem to step away.

I was unnaturally calm when they finally came for me. I knew they would recognize the signs. But it didn't matter now. I walked forward, resigned to my fate.

What I didn't expect was their response. The throne room was full. They all gasped when comprehension hit. But my father, and each of those present, seemed almost pleased when they saw me. They had no idea there was a human growing in the belly my hands cradled. I listened as their voices began and then rose, clamorously discussing the news and what it could bring. I cringed as their words turned to the possibilities, the power I might pass down, the strength the new one might bring.

"WE WILL LEAVE AT DAYBREAK," Grey informed Ruby as I read. The news brought on nothing but worry, so I went back to the book.

EVENTUALLY, *my father did seek to find out who the father was. I refused to tell him anything, and he could not force me in my condition. I could see his plans already forming. I was almost happy it would not be powerful—it would be half human and unmagical. I wondered if it could even be brought to term, I was ill so often. The elders discussed it constantly—it was so unusual to be sick, but it must have been a result of the pregnancy. Several of them were assigned to watch me, and I had to listen to their incessant chatter. They seemed thrilled not to know how or when I had gotten this way, carrying on about young elves and their quests.*

RUBY'S HAND was on my shoulder, shaking me awake. I hadn't realized I'd fallen asleep. I jerked up, hoping she hadn't seen the journal. It wasn't lying there. I grabbed my pack, pretending to get ready, and sighed when I felt it tucked inside. I didn't remember doing it, but I was grateful I had. I was really getting into the story.

I yawned and stretched then followed her out of the room. I was surprised by the size of the fort. We went down several corridors and passed a few doors before finally coming to a large, open arena where the others waited for us. Chevelle favored me with a smile as I passed him on the way to my horse. I started to command the horse to kneel, but Steed grabbed me about the waist and threw me up. I took one deep breath before we kicked the horses into a gallop and ran from the fort in a pack.

Our pace finally slowed as the way became too treacherous. Massive rock formations loomed over us, loose stones underfoot causing the horses to stumble. The haze was so thick I couldn't see anything but the riders in front of me. I only knew from the strain on my legs that we were heading up, climbing higher into the gray sky and biting wind.

Chevelle rode beside me throughout the day. When we stopped for the evening, he pulled me down from my horse and stayed near as we sat on large stones around a fire. Ruby was telling stories again, and everyone gave her their full attention—everyone but us.

"How do you feel?" he asked.

I shrugged. "Fine, I guess." He seemed unusually concerned. He was also sitting uncommonly close.

He spoke in a low voice, though the others didn't appear to be listening. I had to strain to hear. "I've been thinking about the bindings." I turned to face him, his deep-blue eyes on mine as he continued, "I was thinking there might be another way." He was hesitant for some reason.

"How?" I demanded, keeping the volume as low as I could, my palms pressed to the smooth rock beneath us. *What is he hedging around?*

"If... Well, it seems you may have more control over your thoughts than you realize?" He phrased it as a question. He had to be talking about my secret, but I couldn't figure whether he was trying to be respectful of it, or trying to keep me from getting upset.

I wasn't sure how to answer. But if it helped, if there was a way to unbind me, free my mind and get back the magic... I settled on an "Mm-hm?"

He nearly smiled. "Well, if you were able to... move about..." It seemed to make him uncomfortable, searching for words. "Then perhaps you could find a way around it."

I bit my lip, and he reached up to gently pull it loose. His hand lingered, his thumb tracing my bottom lip. I was definitely not imagining that. Warmth flooded my neck and cheeks, and his gaze followed the flush.

His hand dropped to my shoulder. "Please, Freya, try."

All I could do was nod.

He stood and walked away. I sat unmoving for a moment then finally glanced at the group. They were deeply involved in their conversations, seemingly unaware of the encounter that had my heart in my throat. I closed my eyes and took a deep breath, attempting to move about in my mind.

It was completely frustrating, fuzzy, and wrong. Nothing worked. None of it connected the way it should have. It made me angry and tired, and the maddening fight against it gained me nothing but a buzzing headache.

I sighed and threw myself onto my blankets, away from the group. It was still daylight, and I tossed and turned, unable to rest. I decided to go back to my favorite distraction.

THE TIME CAME SOONER *than any of us expected. Looking back, I suppose it was fortunate. I can't imagine what might have happened if a full birth ceremony had been prepared and how many would have been present. It makes me cringe to merely think of it.*

The elders were there, though. My father and the others waited in the throne room, arranging a celebration. I had read everything I could obtain on the process during my pregnancy and imprisonment in the castle, even finding a few books and scrolls on humans. But nothing prepared me for what happened.

I had been walking—pacing my room with worry, if I were truthful—when the pain struck. It hit suddenly, a stabbing, ripping, horrible thing. My screams called everyone to order, but then it subsided. However, it was only long enough to catch my breath before it was back tenfold. I writhed in agony. Nothing they did would help. I could not control my magic, and it shattered most of the things on the nearby table and twice caught the bedding afire. The elders were frantic, which only frightened me more. I had never seen them agitated.

This carried on for hours. My hair and clothing were drenched in sweat, and I was near surrender. And then, with no more warning than when the first pains came, it was over. A small, sweet child was in my arms.

I drew in ragged breaths as I cleaned her face. I wiped her eyes and they came open, an unbelievable shade of dark green, sparkling like emeralds. She was a beauty. I wasn't aware the room had grown silent until I wiped her ears and heard my own gasp. They were slightly rounded at the tips... almost blunt.

I REALIZED I had stopped breathing as I read, completely engrossed in the story. I reached up absentmindedly to stroke the tops of my ears.

I LOOKED UP, then, at the elders who surrounded me. Their faces were astonished. "She is... human," they said.

I took a steadying breath and spat out, "No." They stared at me

incredulously. I spoke deliberately. "She is elf. I name her...
Elfreda."

MY HEART STOPPED THEN SURGED as blood rushed to my face, my neck. My ears rang. I must have been speaking or cursing. I could hear the sound, but could not make sense of it. Nothing made sense.

I was standing before I knew I was surrounded. Fury and fire swam in my head, my chest, my hands.

I heard them through the buzz. "Frey, what's wrong? What is it? Frey... Frey." And then, more clearly: "Elfreda!"

My jaw tightened, and my teeth ground together.

Comprehension crossed Chevelle's face as he saw the book on the ground between us. He reached for it.

"Touch that book and you die," I hissed.

He froze, staring me straight in the eyes. I was fighting for control, struggling to find my thoughts.

Then I saw him flick a glance at Ruby, and I knew. They knew. And it was all true.

Suddenly, I couldn't catch my breath.

"Please, Freya, stay calm," Ruby pleaded. They were circling me, their arms outstretched as if to catch me... or cage me.

Black spots floated in my vision. My head screamed. The sound of metal bands snapping echoed through a scraping, screeching noise inside my mind. I pressed my palms against my temples. I didn't know I was going down until my knees hit the hard rock. I held myself there, refusing to give in.

They argued frantically. "Knock her out. Do something. She's going to crack."

Yes, crack was a good word for it. I felt as if I were

breaking in half. No, I was being torn.

I sensed someone close to me, Ruby no doubt. She would drug me. I didn't want that. I didn't want that ever again. I slid from the pain, reaching out. I found nothing but the horses, but I would take it. I left my body completely.

My entry was so furious that it startled the horse. I held him there, but when he raised his head from grazing, he was facing them. They were standing, kneeling, surrounding my limp body. I watched them and the horror on their faces for an immeasurable moment. It was too much. It was all too much.

A raw, unbearable ache crushed my chest, and I gave in to it, accepted it. There was nothing else I could do. I sighed, melting back into my own mind. It was quiet there, and I wondered if I had cracked. But then it occurred to me that maybe I had been the cause of it. I was resigned—the fury was gone, and so was the screeching, the pain. They had said the binding was dangerous...

There was a collective sigh as they realized I was back. I heard someone beside me, and a flash of anger swept through me, lighting a flame at whoever it was. *So maybe the fury wasn't completely gone.*

I suddenly remembered the pages I had burnt in the briar patch so long ago—I'd burned them before I'd read them. My eyes flashed open. I sat up, ignoring my spinning head, but the book was already gone. I glared at Chevelle. It must have been dreadful, because he nodded and backed away, his mouth tight.

"Oh, Frey." Ruby's voice was low and soothing.

I grimaced as I turned to her, not at all wanting what I was about to say. "Go ahead." I closed my eyes again as her jaw shifted.

15

The dreams I had then were the most dreadful of my life. I jolted awake and shuddered at the images I could not beat down, my mother screaming in agony, her body tearing and breaking from the magic inside, fire, blood, betrayal.

Ruby was there, waiting for me.

"Where are the others?" I asked, my voice hoarse.

"They've set up a perimeter."

It was all I had to say. I felt empty, alone. It was dark—even with the dust, I'd not slept through the night. I sat up, curling my legs against my chest, and wrapped my arms around them, pulling tightly.

Though I didn't speak, I occasionally glanced or glared at Ruby. She sat, immobile, watching me.

It was morning before she broke. "You have your fire back."

It hadn't occurred to me. I held my hand out, flicked a flame above my palm, then promptly extinguished it. I tried moving a stone from the ground to no avail. *Just fire*. I sighed. But Ruby looked hopeful.

The group approached warily, keeping their eyes on me. Chevelle hung farther back, avoiding my gaze as he hovered near the edge of the mist. Steed led my horse to me. I didn't think I blamed him—he seemed to be involved by chance— but I hadn't fully decided yet. I was too occupied by my anger at Chevelle. It might have been irrational, but it felt as if he lied to me again. He'd been there before, when my mother was killed. He had known all of it, and he'd kept it from me. He had bound me from using my magic because I was dangerous, a deadly threat. I wasn't even wholly elf.

As we rode wordlessly through the cold stone landscape, my thoughts twisted and writhed as they were a pit of vipers. In the end, I'd decided I wasn't really that shocked about being half-human. It explained so much about myself, my clumsiness, lack of skill, and the fact that I never quite fit in. What took me by surprise was the betrayal I felt. In all the years I'd lived in the village, I'd never counted on anyone the way I had done with the group, and especially Chevelle. My chest was heavy.

The rest of me wanted everything to burn.

Struggling with my reactions kept me distracted from the ride. It was steep and rocky, with a haze hanging in the few spiky trees. When we stopped for the evening, the men quietly set up a perimeter, except for Chevelle, who was watching me as I glared back at him. I chastised myself for expecting more from him. He was my watcher. He'd volun- teered to help Council bind me. He owed me nothing. But it didn't stop the hostile glower I was sending his way.

Ruby stepped in front of him. "I'll stay with her."

He didn't reply but merely turned from her to walk into the haze.

I was still fuming when she faced me, wearing a self-satis-fied smile. She practically danced forward to plop down in front of me. "I have something for you, Frey."

I simply stared at her. She was harder to stay mad at. I expected her to be a pain—it wasn't as difficult to accept that she'd kept the truth from me.

She extracted a small package from beneath her cloak and passed it to me. I pulled the material aside and saw the V etched into the cover. I wondered what Chevelle would do if he knew she'd given it to me.

She answered my curious gaze. "It's yours, and I think you should be able to read it."

I could do nothing but nod. It didn't matter. Her expres-sion made it clear that she considered herself forgiven. She faced the direction Chevelle had gone and left me to my discoveries.

I EXPECTED *fury from my father. He never failed to disappoint me. He saw the child, as he called her, as an opportunity. I shouldn't have been surprised. After all, had he not stolen my mother for precisely the same purpose, to experiment with power? He did, however, concern himself with where I'd found a human.*

I refused to tell. The only gift I could give Noble was his safety. I laughed bitterly as I remembered that was how I'd convinced him to stay. I'd promised him protection, but it was a false promise.

Eventually, one of the servants slipped, revealing they had seen me following my sister. And just like that, she was to blame for the entire ordeal, even though she'd never known. She'd been still searching the empty camp for trinkets and trifles. At least I was off the hook.

I SURPRISED myself by being so slow. Of course, her sister would have been Aunt Fannie. For a flash, I felt sympathy for Fannie, but it passed. Just because life had given her sour grapes didn't mean she had to stomp them into wine and get drunk.

I wondered whether Fannie had known all along, but that was hard to discern. I did know that she had been bound, as I was.

THE ELDERS WERE a different story altogether. My father had given them orders to protect me and the child, and even though they followed through with them, they persisted in chattering about their concerns. The humans frightened them unreasonably. They constantly fretted, wanting to keep her—and me—from contaminating anyone else.

I attempted to reason with them, but they turned on me. "You don't understand. You never will! They will consume you. The humans will consume us all." Their hands shook as they spat out the words.

I didn't argue after that. I wouldn't have been allowed to leave the castle, anyway. Besides, it kept her from being paraded in front of so many visitors.

I STOPPED AGAIN. I had been born in a castle. I sat with the journal for a long moment. There was no way to reconcile that information with my own thoughts, no way to fill in what the bonds had taken. It hurt to read the diary, but there was no *not* finishing it. I decided the only way to keep going was if I read it as I had before I'd known the author was my mother. I had to be an uninvolved reader.

MY FREYA HAS GROWN into a stubborn and willful child. She's prone to fits of screaming or crying. The emotion frightens the elders. It comes from her father, yes, but I can't see how it will harm her. The humans seemed to live their lives fine, controlling it well enough.

I FROWNED, hating that I felt like crying or screaming and that I could not step away from the story because it truly had been written of me. By my own mother. Then I remembered the tales of elven grief, how it could become strong enough to overwhelm one enough to take one's life. I felt sick, but I continued.

I RECEIVED a visit from my mother's sister today. News of the child had reached her, and she felt she needed to call on me, now that my mother is not here to guide me.

I was in my room when she arrived. I heard the two quick raps and then one loud knock from her visits during my childhood and instantly knew it was her.

I gushed as my Aunt Junnie came in, grateful for someone who actually felt like family. She wore a simple hooded cloak, seemingly unafraid as she passed the guards at my door. She walked as though she ruled the castle, not as if she were a light elf in the center of a dark lord's rule.

She confessed to me a secret her family held, a power I had not known from my mother. They had kept it from my father, though he had stolen her after hearing a rumor of it. She passed to me many details of her sister, of the family... my family. She'd risked so much by coming here to help me, to help my child. I would owe her.

I HAD to stop reading as betrayal ripped through me again. *Junnie.*

Ruby laid her hands on mine, which were trembling, but I would not take the dust again.

Tears streamed silently as I drifted, the ache in my chest only dulled by exhaustion. I felt weak when I woke, but I was silent about the pain as we continued the journey. Yearning to avoid my thoughts altogether, I spent much of the day in the mind of my horse.

IT WAS evening again when we stopped. I barely noticed the group's mood—though quiet, they seemed anxious and kept the perimeter close. Ruby brought me the book again, and I took one long, deep breath before I started back to it.

FREYA IS GROWING AND STRONG. She has amassed a following of sorts, though I suspect it is somehow connected to her frailties. There is something endearing about it, but some of it worries me. She doesn't seem to be able to hear as well as she should through her rounded ears, and her voice is oddly alto. She is a beauty, though, her unusual features earning her extra attention. The elders express their anxiety again that the humans will consume us, but my father is already discussing arranged marriages, even mentioning Rune's son, of all people. He'll do anything he can to gain power from her.

IT WAS hard to read my mother's diary. I had so little memory of her, but it had not diminished the loss I had felt all along. Her writings went on until they became more erratic, answering questions I didn't want answered.

MY FATHER HAS TAKEN Freya from me. He has assigned her tasks, and Rune watches over her, testing her. It's just as Junnie feared— just what he'd done to my mother. I will find a way to stop him.

◦∾◦

THE ELDERS ARE KEEPING Freya now. Guards have been assigned to me. Like a prison.

◦∾◦

I KILLED three guards to get to her. We only had a moment before I was torn away from her, yet I feel I got the message through.

◦∾◦

SHE CAME to see me last night. I don't know how she got past the guards. But I begged her to keep our secret, for her protection...

. . .

AND THEN SEVERAL pages were torn from the diary before it continued.

IT WAS AN ACCIDENT. *A product of her temper, her human emotions. They were testing her, a servant told me. Anvil was holding her back physically, Rune with magic. She snapped, and they saw her power. Some denied the possibility, but not my father. He has attained his prize, that which he has always coveted. I will stop him.*

THE PLAN IS FORMING, *but I am unsure whether it will work. I know I cannot defeat him and his guard alone. But I must protect my Freya. I must protect us all. It is the want of power that will consume us. The want.*

THE SCRIPT WAS SHAKY, many of her words hard to decipher. It felt ominous.

I HAD *no choice but to escape. I would need a distraction to have any chance. I went to the village to find my young Noble. I didn't expect what was there.*

On my way in, I found the spot where we had met on so many days. I almost didn't recognize it, bare of growth, the dirt patted down from years of wear. And then I saw him, the man in tattered clothes, hunched over with his face in his hands. He heard me approach and raised his head, the awe all that was recognizable.

"You're back." *His voice was trembling, feeble. It was my Noble, young no more. He had been waiting for my return.*

He was an outcast of the village—no one believed his tales of magic, the mysterious woman he claimed to meet here. He confessed to spending years trying to find me. He'd thought I was angry with him and that was why I'd not returned. He was afraid to leave this spot in case I were to change my mind and forgive him for whatever he'd done.

I pushed the guilt aside when I recalled why I'd had to come here. For my Freya, to save her. What my father had done to me, to my mother, I would not let him do to her.

I approached the grieving man and reached out to him. As I held his hands, I closed my eyes. I could not watch as I snapped his neck, the way I had with the small boar as my first show of magic to him so long ago. I placated myself by remembering he would soon be gone, his life so short.

I held him until the daylight began to fade then carried his life-less body into the village as proof they would be attacked and killed, proof they must fight the elves. It was not hard to incite a riot. They were fearful creatures. I convinced them to raid the castle and gave them direction.

And then I returned. I knew I would have time to prepare. They would be slow to gather and make the journey. I was thinking of Noble as I resolved to wear the dress meant for our wedding, with its dramatic shape and deep meaning. I remembered when he'd given it to me, explaining the white stood for innocence. I had stifled a giggle then. I could find no humor now. Yes, it would be fitting.

I KNEW WHAT WAS COMING, but what I had read so far was much more horrifying than I'd expected. I didn't want to continue. I couldn't believe that I had been so stupid as to forget it was my mother who had destroyed the Northern clans and taken the families from everyone I knew. As they stood protecting me, the betrayal I'd felt before was gone. In its place was a new hurt, a heart-rending sorrow.

They heard my sobs. I was aware of their eyes on me before they uncomfortably turned away again. Chevelle approached me warily as I lay curled in a ball on my blankets, the book positioned in front of me. He tossed it aside, but I no longer cared. He sat behind me and pulled me into his arms, holding me as I wept. It felt more right than anything had been in a long, long time.

I AWOKE WITH NEW RESOLVE. I stood, prepared to make things right, but something was off. The group surrounded me, tense. I glanced at our surroundings but couldn't see why.

And then, from nowhere, I was thrown into the air. I landed hard against my back. I slid down a wall of stone, barely managing to stand when my feet hit earth. Ruby was suddenly in front of me. I threw my hands back to steady myself on the stone barrier behind me. I didn't look to see where I was, though, because just as I'd regained my footing, I heard the howls.

Before the next breath, a new sound—a closer sound— filled my ears: *shoosh, shoosh, shoosh*. It took longer than it should have to realize they were arrows. My mind couldn't seem to process the scene quickly enough. Before I could distinguish the threats, they changed. The hands I'd splayed against the wall for support were in bonds. I forced myself to look away from Ruby's back, and her arms stretched out defensively, to see what was holding me.

My breath came then, fierce and gasping as panic took over. Long vines were wrapping tightly around my wrists and reaching for my legs. I burned my right wrist free, fighting to reach my sword before they grew back. Large thorns burst from the vines on my legs and pierced my skin like daggers. I barely had the capacity to hope they weren't poison. I sliced at them furiously, but I wasn't fast enough. There was a flash of lightning, though no storm was near.

A vine wrapped my shoulder, jerking me back. I was trapped. I looked to Ruby, but she could not help me anymore. Beyond her, a line of long, flowing robes marched through the mist. They were coming for us.

The sight gave me strength, or courage, or blinding stupidity. I didn't know, but I gave everything I had. I was trapped against the wall, unable to move, but there was one thing I could do.

The sun broke through the clouds, and I saw precisely what I needed. A shadow crossed the ground in front of us as a hawk flew overhead. The corner of my mouth pulled up in a smile as I closed my eyes to join him.

The scene from above was just as incomprehensible. I focused on one thing at a time. Directly below me, I saw Grey. He was caught, wrapped in vines as my own body was, but there were flames circling his feet. I followed his gaze to find his opponent then dove.

I hadn't planned what I was doing, still running on adrenaline. I decided the fastest course of action was pecking the council fighter's eyes out. It worked. He threw his hands up, covering his face, screaming. But he did not attack me. As I rose to find my next target, I saw the wolves. They were also not being attacked and were fighting with no opposition. I remembered what Chevelle had said. They would not kill the animals.

As I laughed, the hawk screeched, and Chevelle and Steed glanced up at the sound. They were fighting, almost back to back, the bodies of council fighters strewn around them. I surveyed the land, searching for a stronger animal to jump to, something more harmful. I ran through my options, but I wasn't able to find anything nearby. Evidently, the fight had cleared the mountain, so it was just the hawk and the horses. I quickly passed through their minds, urging them to stampede before I returned to the sky.

When I entered the bird again, something was wrong. It wasn't only the bird—someone else was there. The shock of it threw me back to my own mind. My eyes shot open, and I scanned the scene again.

I forgot what I was looking for when I recognized a face hooded in a cloak, fighting against her own. *Junnie.* She stared back at me for one brief moment before she turned to fight some invisible foe.

That moment of shock took the last of the borrowed courage from me, and I drew in, afraid as my body remained encaged in vine and thorns. My legs were wet with blood, arms deadened to the pain and cold. I became aware of an unbroken chant, a voice I didn't recognize, and I turned, stunned again, as I saw Asher. He wasn't in the battle. He stood back, seemingly a bystander as the words flowed from his barely moving lips. Then he ran.

Confusion hit me again as Junnie chased him.

Ruby's whip cracked in front of me, and I knew the advance had gotten too far. And I was tied to a wall. *Why haven't they killed me already?* I waited for the flames, but what came instead was far more excruciating.

I expected to collapse as my body disconnected from my mind, but the vines held me in place. I saw a few final flickers of the battle before my eyes looked toward the sky, rolling back into my head. I had no way of forming a coherent thought, or I might have been afraid.

16

I was surprised, in my dreams, that I wasn't already dead.
For a long time, there was no sound, only disjointed
images. When the sound came, something else was
wrong. It was like I wasn't alone. Someone else was there,
dreaming with me, and I could see their dreams. They mixed
with mine, creating chaos.

There were faces I didn't recognize and those I did.

I dreamt of Steed, winking conspiratorially, which was
mine.

A large and frightening dark-haired man in leather and
armor was not.

My room in the old tree, my mother's pendant casting
rainbows on the bed was.

A long, damp stone corridor lit with torches was not.

There was Junnie, her blond hair shining in the sun as
she greeted me at her door on the west side of the village.
And Junnie, mysterious under a hooded cloak, fighting with
magic and weaponry, killing members of the council guard.

We sat around a fire, telling stories. Someone was ribbing

Ruby. Her eyes narrowed when she replied to him matter-of-factly, "Your mouth is very small. It's unattractive." And her head bobbed side-to-side as she smiled, pleased with herself.

Anvil laughed, and his tongue wagged. He was holding someone by the arm, preventing them from running away. Suddenly, my vision changed, and I was a hawk, attacking, tearing a piece from his tongue.

Chevelle was in many of my dreams. We were sparring sometimes, clashing with our swords. Sometimes, he was pummeling me with rocks. Other times, the moments would have surely made me blush if I could have felt my cheeks. He held my face in his hands, declaring his need for me. "I have wanted you since the moment I first saw you." But the word burned. *Wanted*. He'd used the wrong word.

Occasionally, I watched as a third person. My vision would change, and my perspective went off. When I saw Francine, she was razing the village, slowly tearing it apart. There was fire and wind and destruction as she cackled and taunted the villagers. She dropped them as they ran, sometimes snapping their necks, sometimes breaking a leg so they would have to stay alive to watch their homes burn and their families die.

There was a large man who forced me to do magic, testing me until I was on the brink. He was fierce, with a long scar crossing his brow to touch his cheek. He kept his hair cropped short, probably not wanting to hide any part of the damage.

And my mother was there, though my dreams gave her two names. Her dark hair blew in the wind, her arms outstretched, the pendant hanging at her neck glowing fiercely. Fire, flames, burning.

And then water. Drowning. Over and over and over. Being

away from the repetitive drowning almost made the dreams of being shoved from a cliff more bearable.

I swam around in these impressions for what seemed like eternity. Eventually, they became so familiar that they all started to seem like my dreams, not someone else's.

THEN THE DREAMS STOPPED. No images flickered behind my lids, yet my eyes did not open. The muffle in my ears from the drowning dreams was gone. I could hear more clearly than I'd ever heard. I hadn't found my body yet, but I heard conversations among voices I knew. They were whispers, but they were clear. I listened, hoping to gain clarity, but something was still wrong. Nothing fit. They discussed Junnie and Anvil and Fannie, but those felt like two sets of people now.

They were worried. I could hear the stress in their tones. *How long have I been like this? It seems so long, trapped here.*

I remembered the vines. I tried to feel my arms to see if they were still there. *Is that why I can't move? Am I still tied to a wall? No, no, I'm not tied. Had the thorns been poisoned? Am I dying now?* I worked to calm myself. No—I was getting better, not worse.

I felt light pressure on my forehead, and my eyes flew open instinctively, though I'd had no response from them all the hours I'd struggled to force them open.

It was Ruby. She sighed with relief. "Oh, Frey."

I was suddenly surrounded, and the sight made my head spin. I closed my eyes tightly in an attempt to stop it.

"Get her a drink," someone commanded. I felt the hand in mine then, as it was pulled away and replaced with a glass. I grimaced. I doubted I could hold a glass up, let alone myself.

"Don't worry, it's only water," someone reassured me.

At the word, I realized I was parched, bone dry. I forced myself up, keeping my eyes tight as I concentrated on getting the glass to my lips. They were rough and cracked—I could feel them against the rim of the glass. I wondered if it was dried blood or if I had been down so long that they'd simply split. I drank the full glass and felt it exchanged for another.

I finished it and started to lean back. There was suddenly a pillow behind me, keeping me in a sitting position. It was soft. Everything surrounding me felt warm and smooth. I opened my eyes gingerly. I was in a bed. A very nice bed.

I looked up to see several people leaving. *Steed? Grey?* I fought panic as I wondered if they'd all made it. The worry throbbed in my head, and it felt as if my mind could splinter. I checked the faces close to me for stress but could see none. Ruby's smile was soft.

"How do you feel?"

I was having trouble forming a simple answer. There didn't seem to be a word for it in the disorder of my brain. My silence was answer enough.

"It will pass."

I hoped she was right.

Chevelle was watching me anxiously.

"Is everyone all right?" I asked. My throat was raw, my voice gravelly.

"Are you?" he replied in a low tone.

I couldn't be sure.

He hesitated, almost not wanting to ask the question he knew he must. "Can you tell me your name?"

"Elfreda," I answered immediately. He waited for the rest. *I have two answers, don't I?* "Of North Camber."

It must have been the right answer, because he grabbed

me, exultant, sighing and kissing my skin. He held me with a fierce gentleness that took my breath. His lips trailed my cheeks, murmuring words, careful of wounds as they swept to a temple, my eyelid, the corner of my mouth. He lingered there, unable to resist touching the broken skin of my lips, even if it was only feather light, the barest brush of skin.

He drew away slowly, probably feeling my shock or seeing it in my eyes and realizing his mistake. His expression fell, but he didn't take his hands away. He swallowed hard, waiting for my confirmation.

But I wasn't the other Elfreda, not the long list of binding words that had been my identity for so long. I couldn't seem to reconcile the two lives.

"I-I think I'm just Frey."

Chevelle's hands slid to my shoulders with tension in his grip.

"That's all right," Ruby assured me.

"We will find the others," Chevelle promised, his jaw tight. I couldn't tell if the pledge was meant for me or himself.

The others. I had forgotten, lost for so long in my dreams, the bonds I'd hoped would break, the councilmen we needed to free me. I wished I could think clearly. I tried to remember what had happened but could only see flames.

A FLICKER of movement caught my eye, and I turned to find a hawk perched on the ledge of a balcony. Suddenly, I needed fresh air more than anything.

Chevelle helped me to my feet, and I walked, a little wobbly, to the door. I had been dressed in a vest of dark leather and slim pants with carved medallions adorning my chest, but my feet were bare as they crossed the polished stone floor of the bedroom, at ease in a place they seemed to know. I stepped out into the sun, and I had to steady myself on the stone ledge, not because of the lightheadedness, though I was feeling faint, but because below me, before the steps to what I now realized was a castle, a thousand elves watched me. I sucked in a harsh breath, unable to get my mind to accept what I knew was happening.

I had been so oblivious reading the diary, learning of my mother and her ties to the throne. It had told of my own life and of what I was to become, a reality that would not be put to rights in my broken mind. But as I stared down, the assembled pieces of my shattered self held together by no more than tattered bits of string, I understood.

It was my place. It was part of what had been taken from me.

I heard Ruby behind me. In a low voice, she said, "They have heard of your return. They have come to see for themselves."

Their rulers had burned along with so many of their families. After the massacre, there had been no one. From the dead, it seemed, I had returned.

Chevelle stepped to my right side, placing a familiar weight against my palm. A sword. *My* sword.

I knew what to do, then. I took a deep, steadying breath as I raised the blade into the air. There was a faint pause, the briefest tick before the bird took flight, its wings hitting wind as the shift began, and then nothing could be heard but my name, roared in the song of the crowd below.

Please look for book two in the Frey Saga: *Pieces of Eight*

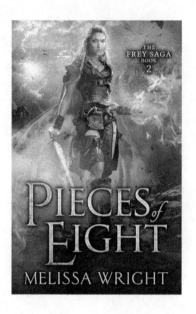

ALSO BY MELISSA WRIGHT

THE FREY SAGA

Frey

Pieces of Eight

Molly (a short story)

Rise of the Seven

Venom and Steel

Shadow and Stone

Feather and Bone

DESCENDANTS SERIES

Bound by Prophecy

Shifting Fate

Reign of Shadows

SHATTERED REALMS

King of Ash and Bone

Queen of Iron and Blood

HAVENWOOD FALLS

Toil and Trouble

BAD MEDICINE

Blood & Brute & Ginger Root

Visit the author on the web at

www.melissa-wright.com